# UNCOVERING LOVE

## J. J. SOREL

Copyright © 2021 by J. J. Sorel

All rights reserved.

No portion of this book may be reproduced in any form without written permission from the publisher or author, except as permitted by U.S. copyright law.

Dear Reader, due to steamy sex scenes, this book is for Adults Only. All the characters are consenting adults.

There is some violence, while not graphically described, certain scenes may still offend.

LINE EDITING  Imbue Editing

PROOF READ  Imbue Editing

> Between the desire
> And the spasm,
> Between the potency
> And the existence,
> Between the essence
> And the descent,
> Falls the Shadow.

T. S. Eliot, "The Hollow Man"

# CHAPTER 1

---

A DARK SHAPE MADE me jump. Creeping along the hallway, I turned sharply and saw it was only my own outline on the wall. I released a trapped breath. Frightened by my own shadow, I was losing my mind. I had to keep looking over my shoulder even inside my childhood home, where I now lived.

After twenty years, I was back with my mother. Not by choice. I would have preferred my flat in Notting Hill. But I lost everything when I walked away— or, I should say, ran away from my marriage. Now I had to start again.

Being Wednesday, my mother was at the local women's shelter where she volunteered. The same shelter that, thirty years ago, had given us a roof over our heads after we'd bolted from my drunken father late one night. I was only ten, but I still remember that crowded, rundown facility very clearly—too clearly— as well as the frightened eyes of those women and children, all of us shivering and clutching tightly to each other. And that sickening antiseptic and stale smoke stench, making it hard to breathe.

Eventually my father died, and we returned home.

I'd followed in my mother's footsteps by marrying the wrong man. Stupid of me, really. Almost a cliché when taking into account the common belief that women attract men like their fathers. Yep. I'd fallen down that rabbit hole, and Kevin, my ex, was more a brute than a bunny.

Realizing I'd forgotten to buy milk, I stepped out again and ran into Gladys, an elderly neighbor.

"Hello, Ainsley, we haven't seen you for a while."

"I moved back last week. Just until I land on my feet," I said.

She studied me with the intense scrutiny of a nosey loner. "Not going well with the husband?"

My legs stiffened. "I left him." I leaned in and pecked her on the cheek. "Must run."

Before another word left her lips, I dashed off.

As I hurried along the main road, I slipped into the convenience store to pick up some milk, and while pitched against the counter, I stared longingly at the row of cigarettes. I'd lost count of how many times I'd given up.

My nerves had the upper hand, and I bought a packet, promising myself they'd be my last. When it came to willpower, mine had gone off on a holiday to some seedy island where the rules were as loose as its tourists.

I stepped outside, stood against a wall by the store, and lit my cigarette. As guilty smoke slid pleasurably down my throat, I observed people scurrying back to their homes after they'd finished their work for the day.

After a few calming puffs, my mood started to thaw. I peered up at the evening star, and just seeing a sparkling dot dancing in the delicate twilight sent a jolt of hope through me.

Tomorrow I'd visit my former agent for acting roles and look for an admin job in the meantime. Or even online editing. My theatre degree had equipped me with skills other than acting. Like most budding actors, I'd flitted from one job to another. That was before I married a violent control freak, and my life became one big fucking melodrama.

Stubbing out my cigarette, I hurried back home. After a foggy-headed week of staring out the window at a wasteland of possibilities, I finally had a plan.

The following morning, I rode the tube to Piccadilly and headed to my former agency. I'd performed in enough supporting roles to justify my being there. Only my physical appearance had changed. Having put on weight, I'd let myself go after developing a late-night-sugary-snacks habit. I sucked it in. Not every role on TV demanded svelte beauties.

After waiting two hours, Jean Sawyer directed me into her office. Black-and-white photos of famous actors and movie posters lined the walls of her high-ceilinged, bay-windowed office looking out onto the busy square. My eyes settled on the winged statue of Eros with his arrow pointed in my direction.

"We haven't seen you for a while, Ainsley," she said.

"I had a bit of a break." I took a moment to channel my acting skills. Confidence to an actor was what a hammer was to a carpenter.

"I've been traveling and doing some writing. I've also performed in a few community plays," I lied.

She stared at me intently through her glasses. "Let's see. You're now forty."

There it was. Too old. The only lines an actor needed were on paper, not on the face.

"Have you got recent photos?"

"I'll arrange a shoot. I just wanted to touch base."

She held on to her chin and studied me. Her lingering scrutiny made my muscles tighten and caused me to regret my disdain for Botox.

"You know something did come in today," she said. "It's a little different." She typed on her laptop. "I take it you need work?"

"Yes." I sat up. "I'll take whatever's there. An ad even." I hated sounding so needy. Maybe once I could have stretched back with a cocky attitude—when I boasted a pretty face, firm tits, and a well-trained voice. Screaming from fear had mangled my vocal cords. Now my raspy tone might work on film but not on stage.

"This isn't to do with being in front of a camera or anything." She locked eyes with me. "Would you be prepared to relocate to the country?"

And get away from my damp childhood home filled with so many ugly memories that I hadn't been able to sleep?

You fucking bet.

"I have nothing holding me here, so yes, I'd be willing to leave—for the right conditions, of course"? I squared my shoulders.

"They need someone pretty urgently, I believe. It only just came in."

"I'm happy to audition or change my hair, whatever. I could use the work."

"This is different from that, although..." She looked at me again. "You might want to change your identity."

My eyebrows rose.

She leaned forward on her elbows. "Look, I'm not going to pussyfoot around here. It's an undercover job. We sometimes get recruited by Scotland Yard. And this one's come up."

"Like MI5 or something?" I asked.

She nodded. "Only I believe this has less to do with government matters and therefore is less dangerous, of course."

I nodded slowly. "Can you tell me more?"

"You'd be required to work as a personal assistant. You'll be given lodgings at an estate situated somewhere in Kent. By the sea." Her mouth twitched into a smile, as though that was something to celebrate.

"Working for?"

"That I don't know. In fact, I've told you all I know."

"Undercover means I have to spy?" I asked.

She shrugged. "If you're interested, you'll be briefed. I believe there's a process. For obvious reasons, they need to keep this as confidential as possible. They asked for a mature person."

I grinned. "I suppose I fit that profile as a forty-year-old."

"So are you interested?" she asked. "I need to keep moving."

I took a deep breath. "How much would I be paid?"

"I believe the person hiring, who'll be your boss, pays well. It would be a full-time position."

"Okay. I'm interested."

She raised a finger. "Let me make a call and I'll arrange for you to meet the officer in charge."

"Officer?" My body tightened.

"Why, yes." She peered at me over her glasses. "I mentioned Scotland Yard earlier."

I released a tight breath and nodded.

"Do you still want me to make that call?"

"Yes."

"If you don't mind waiting out in reception, I'll arrange it for you."

I rose and straightened my skirt. "That would be lovely, thanks."

I returned to the reception area and decided to check my phone. I'd changed my number and only a few people knew it—namely, my mother and a couple of girlfriends, whom I'd been neglecting lately. I wasn't exactly the best company.

Girlfriends were for partying and sharing cheeky details about a new man's bedroom habits. Even dick size. But my ongoing marital issues had become stale and dull. Even for me.

Twenty minutes later, Jean stepped out of her office and handed me a piece of paper.

"Here's the number. She's expecting your call."

I took the slip and nodded. "Thanks."

"Let me know how you get on."

"Sure."

# CHAPTER 2

LEAVING DAYLIGHT BEHIND, I entered the virtually empty pub, and walked up to the bar. An acrid stench of alcohol clung to the air and followed me along.

The bartender, who looked as worn as the surrounding chipped walls, shuffled over. "What can I get you?"

"I'll have a white wine, thanks." I'd stopped asking for a wine list long ago. After leaving my husband, I had little choice but to budget. As a result, I developed a taste for cheap wine.

I settled for a table by a tinted window and waited. The prospect of a job by the sea offered a glimmer of hope and helped me overlook the dingy environment.

A few minutes later, a middle-aged woman stepped through the door, and I knew straight away she was there for me. Wearing men's clothes, she walked as though weighed down by a heavy weapon.

I stared up as she stood before me. "Ainsley?"

I nodded.

She held out her hand. "Detective Chief Inspector Somers."

I stood up and shook her chubby hand.

Staring down at my wine, she said, "Just give me a minute while I grab a drink."

She returned, pulled up a chair, and after taking a swig, said, "I believe you're an actress?"

"I am."

She studied me for a moment. "Would you be prepared to change your appearance?"

I nodded. "Have you got any particular look in mind?"

"Someone with a professional appearance. I'm told you've worked in admin."

"I have. It's been a while though."

"The role looks pretty straightforward." She removed a document from her satchel and handed it to me. "The duties are outlined here."

I read the following tasks: running errands, ensuring staff needs are seen to, sending correspondence.

"Is it a man or woman I'd be working for?" I asked, searching for a name on the piece of paper.

"It's a male." She studied me. "Does that matter to you? You'd be required to stay there."

I shook my head. "Is this dangerous? Or, I should ask, is he dangerous?"

"Not from what we've observed. He's a recluse, and his record's clean. But he's also filthy rich."

"Meaning?" I asked.

"The wealthy are often good at avoiding the law."

"Why aren't you sending a policewoman? Someone trained?"

"We did that, but she had to leave. She got pregnant." She took a breath. "Look, to be honest, she found nothing on him. I need an actress. A honeypot."

My head jerked back. "Forget it." I went to rise when she touched my arm.

"Wait. Perhaps I should've chosen my words a little more carefully." She pulled an apologetic smile. "The man's inscrutable. That's why I'm looking for an actress. Someone who can make conversation. An actor should be good at that. Someone a little fascinating. You know, who might help him open up."

I sat again. "I'm not sure if I can make myself that fascinating."

"You're highly educated—well read, I imagine, going on your degree. You've been employed as an actress. Something tells me you'd hold your own in a conversation."

"But my fascination with French literature's hardly going to turn him into a chatterbox."

She smirked. "No, but you're a beautiful and intelligent woman."

I knitted my fingers and quickly tucked them away, after seeing the detective looking at my chewed nails.

"I know about your ex—that you've got him on a restraining order —and that you're living with your mother."

My brows knitted. "You got that in just two hours?"

"That kind of information isn't hard to find. Especially since you've reported him on a few occasions. He sounds like a fucking pig."

"He is a pig." I cocked my head. "No offense."

"None taken. He's a dirty cop. We all know that. He's being investigated."

"Well, this time, I hope they find something and throw away the key. He's obviously got lots of buddies in high places."

"Has he been near you lately?"

"He's stalking me." I swallowed tightly. "But I can't prove it. That's the problem."

"Yeah, the fucking system stinks. We can't touch them unless they do something."

"Yeah, like murder their exes, or beat the crap out of them." I puffed a frustrated breath.

She responded with a sympathetic smile. "This job will offer a double layer of protection. We'll be watching over you, and your whereabouts will be hidden."

"So am I allowed to know your interest in this rich recluse?"

"Not until you've agreed to the job."

"But how do I know he's not a cold-blooded murderer?"

"Let's put it this way: He's only a suspect. Constable Davies, our last undercover, wasn't at all threatened. He just keeps to himself."

"That's something, I suppose." I finished my wine. "How long have I got?"

"Until the morning. There are two others. But they're not as well educated or as beautiful."

"I'm not that good—I've stacked on weight, and I've got permanent bags from not sleeping."

"You're still beautiful." Tilting her head, she asked, "Why a cop?"

"What do you mean?" I asked.

"Why did you marry him? A woman like you could attract anyone."

I shrugged. "All the regular clichéd reasons. He was ruggedly charming."

I didn't wish to admit that I once had a thing for rough, bad-boy types. One after another. All fucking mistakes.

"I get it. Women like rugged men. They're not always good men, however."

"Tell me about it." I sighed, staring down at my fingers. "It wasn't until we married that he became a vicious, controlling monster."

She shook her head. "If only I had a pound for every time I heard that. I'm going to make it my personal mission to have your ex watched."

I rose. "Okay. I'll give you an answer in the morning."

"One thing, please: not a word about this to anyone—your mother included."

# CHAPTER 3

THE AROMA OF ROAST beef filled the air. While stress robbed some people of an appetite, it did the opposite for me—and although I'd only been home for a short time, I now struggled to get into my clothes.

"Is that you, Ainsley?" my mother called out.

I walked into the kitchen where I found her preparing dinner. "That smells nice."

She lowered the tray of beef, roast potatoes, and carrots onto the bench. "I picked up a nice cut at the market this morning."

I went to the fridge and grabbed the six-pack. "Do you want one?"

Wiping her brow, she nodded. "Why not?"

I pulled two bottles apart and handed her one.

"So how did your interview with the agency go?"

"Okay, I suppose." I swallowed some beer. "They might have a few bit parts and commercials."

"That's nice." She looked concerned. "Will it be enough though?"

"I've also applied for an admin role."

"You're such a clever girl. Have you thought of getting a lecturer's position? You love your books."

"I'd need a doctorate to do that."

"Well then, keep studying, love. You can stay here." She smiled and the lines around her eyes deepened. Her need for company pounced at me, and I swallowed tightly.

How would she take me moving so soon?

We sat at the dining table for a change instead of in front of the television. I carved the meat and placed some on a plate for my mother along with potatoes and carrots.

My mother wasn't the chattiest of people, so we ate in silence, which worked for me. I had a lot on my mind.

"You seem a little distant tonight," she said.

"Why haven't you ever married again?" I asked suddenly, having no idea why that popped out. Perhaps, subconsciously, I didn't wish to see her alone, especially now that I was contemplating a move.

She took a sip of wine and cleared her throat. "I didn't trust myself to get it right."

Even at sixty-two, my mother was still pretty. Unlike me, she was slim with dyed blonde hair. We did, however, share the same green eyes.

"Not all men are like Dad was."

"I know, sweetheart, but I'm a pushover. The charming ones with the quick tongues are so damn attractive to me." She looked down at her plate. "There's Roger. You know, the handyman at the shelter."

"Oh? I don't know about him."

"I thought I mentioned him. Anyway, he's asked me out." She chuckled. "We sometimes meet in the kitchen for a cuppa. He's a little younger. But I don't know."

"Why don't you try?" I asked.

Her mouth stretched into a grimace. "Oh, I don't know, love. It's been so long. When did your father leave?"

"When I was ten. Thirty years ago."

"It's been that long, then."

"You haven't had a boyfriend?" I asked. "Even in secret?"

"In secret?" She cocked her head. "I wouldn't hide it, darling." She continued to cut her meat. "Who knows? I might go out on that date with Roger." She put down her utensils and peered up at me, wide-eyed. "I think I'm scared."

"What's his story?" I asked.

"He's a widower. When his sister ended up at the shelter, he was so taken with the great work they do that he's now volunteering, like me."

"Then you've got something in common. Is he handsome?" I asked.

She chewed on a carrot and swallowed. "Oh yeah. Very."

I opened my hands. "Then why not?"

"Who knows, I might say yes." Like a cloud drifting over the sun, her smile soon faded.

I understood. That would have been me too. I wasn't sure how I would ever be with a man again after what my ex did to me.

"Are you scared because of Dad?" I asked.

She shook her head slowly, and unconvincingly. "And what about you, Ainsley? You're so pretty. Why not try that online dating? Brenda's Shelly met her fiancé, a lawyer, that way. She sounds very happy."

"No way. I'm not that desperate."

She patted my hand. "You'll meet someone when the time's right. And this time he'll be a good man. Estelle told me."

"You haven't had your cards read again?" I asked, unable to understand my mother's fixation with the occult.

"I did. She told me that you're going to meet a very wealthy man, who lives in a big house by the sea."

The wine I'd just swallowed was close to splattering on my chin.

"Are you okay?" she asked.

"Go on." I wiped my lips.

"Just that he'll be the love of your life. You'll have children."

"At my age?" I laughed.

"Women can conceive up to forty-five."

I released a breath. "My chance came and went."

Her eyes shone with sadness. "That was plain bad luck. You married a brute."

I saw myself in our cramped Notting Hill flat. Kevin came home and planted me a stomach-churning, sloppy kiss. Like every night, he stank of liquor and cigarettes. I'd just discovered I was three months pregnant, and my moment of elation soon turned to terror.

At the age of thirty-five, pregnancy came as a surprise. I'd had unprotected sex before—too many times in my wild, impetuous days—and never got pregnant, so I never expected to conceive.

All it took was one push against the wall, hard enough for my tooth to cut into my lip, and that was that.

I sighed. "So what else did Estelle say?"

"That he would be tall, dark and handsome. A gentleman. And that you would become a grand lady."

I laughed. "Does this Estelle write for Harlequin by any chance?"

My mother's lips twisted into a grin. "Oh, you always were a cynic. It never hurts to dream."

What happens when that dream turns into a nightmare?

I rose and pecked her on the cheek. "Thanks for dinner. I might go and read for a while, then turn in, I think."

I tossed and turned while I lay in bed. I didn't normally sleep early, but I'd decided on an early start so I could apply for more jobs that didn't involve some weird cloak-and-dagger act. That was despite a curious itch to learn why this reclusive, wealthy guy was being investigated. And staying by the sea would be a nice change from this smoggy city.

It must have been around eleven when a knock came at the door. I ignored it but it became insistent.

I snuck a peek out the window and saw my ex, Kevin. "Shit," I muttered.

I grabbed my dressing gown and ran downstairs where I met my mother. She shook her head and crossed her arms. "Should I call the police?"

I nearly laughed at that. "Like that's going to help. Just grab your phone."

She went to the door. "Go away," she yelled.

"I want to talk to her. I know she's in there. I'm not going anywhere," he said, banging on the door.

I rolled my eyes and exhaled a breath. "I'll have to talk to him. He'll wake the neighbors."

Opening the door with the chain still intact, I spoke through the crack. "What do you want, Kevin?"

"I want to talk."

"You're not meant to be here."

"You're my fucking wife. I have a right."

"No, you haven't. Go away. We have nothing to say."

"Let me in. I won't hurt you. I promise. I just want to talk," he said.

My mother stood close by with a broom. I nearly laughed, though it was anything but comedy. My pulse raced like mad.

"Last time we tried to talk, you broke my arm," I said. "I'm scared of you."

"That's because you don't listen to me."

I turned toward my mother and whispered, "Call the cops."

She rushed off.

"We're calling the police right now. So you better go. You shouldn't be here."

He came so close to the door I could smell the booze on his breath. My stomach turned upside down. What had I seen in this bastard?

"Go away and don't come back."

"I won't sign the divorce papers unless you talk to me," he said.

"We can meet in daylight with a mediator," I said.

"I love you." His voice trembled and pity shuddered through me as I suspended the hours of pain and torture this man had inflicted upon me.

Kevin was born on the wrong side of town and was a victim of a turbulent upbringing. Like my father, his dad had turned to alcohol.

Only his dad was more violent than mine had been.

I went to undo the chain, when I experienced a flashback of the times he'd lulled me with tenderness only to descend into a demoniacal rage.

"I'll only talk during daylight, when you're sober and there's someone in the room to protect me."

His groveling scowl soured. "You're a fucking spoiled bitch. You're a slut who's fucked half of Notting Hill."

"That's all in your head. You're paranoid. You need help. You've stopped taking your meds again."

"I don't need them. It was living with you that made me go crazy. I couldn't trust you."

"That's bullshit. Now go away. You're waking the neighbors."

A police car arrived, and my shoulder blades unlocked.

Conceding defeat, he lumbered off, hunched over and pushing past the young policeman.

As the uniformed cop caught up with him, Kevin pointed his finger into his face and roared at him. The policeman's colleague then joined them while talking on his phone.

They pushed Kevin into the car and drove off.

I knew what would happen: They'd drive him home, and nothing would come of it. He'd invent some story that I'd caused all the problems. That I'd riled him by fucking other men under his nose.

Cheating was never my thing. One man was enough. Only with Kevin, after the honeymoon period, the little tenderness we'd shared degenerated into rough sex. The only way he could get an erection was when taking me by force. Violence turned him on.

In the beginning, I confused that for passion. I liked him ripping my clothes off and fucking me so hard my eyes watered. But that soon lost its appeal. One push too many against a door or a wall and desire was soon knocked out of me.

# CHAPTER 4

A FEW DAYS LATER, I drove through a towering filigree gate scrolled with the title Starlington. Across the sprawling grounds stood a commanding Georgian mansion that glowed like a jewel in the sunlight. I read that as a good omen. A dark, Gothic structure with an ominous cloud spitting vitriolic lightning would have sent me running.

All night, I tossed and turned, my imagination conjuring up a windswept, secluded mansion staffed by some creepy hunchbacked butler. Much to my delight, however, the bluestone estate was more Downton Abbey than Northanger Abbey, taking me back to when I performed in period dramas.

At least this time I had the main role and wasn't required to swan around in a strangling corset. So why did I have to keep reminding myself to breathe? Pretending to be someone else on camera was one thing but playing a fake role in real life posed a real moral dilemma.

"So you're convinced this Daniel Love's guilty?" I asked at our last meeting.

She responded with a shrug. "That's what we need to find out."

Early for my interview as pretend personal assistant to Daniel Love, I remained in the car and lowered the sunshade. Peering into the mirror, I adjusted my unmagnified, tortoise-shell glasses, and studied my face. Those glasses made all the difference, as did my new black wig styled in a bun.

The glasses offered a shield between the old me and this new, eagle-eyed, efficient me. No loose threads or wrinkled clothes. All pristine and pressed. Unlike the real me, who rarely picked up an iron.

I'd even opted for higher heels than normal. Maxing out my credit card, the slick, black stilettos came as an added expense to what I'd been allocated. It was as though I was learning to walk again in those new shoes. To avoid wobbling, I had to push out my ribcage and walk as if a stick were up my ass.

After Kevin's late-night visit, I quickly decided to accept this role, even without reading the contents of the folder. So the following day, I met with the detective at the same venue as our first meeting, and passing me a new phone, she explained, "You need a new name. Like now. So I can get your documentation in order."

"How's Scarlet?"

She scribbled that down. "Surname?"

I thought about it for a moment. My favorite book came to mind. "Scarlet Black."

Her eyes narrowed slightly as she studied me in my new black, shoulder-length wig. "Maybe a tad theatrical. But it suits your new look."

"I like it. It's miles away from Ainsley Alcott."

"You'll have to get used to your new background."

"Will he want to know all of that?" I asked.

"He might. Remember, we need you to strike up conversation. The more personal, the better. You need to get into his head. Get close."

I bit into a nail. "I'm not going to sleep with him."

"We're not expecting that. We would've hired a prostitute." She smirked. "You need a backstory. As an actress, you must have invented a few of those."

I nodded reflectively. "Can do. I live in fantasyland most of the time."

"Good. Only be consistent. My sources relate that he's deeply suspicious and guards his privacy. He has a profound hatred of the media. Especially lately." She raised an eyebrow. "He'll run a background check."

My spine stiffened. On stage, the challenge of being someone else thrilled me. But in real life, it had me chomping at my fingernails. "He won't find anything. Won't that be a problem?"

She shook her head. "By this afternoon, Scarlet Black will be a living, breathing entity with a clean past. A white, picket-fenced upbringing, public education. Never married." She stared at me with the makings of a flirty smile. "We could make you gay, if you like. That would remove the possibility of him trying it on."

My face pinched. "You think he'd hit on me?"

"Maybe. He is a man." She cocked her head. "I'll leave this with you. You've got one day to get into character and study your background. I'll get tech to fabricate records so that Scarlet Black's past is traceable." She tapped the manila folder and passed it to me. "Make sure you memorize it."

After she left, I stared down at the manila folder, trying to quell the sudden rush of nerves. It wasn't any different than roles I'd taken in the past, only this was real life and not make-believe for entertainment.

I ordered another drink so that I could learn a little more about Scarlet Black.

Born July 2nd, 1981. As my mother's birthday was also in July, I knew that would make Scarlet a Cancer. I'd been influenced a little by my mother's daily fixation with horoscopes—only because I suited my Scorpio profile to a tee. I Googled Cancer: loyal, protective, intuitive, and sensitive. Loves being by the water. Negative traits: moody and vindictive.

I flipped open the file and read:

Educated at St. Paul's West London. Never married. Didn't go to university. Parents dead. No siblings. Employed in the public sector in health admin until six months ago. Needed a change. Travelled to Australia. Stayed in Sydney with an aunt. Recently returned. Owns her own flat in West London but was wishing to relocate to the coast. When this position came up, she saw it as a great opportunity to realize that dream.

I shut the folder and stared out the window. Scarlet Black, the loner. Mm . . . not a far cry from Ainsley Alcott.

Positioned on a hill, the estate boasted an unobstructed view of the silvery ocean shimmering under a delicate beam of light. The sun, enshrouded by a wispy cloud, resembled a veiled lamp.

I stood by my car and soaked in the atmosphere. Salty, fresh air smacked my face, doing more to revive me than the coffee I'd had at a café in a charmingly rustic village.

I wiped my palms and inhaled the fresh air to quell my nerves. I was still twenty minutes early, so I decided on a stroll around the grounds.

When my heels sank into the grass, I reverted to the path, and instead of walking to the columned entrance, I headed in the opposite direction to stretch my legs.

I arrived at the back of the manor, where in the distance, I spied a building flanked by weeping willows.

The miniature-spired structure looked like something out of a Gothic fairytale. Rippling at its feet was a pond, where swans glided through the spiky-gabled building's reflection.

I almost expected to see flittering fairies pursued by a witch on a broomstick.

Seduced by the beauty of my surrounds, I sucked back the heady, earth-drenched aroma as I would fresh coffee beans. My cheeks, massaged by a sea breeze, warmed.

For a minute, it felt as though I'd fallen into a Daphne du Maurier novel, which made me smile and helped me forget the task at hand—uncovering Love. That was the title of my brief. At the time, I chuckled, given that love was such a mystery to me. A play on words, considering that the client's surname was Love.

Client? Lord of the manor? Or murderer?

A pair of dogs suddenly charged at me, barking and growling with threateningly sharp teeth exposed.

I then suddenly stumbled back and fell into a large, cushioning frame, as pine cologne wafted up my nose.

Everything seemed to go in slow motion as I remembered my wig. Luckily, I'd pinned it down and lacquered my bun into a sculpture, every strand glued down.

Startled, I lingered in his hold, lost to his masculine scent, before he helped me back to my feet.

I turned and was met by a tall, broad-shouldered man. Wearing a cap and tweed jacket, he suited the place.

"Sit," his deep voice filled the air, and answering his command both dogs sat with wagging tails, suddenly happy to see me.

I straightened my skirt, touched my bun, then gazed up at him, uttering an apology.

Taking a steadying breath, I cleared my throat. "I'm here for the PA role. I'm early." I smiled tightly. "I thought I'd take a look around."

He brushed his shapely lips with his tongue, which I hoped he hadn't seen me noticing. As he studied me, his tanned brow remained furrowed, and his dark, penetrating eyes held me captive, making me feel naked.

I squared my shoulders, reminding myself I was a confident, cool, and capable woman. Handsome man or not, I was playing the role of a woman who didn't swoon, ruffle easily, or bat an eyelid.

I just wished my heart would stop pounding—a visceral response I could no longer blame on the dogs.

He held out his hand. "Daniel Love."

I shook his large, fleshy hand and electricity sparked through me.

He seemed older than his thirty-two years, and he was nothing like I'd imagined. The only images online, recent press photos, showed him on a yacht wearing shades.

"Oh . . ." spilled out of my gob. Improvisation classes might have prepared me for the stage, but not for such a strikingly handsome man as Daniel Love.

"I'm to report to you, I believe."

"You must be Ms. Black."

I nodded with a quivery smile. "I have a tendency to arrive early for appointments."

His chiseled features remained stuck on serious mode. Something told me this man didn't smile.

"That's a good habit. I detest tardiness," he responded.

His lingering gaze churned my breakfast. I prayed a stray red hair hadn't escaped. Considering the hair net and lacquer, I reminded myself to chill and returned a faint smile.

"Follow me, then," he said, walking ahead.

His stride was long and assured, while I teetered in my new heels, scurrying to keep up.

I climbed the stairs to the entrance and, staring down at my feet, I was met by a red-and-earth-tone mosaic of the sun that could have been crafted by ancient Romans.

I remained respectfully quiet, even though my normal nervy, babbling self would have chatted all the way. Making Scarlet a woman of few words would at least avoid gaffes.

When I stepped through the door, a plethora of colors and textures came into view. I'd been in stately homes before, while on film shoots, but nothing compared to the opulence of Daniel Love's world, which was filled with walls covered in silk paper, gilt-framed art, carved ceilings, and a stained-glass window beaming a kaleidoscope of geometric swirls that defied words.

The handsome dogs, meanwhile, followed at Love's feet, flanking his tall figure as though placed there for a photo. Everything about that place was photogenic, including the man I was about to spy on.

Without looking at me, he pointed to a yellow room. "Wait in there."

Before I could respond, he ascended the winding staircase.

# CHAPTER 5

THE SUNNY ROOM'S BRIGHTNESS was accentuated by its lemon walls. Paneled glass doors opened to a courtyard vibrating in color. Violets, begonias, and cornflowers flourished in terracotta pots, behind which, lush green meadows rolled on and on.

I sat down on a crimson sofa. The silky fabric glistened in the sunlight, making my grey skirt look cheap in comparison.

As this was only an interview, I wasn't ready to splurge on a new wardrobe. The shoes had been a necessity. I couldn't exactly arrive wearing my trainers, and all my other shoes were in a sad, shabby state.

My eyes settled on the vivid abstract painting hanging over the marble fireplace, where lilies in a crystal vase radiated a sweet, elevating perfume.

I'd finally found a steady breath when an elderly woman entered.

Wearing her white hair in a chignon, she exuded effortless elegance and carried herself with a dignified air of authority.

I went to get up when she motioned for me to remain seated.

"I'm Elizabeth Love."

"Pleased to meet you," I said.

She stood at the fireplace. "I trust you found us easily enough."

"Yes. It was very straightforward." I smiled. "I stopped off at the village for instructions."

"Good." She paused for a moment. "You'll be reporting to me for anything you may require."

I nodded slowly. That sounded like I had the job.

She gestured. "Follow me into the office and we can talk there. I'll arrange for tea."

"I'm fine. I don't need anything, thank you." I rose, and her eyes travelled up and down my body. I adjusted my skirt, which had ridden up again. I'd put on weight, and it hugged my body a little too snuggly.

I followed her to the back of the house. The hallway along the way, spotted with doors, seemed to go on forever.

We then entered a room that looked out to a thick wood. The trees were so tall they speared the clouds. Looking like it had been there since the dawn of time, the forest made for a perfect view, especially for someone who'd been living in a concrete jungle for too long, like I had.

I inhaled a calming lavender perfume coming from the large thriving bushes just outside the window, which Elizabeth closed.

"It's a brisk morning," she said. "Not like yesterday. The heating system remote is here if you need to make yourself comfortable."

She spoke as though it was my first day and not an interview.

I peered at the leather-lined desk with a green banker's lamp. Everything about that room screamed money and fine taste, just like the rest of the house—not least, the eclectic art collection of seascapes, landscapes, portraits, and abstracts, all thoughtfully positioned.

"You come highly recommended by the agency." She studied me closely. "Your duties are here." She tapped a folder. "Just standard administrative tasks—making sure the staff are looked after and paid on time, paying of accounts, running errands. Pretty straightforward."

I nodded and smiled tightly. "I'm very organized." She was making me nervous by lingering her focus on my outfit. I had to ask. "Dress?"

"Tidy. Modest."

"I'm pretty beige." I giggled. Now that was a first because I loved colorful clothes. "Is this type of outfit okay?"

"It will do."

The wealthy and their designer tastes.

"During the week, you're to live on the premises. And you must sign a non-disclosure agreement. After Charlotte's disappearance, the media's developed an unhealthy fixation with my son."

"Oh, I see."

"You look mystified," she said.

"I must admit, I am a little. But it's not in my nature to pry." Of course I'd heard. But I decided to play dumb. And I was dying to know more about the missing wife—other than what I'd been briefed. "I don't pay much attention to the news."

"The last thing we need is a nosy employee. It's imperative that you keep to yourself. No visiting friends."

What friends? They all bailed after I married my controlling husband.

"I can leave on the weekend?"

"If you want to stay in London, that's your call. But as I said, no gossiping. We will hear."

I took a deep breath. Her unblinking stare had me clenching my fingers. I released them and let my arms hang loosely. Body language needed adhering to. And I sensed it would be difficult hiding anything from Elizabeth.

"Is it okay if I choose to remain here on my days off?"

"You can come and go as you like. The weekends are yours." She lifted her chin. "I'll show you your room."

The bedroom happened to be next to the office. Elizabeth turned a brass knob and stretched her arm for me to enter.

The room had blue accents and appeared larger due to glass doors that opened out onto a cobbled courtyard with a table and chairs surrounded by flowerpots.

Watercolors filled the sky-blue walls and a queen-size bed sat in the middle.

"You should be comfortable here."

You think?

It would be like staying at a five-star hotel. The eye-popping aesthetics alone were enough to give me goosebumps, especially after the drabness of living in an area where most people subsisted on pensions.

She opened a door into a walk-in wardrobe. "There's plenty of space." She pointed to an antique dresser with a round mirror.

The other door led us into the bathroom, where a shower, a bath, and marble surfaces glistened. I breathed in the rose-scented space.

So this is what billionaire luxury looks like.

For a moment, I even wondered if I could withdraw from the undercover element and just take the job as an administrator.

But then, a deal was a deal. And my natural curiosity itched to learn more about Daniel Love—if his officious and eagle-eyed parent, who spoke like she belonged to 10 Downing Street, would enable that.

I stepped out of the bathroom. "This is so lovely. I'll be more than comfortable."

She clasped her hands. "Good. Can you start tomorrow?"

My eyebrows merged. "So I'm employed?"

She nodded.

Although pleased, I was disappointed that I wasn't interviewed by Daniel Love. If only to get another look at that exquisite male specimen. I wondered if they had Greek or Italian in them because he really fitted that tall, dark, and handsome description.

I followed her back to the office, and Elizabeth handed me an envelope. "Read over it, sign it, and we will see you here tomorrow at nine."

# CHAPTER 6

AFTER SOAKING UP FRESH sea air for a week, I nearly choked from the city's pollution. It felt like I'd stuck my head in a garage with the door closed.

I made a dash to meet Detective Somers. I was running late, as I'd spent the morning shopping with my mother, who had more fun than me. I ended up buying two blazers, interchangeable skirts, and five shirts.

"I'm sorry I'm late," I said, taking a seat in a quiet café at the back of a laneway.

After we got our coffees, the detective looked me up and down and nodded. "That new hair color suits you. Goes with the name."

I touched my black wig and chuckled. "I figured someone called Scarlet Black needed to go dark." I'd borrowed two wigs from my former theatre department. At least I could wear the bob after hours and the bun for work.

"Congrats on getting the role," she said.

"Thanks. I really needed it, especially to get away from town."

Her eyebrows knitted. "Have you seen your ex again?"

"No. He hasn't even tried to call, which is interesting."

"You won't be hearing from him for a while."

"Did you have a word with him?"

"I sent someone from the Integrity Unit to have a word."

I sat up. "So you know he's on the take?"

"He's suspected of it." She stretched out her legs and crossed her arms over her paunchy belly. "But he hangs out with some pretty powerful cops. I'll see to it that he keeps his head low. We can't have the prick sniffing around."

"I just don't want him hassling my mother."

"He won't." She looked down at my shopping bags. "You've got yourself some new clothes."

I nodded. "I've given my credit card a good workout. That first pay cheque can't come quickly enough."

"I can lend you some cash if you need," she said.

"Thanks, but no need. My mother helped."

"You've kept this from her, I hope."

I played with my cup. "I have. Just the bare bones. She's curious about who I'm working for and their extravagant lifestyle."

"Mm . . . people have this unhealthy fascination with the rich and powerful."

I thought of what I'd seen so far and asked, "Are the Loves that powerful?"

"Can't say. Like most wealthy families, they keep their affairs tight to their chest. Their staff are under strict non-disclosure contracts."

"I signed one of those." I grit my teeth at the thought of being exposed. Recalling my trembling hand when signing, I prayed Elizabeth hadn't noticed.

"You'll be very discreet. No talking to pals, your mother, and definitely not the staff. That said, you need to cozy up to one or two of them. Share a few drinks at the local. Tongues tend to loosen after a few pints. But not yours." She lifted a finger.

I nodded. "I get that his wife disappeared during a yacht trip. I got that from searching online. It was easy to find. From what I read; the case is closed. Police are no longer questioning the husband."

"That's right. We have nothing on him. But the wife's family is pressuring us. They're convinced he did it."

I thought of Daniel Love, whom I'd only seen once. Although he didn't say a lot, he didn't come across as a wife murderer.

"The captain of the yacht heard them arguing, corroborating reports from staff members of the couple's constant arguing. There's a powerful motive right there. Despite being married for eighteen months, he'd still lose a tidy sum at settlement."

"They didn't have children?" I asked.

"No."

"And a body hasn't been found?"

The detective shook her head.

"Do you think he pushed her over?"

"Maybe. According to Love, they went to bed separately. He didn't hide the fact their marriage was on the rocks." She raised a brow. "Maybe that's where Charlotte Love ended up."

I smiled faintly at her dark humor.

"Anyway, by morning, she'd disappeared."

"And the captain?" I asked.

"He didn't hear or see anything unusual apparently."

"'Apparently'?" I asked.

She shrugged. "He could have been paid for his silence. Money speaks louder than the risk of perjury."

"So what are you expecting me to find? And how can that be used as evidence?"

"Great question. Here's the thing." She picked at her nails. "As much as we'd obviously like to know what happened to the wife, we're more interested in Love's activities. A Russian drug cartel has been linked to that property. We need you to get into Love's private computer."

My mouth fell open. "So, it's not so much about his missing wife?"

"That's right, although I'd still be interested in anything you might hear about that."

"Isn't this MI5 territory?"

She smiled. "They're more focused on terrorists. Drugs and trafficking of weapons are left to us, largely."

I nodded slowly. "Drugs? He's involved in trafficking?"

"We're not sure. The Love family is worth about ten billion."

I whistled. "Is it too soon to ask for a pay raise?"

She smiled. "I want you to keep your eyes and ears open. Don't do anything too risky. Don't blow your cover."

"What kind of drugs?" I asked.

"We're talking crystal meth, plus guns and other weapons."

She passed me a phone. "This is only to be used to communicate with me. Send whatever you find out through this device."

· · · • · • · · ·

I CLOSED MY LAPTOP and finished for the day. Like each day so far, the work had been straightforward, consisting of simple tasks, like paying bills and making sure the accounts were in order.

I peered out the window at the astonishing beauty before me. My attention, as always, was drawn to the wood, where thick iridescent greens seemed to vibrate under the sun's rays.

The day was warm, and I decided to venture out beyond the estate to the cliffs and the beach.

I headed over to the west wing of the house, where Elizabeth lived, and knocked on her door.

"Come in."

I found her sitting at her desk.

"I've finished the wages and wondered if there was anything more for today."

She shook her head. "It's past five, I believe." Just as I was about to leave, she added, "Since you're staying on this weekend to help, you can have Monday off."

"It's all good." I smiled. "I'm happy for the extra work."

I thought of the double pay, stipulated in my contract, for working weekends, which brought a big smile to my overdrawn bank account.

"Good. We're not expecting the guests until after two. I just need you to keep an eye in the kitchen and make sure the afternoon tea is served. After that you won't be required. Just remember to use the servants' entrance. Also, have Stephanie give you a tour of the house. Upstairs is out of bounds. Only those authorized are allowed up there."

I nodded.

"Right, then." She looked away and I left.

Although I hadn't really gotten to know her, given her reserved nature, Elizabeth didn't strike me as a bad person, even if I'd yet to see her smile.

I changed into jeans and a loose cotton shirt, then headed off to the beach for a walk. I'd been promising myself a sight-seeing tour, especially a visit to the famous white cliffs that I'd only ever seen in photos and film.

Now in my second week, and with my duties well and truly honed, I finally felt comfortable exploring the surrounds. I'd almost forgotten my mission, and having grown so fond of my new job, I wished that side of the arrangement didn't exist. Despite that fact, Daniel Love fascinated me. For someone so rich, there was little about him on public record. He seemed to fly under the radar, which either meant he was a recluse, or he was hiding something.

Traipsing through the enchanting wood, I took tentative steps, watching out for hidden burrows. The last thing I needed was a twisted ankle. Sun-dappled leaves glowed, and the dewy salt air smelled of decomposing leaves and earth. The closer I got to the sea, the more tangled the scratchy scrub became, feeling like gnarly fingers clawing at me.

Despite my daily walks, I hadn't made it this far yet. I had, however, discovered a swimming pool, a fragrant oasis that could have competed with the Royal Botanic Gardens, and green rolling meadows that I half-expected Julie Andrews to appear in, hitting a high note.

As an estate, Starlington boasted a solitary but majestic presence sandwiched between a restless sea and curvaceous terrain. The landscape offered no reminder whatsoever of humanity other than its occupants, who seemed to keep to themselves when they weren't working. And for the first time in years, I didn't have to keep looking over my shoulder. The healing power of nature had proven a balm to my spirit.

I descended an ancient rocky stairway that might have been built by the Romans. The steps led to the bay, where I spied a secluded beach surrounded by rocky walls and partly submerged rocks resembling modern sculpture.

Like a child at a theme park, I couldn't decide which to discover first, the bay or the cliffs. I decided on the latter and took that path upwards instead.

Lost in thought and panting from the steep incline, I was startled by barking dogs. When I turned, I discovered Daniel Love towering over me.

We hadn't exchanged a word since I began working there, despite seeing him from a distance.

It took me a moment to gather my thoughts and a faint "hello" tumbled out. His dark, mesmerizing eyes had this uncanny way of overwhelming my senses. "I thought I'd take a look around. I've never visited this part of the coast before."

He nodded slowly as his gaze burned into my face. Pointing out to sea, he said, "That's France over there."

"Oh, really? It's so close. One just needs a boat."

"It can be rather treacherous."

"I'll try and pick a calm day." I chuckled.

When his lips didn't move, I assumed he didn't do jokes.

As we kept walking, his dogs ran ahead and he called out "Zeus" to the large red-haired hound.

"Come." He crooked his finger. "If you keep taking this path, you'll get a good view of the cliffs."

"Okay." I followed along in tense silence. Small talk was never my strong suit. And he didn't exactly inspire conversation either.

We reached the peak of the cliff, where wind soared through me. I brushed my fringe away from my face and noticed him staring at me. I prayed that a red hair hadn't escaped my bob.

I regarded the chalky white cliffs contrasting with, and thus intensifying, the blueness of the ocean. "How magnificent."

A glimmer of a smile touched his lips. "It always surprises me. The colors change depending on the time. At night it's bewitching." He turned to gaze at me again, and I swallowed tightly.

This man was intense with a capital "I."

Returning my focus to the ocean, I watched a wave smashing against rocks. My heart had finally settled after the climb. Or had it been Love's magnetism that made it race?

Wearing cream-colored chinos and a white linen shirt that showed off his tanned Mediterranean features, Daniel Love was so handsome he reminded me of a movie star.

Yet his eyes were remote. He looked out in the distance, then his gaze returned, landing on my face and heating it up from his penetrating stare. I don't ever recall blushing like that before. I even forgot to breathe.

Despite his smooth, healthy complexion, in his eyes I read an old, world-weary soul.

He'd lost his wife, I reminded myself. It made sense that he was morose and distant.

As the wind flapped his shirt about, the sight of his muscular chest covered in a smattering of dark hair flushed me with even more heat.

I had a sudden urge to feel a man again. After being frozen for so long, I'd become a hot-blooded woman again.

Just because I hated men didn't mean I hated sex. The conflict was that I only liked sex with men. And that was unreasonable anyway because it was my choices that I didn't trust. Not men.

The last time I'd had sex, Kevin forced me onto the table and bent me over. He saw it as a moment of passion. I saw it as rape. That was a year ago, when he'd arrived unwelcomed one night, after I'd thrown him out.

As my nipples tingled, I took a calming breath, telling myself the cool air was responsible and not my new boss. But still...

Why does Daniel Love have to look like Theo James?

"Were your parents into Stendhal?" he asked out the blue.

He'd caught me off guard, and it took me a moment for my brain to catch up. "Yes, my mother loved Scarlet and Black."

I hoped he hadn't noticed my hesitation. Although my mother would never have heard of that author, I studied him. After appearing in a play adapted from Madame Bovary at college, I fell in love with nineteenth-century French literature.

Considering I was meant to be invisible and ordinary, I regretted my name choice. I hadn't thought it through because Scarlet Black didn't sound like the title of someone who'd lived an unexceptional life.

"You've read Scarlet and Black?" he asked.

Channeling the actress, I shook my head, which almost pained me. I loved that book so much the cover had nearly fallen off.

"We've got a copy in the library, an earlier edition. The title is now more commonly referred to as The Red and the Black, I believe," he stated.

"So, it's a book you've read?" I couldn't help but ask. Curiosity had the upper hand.

"I have. When I saw your name, I had to look twice. I could only assume it was either a coincidence or an invented name." His slight raised brow made my breath hitch.

My inner actress had suddenly lost control of visceral responses as blood drained from my face.

"No. Just a coincidence." I smiled.

Now he was really staring. So much so that I noticed his eyes had gone a soft chocolate brown and I had to take another calming breath to avoid melting in front of him.

His gaze lingered to the point of intrusiveness. Had he noticed my wavering response? Could he tell I was bullshitting?

"It's a great book," he persisted, much to my chagrin. "I read it at Oxford."

"Oh, you studied literature?" I already knew that. But this was a good way in.

He nodded and looked away again.

"It seems like reading's becoming a forgotten pastime for many," I said.

"Has it for you?" He turned to me again.

"I like to read. Mainly light romance," I lied with a chuckle. I couldn't exactly admit to my passion for French literature. Not now. I mean, Stendhal was to the French what Tolstoy was to the Russians.

"You're staying on for the weekend, I'm told."

I nodded. "I don't have much going on in London."

"No friends to catch up with?" he asked, tilting his head with a hint of a smile.

"Yes. But they're all married," I lied. Clearing my voice, I added, "I'd like to maybe look around the region." I pointed at the beach. "I might even take a dip. It's meant to be a warm weekend."

"There's a swimming pool at the house. You're welcome to use it."

"I wouldn't be intruding? I like swimming. Especially in the warmer weather."

"Make yourself at home around the grounds. Only . . ."

My brow creased. "Only?"

"I'd prefer it if you stay away from the folly."

"The folly?"

"That's the ornamental building by the pond."

I nodded slowly. "Oh. That's a folly."

"My great grandfather built it. That's why it's still there."

The last bit trailed off and I had to strain to hear it.

"You don't like it?" I had to ask.

"It's a private space." His slight flinch piqued my interest in that quaint little building.

"I'll make sure to stay well away."

"Enjoy your walk." He nodded, then turned away.

Walking with liquid elegance, he whistled for his dogs and off they went.

I remained put, hoping for the vigorous wind to blow some sense back into me.

This role had already become a challenge, despite an easy-on-the-eyes boss and the breathtaking beauty of Starlington.

Improvisation was fine around men who didn't look like Daniel Love, but his penetrating stare made me shiver as though I'd been stripped naked. Although a difficult man to uncover, he had not only stirred my hormones but also my intense curiosity.

# CHAPTER 7

I DECIDED TO GO down to the beach for a swim before the guests arrived. Although it was risky, I tucked my red mane into a hat, which came as a great relief since my head itched from wearing a wig all day.

Being a small bay in a secluded area, the beach was all mine it seemed as I slipped off my sandals and enjoyed the grainy sand massaging my soles.

I removed my clothes and hat, laid out a towel, and ran into the water. Swimming was my exercise of choice. I hated pounding treadmills and lifting weights or attending shouty fitness classes. And I always felt great after I swam.

I dived under, and following a cold, breath-catching shudder, I acclimated and swam out past the large jutting rock.

As I floated on my back, enjoying weightlessness, a sudden sound of splashing snapped me out of my daydream.

I peered over and noticed a man with dark hair swimming freestyle. Despite him being some distance away, I became paranoid that the swimmer was Daniel.

What if he sees me?

I hurried back to the shore, and although the swimmer was far away, I scrambled for my towel, rubbed myself down, and quickly tucked my hair under the straw hat.

With a potential embarrassing incident averted, I lay down on my towel and soaked in the sun.

A visit to a hairstylist was imminent, as I reminded myself that my hair was a small price to pay for a job I'd quickly fallen in love with. At least I wasn't looking over my shoulder and jumping at shadows. The only downside was that I needed to stay in touch with Detective Somers to give regular updates.

Lowering the straps of my bathing suit and turning onto my stomach, I pushed that nagging thought aside and stretched out like a lazy cat in the sun.

I heard panting and noticed my boss's dogs charging over as I turned to look. He was close behind. Quickly readjusting my straps, I pushed down my hat, making sure my hair was out of sight.

I was grateful that the swimmer had appeared when he had. It was a close shave. I'd nearly blown my cover.

He looked over at me and I waved.

"Good morning, Mr. Love."

He nodded. "Morning."

Bare-chested and wearing knee-length shorts, he had the physique of a Greek god with that tanned muscular build.

"You've been in?" he asked.

"I have. It's cold but invigorating."

"In the warmer months, I prefer the sea to the swimming pool," he said, his lingering gaze moving over my half-exposed body.

"All that chlorine can't be great." I grinned crossing my arms. His eyes had this way of making my nipples tighten.

"It's a saltwater pool," he said, his mouth curling slightly at one end.

"That sounds healthier." I squinted from the sun as I looked up at him.

"In I go then." A half nod, and he was off.

I sensed Love was either shy or reserved. I couldn't decide which. I detected a hint of arrogance too in the way his brow creased slightly when I spoke, as though he was judging me. But that could have been me jumping to conclusions about this rather mysterious man.

His dogs splashed about in the shallows as he dropped his towel.

When he lowered his shorts, I was close to having a seizure. He looked so hot in his speedo briefs that I turned into a salivating wreck.

He had long, lean, muscular legs and a chest that made me drool. I had to look away to repress a rush of hormones.

Even if he weren't my boss, a man like that would never go for a woman like me. And why was I even thinking that?

• • • • • • • • • •

BY AFTERNOON, THE GUESTS had arrived. I counted a dozen. Mainly couples. All dripping in wealth. Men with Rolex watches and bespoke blazers and women with big flashy diamond rings that dazzled like their super-white teeth. They clipped their words, barked orders, and had the staff racing around, answering to their many needs—or, I should say, demands. They seemed like a helpless lot.

I helped them connect to the Wi-Fi and find outlets for charging their phones while ensuring their tea had been served and nips of whisky were to their taste.

A young, bubbly, blonde woman hovered around Daniel, who looked bored or didn't seem to return her enthusiasm. But he gave her the attention she sought by nodding his head as she giggled and chatted, tapping his arm every now and then.

Elizabeth Love approached me. "Right, everything seems to be in order. The caterers have their staff circulating now. So you're free to leave."

"Thanks. I might go out to the village. Feel free to text me if there's anything you need."

"We should be fine for the night. Remember to use the servants' entrance."

"Of course. I'll be sure to stay out of the way. I'll be here tomorrow if you need help," I said.

"I'll let you know if we need any administrative support. Tomorrow's the faux hunt day." She pulled a face, which was the most personable she'd been so far.

I couldn't ignore that. "Faux hunt?"

"As you might know, fox hunting's been banned. I can almost hear my late husband's grumbles." She smirked. "We still like to uphold the tradition with our stable of horses. And it's nice to see everyone in gear. It brings back some exciting memories."

"I'm sure it must." I would have liked to have listened to more about her life, as I'd become fascinated by the Loves—mainly because of their reticence to share any personal details. The more mysteriously people behaved, the more my curiosity piqued.

Stephanie, who was the head of the kitchen, had the night off, due to the caterers bringing their own staff. So when she suggested we go to the local pub for a meal, I jumped at the idea. Although I'd visited the old fishing village for supplies, I'd yet to hang around and soak up the local atmosphere.

Jack, the cook, dropped us off so that we could have a few drinks.

"Now don't do anything I'd do." He chuckled as we climbed out of his SUV.

Stephanie, who I assumed was in her late forties, said, "Here's hoping." She gave me a wink.

I liked her.

She pointed ahead. "The Black Swan. Our local bar."

I followed her into the inn, which smelled of centuries past. I visualized carriages stopping there, wenches with ballooning breasts carrying jugs of beers, and boozy, red-nosed men pinching their asses.

"Inside? Or outside by the pond?" she asked.

I shrugged. "It's a nice evening, how about outside?"

We settled on a table facing a pond, with a view of a lighthouse and harbor.

"This is lovely," I said, taking a deep breath, something I'd been doing a lot since moving there.

After we'd gotten our drinks and food, we settled back and stretched our legs onto the bench seats.

"So how are you finding it?" she asked.

"I love it. It's easy work. Have you been here for long?"

"Ten years. I started here with my husband. He worked in the stables, and I worked as a maid for a while."

"He's still there?" I hadn't met the ground staff yet; I'd only seen them from a distance.

"He died two years ago."

"Oh, I'm sorry."

"Ah . . . it's okay. He was an asshole."

Another one?

"He drank himself to death." She let out a deep breath.

The lines on her face showed a woman who'd had her share of struggles. I recognized that same battle-weary glint I'd seen in my own eyes.

"I know how that feels," I said.

"Oh, you've been married to a jerk as well?"

I had to collect my thoughts. As much as I appreciated her openness, I needed to play my role.

"No. But I had a horrible boyfriend once." As that left my lips, I reminded myself that Scarlet Black needed a consistent back story.

On stage, it was easy to be someone else, but, as I was quickly discovering, in real life it played havoc with my conscience—especially with someone like Stephanie, who was supportive and friendly.

"This should be an interesting weekend," she said.

"You say that as though it's unusual."

"It is. It's the first time they've had guests since Charlotte—or Charlie, as she liked to be known—disappeared."

"That's Daniel Love's wife?" I asked, munching on a fry.

She nodded. "Was his wife. I'd say she's dead."

"So what happened?" Although I knew the story, I still wanted to hear her version. If only to feed something to the detective. To keep her off my back.

Stephanie wiped her lips. "They were on their yacht on the Riviera, and according to what I've heard—not from Elizabeth or Daniel, of course—they've remained deathly silent about it. Unsurprisingly." She raised an eyebrow. "The official version is that she must have fallen into the water and drowned."

My brow creased. "You sound a little unconvinced?"

"Charlie was a strong swimmer. She swam laps every day. There's suspicion around Daniel because they hated each other. They didn't even hide it."

"Why did they marry?"

"Word has it, she was forced into marrying wealth."

"He's not exactly ugly," I said, twisting my lips into a smirk.

She giggled. "No. He's fucking gorgeous. But seriously pent-up. He's got a lot of issues. He paints, you know?"

My head jerked back. "Really? I would've thought he was your traditional billionaire. Whatever that means." I laughed. "How does he make his money?"

"He plays the stock market. That's apart from inheriting a truckload of dough. They're old money, so to speak. Never any peerage though. There's a fair bit of dirt on the Loves. Or so I'm told. Mainly the men."

"Where did you hear all of this?"

She shrugged. "It's a small village. The Loves go back generations here."

I reflected on my boss's relationship with his late wife.

"What was Daniel's wife really like?"

"She was a bitch. She'd have these temper tantrums. To be honest, I don't miss her. I'm pretty sure he doesn't either. He seems a little more settled lately. Even with the police on his back. The newspapers have stopped for now, so things have quietened down."

I nodded reflectively. "Did they fight in front of the staff?"

"Not really. But they slept in separate rooms. Holly, the upstairs maid, used to hear them arguing all the time. They just weren't well matched. He was too old-world. And Charlie was celebrity obsessed. Just young, I guess. Elizabeth couldn't stand her."

"But Daniel's not that old," I said.

"No. But he might as well be." She tapped her head. "In looks, he's young, but he's different from most men his age, I think. He's only thirty-two."

"I wonder why he married her." I lifted the bottle of wine. "Another?"

She nodded. "I'm sure he asked himself that question." She lifted her glass to her mouth. "In any case, she was bonking Tyson."

"Who's Tyson?"

"He was her bodyguard."

"A bodyguard?"

"They employed one after things went missing in the house—mainly Charlie's stuff: designer clothes, handbags, perfume."

"And she was having an affair with him?" I asked, taking a sip of wine.

"They were spotted in the folly."

"Oh, the folly. That's out of bounds, I've been informed."

"There's a big story there," she said, offering me a cigarette.

I took it and she lit me up. "Thanks," I said, blowing out some smoke.

"It's pretty tragic," she continued. "No one knows the full story. It's never been told. But I believe someone died in there, and that no one is allowed near it."

"Only Charlotte used it as her love nest. That must have gone down like a ton of bricks."

"I'm not sure if Daniel ever knew. Jarred, that's my late husband, spotted them."

"And he didn't tell Daniel?"

She shook her head. "Sworn to secrecy. Charlie paid him off."

"But maybe somebody should have said something."

"I think they knew about Charlie and Tyson. At least, Elizabeth knew. She doesn't miss a thing."

"I've noticed." I smiled. "I don't get a bad vibe about her though."

"No, Elizabeth's a good woman. She's spent her life protecting Daniel."

"What happened to his parents?"

"They're dead. The official story is they died in a car crash."

"Official?"

She shrugged. "Mm . . . went poking around and there wasn't anything about the accident. But look, it's such a great place to work. And I'm getting older now. I appreciate having somewhere to live with such generous conditions. One just has to keep to oneself. They're intensely private people. We all had to sign non-disclosure agreements."

"So what happened to Elizabeth's husband, Daniel's grandfather?"

"That too isn't spoken of. They change their staff regularly. I've been here the longest. As soon as someone starts snooping around, they get rid of them."

I took a deep, troubled breath.

"What about you, Scarlet? What's your story? Any kids?"

I looked down at my bare fingers. "Nope. Haven't met the right man."

She pulled a sympathetic smile. "We tried." She ran her finger around the rim of her glass. "I miscarried. Then he'd get so sozzled he couldn't even get it up." Her mouth turned up at one end. "Sorry for being crass."

"No. It's fine. What's that saying? While it's hard to find a good man, a hard man is good to find."

She'd taken a sip and had to squeeze her lips. After swallowing, she laughed. "That's so fucking true. But seriously, I haven't found one."

"Neither have I," I said.

"You're a stunner. I don't get that."

I laughed. "Now you're being nice."

"No. I mean it. Jack keeps giving you the eye."

"Mm . . . not really my type."

"No. You could do better. How old are you? If you don't mind me asking."

It took me a moment to answer. "Thirty-five." Admitting to that younger age felt odd.

"I'm forty-five. There's always Randall, I suppose. He's pretty cute. He works as the gardener. We've already gone out for a few drinks." She smiled.

A few hours later, after I'd drunk more than usual, we left the pub, giggling and sharing silly stories about men we'd liked over the years before clambering into a taxi back to the estate.

# CHAPTER 8

"I WISH WE HADN'T come," I heard a woman standing close to the servants' entrance say.

"He needs our support," the man replied.

"Charlie was my best friend. Her family's convinced he did it."

He stubbed out his cigarette. "Let's go back in. Just be nice."

I snuck off before they spotted me.

Having been around violent men for a good part of my life, I'd almost developed a smell for that seething disdain that they often hid behind a charming smile. Then that one drink too many, and bang ... all hell would break loose.

I didn't feel any of that around Daniel. Or was I just dazzled by him?

Although it was midnight, I felt restless. Alcohol always kept me awake. In the background, I could hear the faint sound of piano and people laughing and chatting as I entered through the kitchen.

I made my way to my bedroom, which wasn't far from there. After turning on the lamp, I tossed my bag on the gilt-framed turquoise armchair. It was still difficult getting used to that tidy, opulent bedroom, especially for someone messy like me.

Reaching into my bag, I pulled out a pack of cigarettes and stepped out onto my own private courtyard.

The forest looked so enticing under the shroud of night that I decided on a walk.

With each step, a rich honey scent followed me along. After the stench of the city, the dewy air wafted like an exquisite perfume leaving its damp mark on my face.

Lit up by the moon, the path was easy to navigate as I took myself into the wood, where the sound of breathing trees, insects, and a hooting owl reminded me of a soundtrack I'd downloaded to help me sleep. Now, nature's orchestra performed a variety of soothing sounds on a nightly basis.

Treading carefully, I clutched my arms as leaves brushed my skin like damp fingers.

Once I got to the clearing, I saw the sea with the moon rippling on its surface, painting a stairway to the heavens. I pictured passing ships in the night, which stirred my passion for history. Swept away by nostalgia, I sighed at the beauty before me as I breathed the salty air caressing my cheeks.

"It's a lovely night." A deep voice arrived as though transported by a gentle breeze.

I snapped out of my reverie and turned to find Daniel Love standing close.

"Oh," shot out of my mouth before I could respond coherently.

"I hope I didn't startle you." He peered down at me.

"I'm always a bit jumpy in the dark," I said with a nervous chuckle. "It was such a beautiful night I couldn't resist a walk."

"Yes, it is a perfect night," he said.

Under the moonlight he seemed taller. His shadow-drenched face revealed another man. An older version of Daniel Love. He still made my heart race, especially with those trapping eyes.

"Have you always lived by the sea?" I asked.

He nodded. "I couldn't be anywhere else. The sea runs in my veins."

"I've heard that said before from people who live on the coast. It's pretty magical, although I imagine it can get blustery."

"It does. The roaring wind can be haunting at times. Sometimes, if you listen carefully, you can hear voices." His mouth twitched into a half-smile. "When I was a boy, I thought it was the howls of men lost at sea."

A cool finger touched my soul. I suddenly saw a lonely, sensitive boy staring out his window. Full of fear. Full of wonder.

"Storms are exciting—from a distance, of course." He half-smiled again. "I love watching them."

I nodded slowly, taking him in. So far, I'd uncovered a romantic, which only made me want to know more about him. He certainly didn't strike me as a wife killer. Instead, I saw an enigmatic man, perhaps bound by secrets, or perhaps sensitive and therefore reclusive.

We heard rustling and I jumped.

"It's probably a fox," he said.

"He's heard about the hunt tomorrow and is looking to escape." I chuckled.

"You're against hunting?" he asked.

As my sight adjusted to the dark, and with the moonlight acting like a moody lamp on his handsome features, I caught his eyes softening slightly, as though we'd entered that friendly chat zone.

I chose my words carefully. "I'm not into the senseless slaughter of animals, especially if they're endangered." Ainsley hated foxes. But this was Scarlet. A gentle, nature lover, more at home with David Attenborough documentaries than noisy bars.

He nodded slowly as his gaze remained on mine. I was grateful for the darkness because my face scorched. Another first. Ainsley stopped blushing at the age of sixteen.

"It's a tradition. We don't hunt foxes though. That's been outlawed."

"You don't approve of hunting?" I asked.

He shook his head. "Like you, I detest blood sports. As a child, I would try and divert the hounds by placing food around the grounds."

"But wouldn't that have stimulated them?"

"That kind of logic hadn't made it to my child brain yet."

I smiled. It was the warmest he'd been so far.

"In any case, foxes serve an important role in culling rabbits," he added.

"I suppose they do. However, they come scrounging around in the city and make a mess of our rubbish. So . . ." Oops, too much information. I looked up at him. "Why, if you don't mind me asking, do you still have the hunt, then?"

"If it were up to me, I wouldn't bother with it. But it's for my grandmother's sake. It's tradition that goes back centuries here at Starlington. This estate goes back to the feudal times."

"It's been in your family that long?"

"So I'm told," he said.

"I must admit, you seem like someone from another time."

A faint smile grew on his face. "Then you're very perceptive because I tend to favor the past."

We stared into the distance in silence, surrounded by the forest's murmur while bathing in pearly light.

Would my heart ever beat normally around him?

If only he didn't keep staring at me with that scorching gaze. I even started to wonder if I reminded him of someone by the way his eyes held mine.

When a woman called out his name from behind, my knees were so weak that, as I turned to see who was there, I lost my balance and fell into his arms.

Seconds stretched. It seemed like I remained there for ages. My nose landed close to his neck and caught a whiff of his drugging manly scent.

When the female's voice neared, I sprang out of his arms.

"Oh, I'm sorry. I . . ." I touched my head and my wig shifted. I quickly adjusted it. "I think one of the guests is looking for you."

"Yes, unfortunately." He sighed. "That's Camilla. She's a friend of the family. Which is why I came out here."

"To hide?" I asked.

He nodded. "She tends to get a little rowdy."

Daniel's frown from earlier after I'd released myself from his arms still remained.

Had he noticed my wig move?

"I better get back," I said, telling myself that women often wear wigs. Maybe he'd think I was bald. Ew. My vanity seemed more concerned than the threat of my cover being blown.

As I walked away back to the house, I sensed him staring. I turned for a last look, his eyes burned into mine. Trembling limbs made it hard to move after that. My armpits were drenched.

Along the path, I ran into the blonde woman I'd seen flirting with Daniel that afternoon, whom I assumed was Camilla.

"Who are you?" she asked. "What have you done with the lord of the manor?"

"I'm here," he said from behind.

"Oh, there you are. Are you flirting with the staff?" she asked.

"Come on, you should get back inside before you stumble," he said.

He cast me a passing glance as he helped her along. In her high heels, she wobbled all over the place.

"She's a bit fat. I didn't think that was your type. And she's old." Her shrill was unfortunately audible.

"Shut up, Camilla," Daniel said.

"But really, Dannie, a commoner?"

"I said, shut the fuck up."

"Ooh . . ." She giggled.

I hurried off. I couldn't decide what disturbed me more: my wig moving or her insults.

• • • • • • • • •

THE FOLLOWING MORNING, I sat outside in the sun, enjoying freshly baked scones and a pot of tea, all delivered to my room by Holly, the maid.

As I finished the last scone, laden in melty butter and delicious homemade jam, I recalled Camilla's swipe at my weight. Stress revved my appetite. And what with Kevin poking around threatening me at every hour, food, alcohol, and cigarettes beat going to a counsellor. I'd tried one once but hated all the questions about my father. I preferred to bury my upbringing rather than relive it. A cop-out, for sure. But I wasn't the most courageous when it came to facing up to my demons.

By early afternoon, the house was alive with people. Lunch had been served, and although I'd offered to help, my services weren't required so I headed outside for some sun.

A sea of red and black jackets congregated on the vibrant green lawns. The color was so pronounced, I squinted in the afternoon glare.

From a distance, I spied Daniel Love dressed in a red riding jacket that looked stitched on, molding onto his broad shoulders, and striking against his dark hair and tanned features. I would have danced naked over a flame to get a photo of him, especially in those fitted pale riding pants. With that elegant stride, his muscles flexed in all the right places.

I couldn't take my eyes off him, nor could the females.

Camilla ran up to him and hooked her arm in his. Nobody could blame her for chasing the lord of the manor, especially when he looked like that.

I sat on a marble bench and watched as they mounted their horses.

Riding a white stallion, in that blood-red riding jacket, Daniel Love painted the consummate leading man. It felt like I'd fallen into a Georgette Heyer novel.

# CHAPTER 9

"WHAT HAVE YOU GOT for me?" Detective Somers asked.

"Not a lot." I gulped down some water, maintaining a blank expression. "To be honest, Daniel Love's difficult to read. We've had a few conversations, but I don't get wife killer."

"People kill for all different reasons. Everyone's capable." She raised an eyebrow. "Rage messes with a person's head. There's not one clear profile of a murderer out there, other than the psychopaths, of course."

"I get that. But he isn't nervy, as one would be if they'd killed."

"That doesn't tell you anything. He could just be cool, calm, and collected. Those are the worst kind of murderers. They're harder to read."

I shrugged. I just couldn't believe he'd done it. Or was this sudden irrational crush clouding my judgement?

She stretched out her chubby legs. "You're not falling for him, are you?"

I shook my head almost too vigorously while my cheeks fired up. "Why would you say that?"

"You seem to want to protect him. And he's a handsome son of a bitch."

"I like him, sure." I fidgeted with my coaster. "He's respectful and doesn't speak down to me. Although he could come across as arrogant, I think he just doesn't suffer fools. And he never smiles."

"He's glum, you mean?"

"Yep. Unsurprising, considering his wife disappeared a year ago." I tilted my head. "Wouldn't you say?"

"What have the staff said?"

I crossed my hands. "That the marriage looked broken. That they were very different. And that Charlotte only married him for money. There were whispers she was having an affair with the bodyguard."

"Okay. That's good. Can you get to his computer at all?"

"It's upstairs and I'm forbidden to go there."

"See if you can find a way."

"But what good will that do?" I asked.

"IT are still getting signals between the property and a cartel that we're watching."

"He's filthy rich. Why would he need to import drugs?" I asked.

"The rich like money."

"I'll see what I can find. To be honest, I'm getting a little tense about this arrangement."

"Why? You're being paid well and you're miles away from your shitty husband."

"Ex," I corrected. Those divorce papers were waiting for his signature. "He's now harassing my mother. You promised to protect her."

"He's a rogue cop."

"And?" I asked. "That's even a better reason to arrest him."

"We're working on it. The prick has a wall of pals in the force. I'm doing what I can."

"You need to do more. I don't want him coming to my mother's house."

"I'll send someone out there to keep an eye. And we'll have another word with him."

I'd heard enough at that point and left the detective to finish her drink at the same bar where I'd first met her. Weighed down by the knowledge that I'd lose my job as admin should I resign from my undercover role, I entertained confessing to the Loves. That made me crumble at the thought of admitting to such a devious scheme.

My next errand involved a hairdresser. Following that wig fiasco, I'd decided to chop off my mane.

After hovering about for five minutes or so at the door, I just couldn't cut my hair. It was my best feature.

Trudging back to my car, I conceded defeat. The wig would have to stay, even though the wind felt nice in my hair.

I was already missing the rugged coastline. The sea, along with the intrigue of that estate, had gotten under my skin, and despite the tenuous nature of my employment, I managed to sleep well for the first time in years.

There weren't too many great memories for me in that clogged-up, smoggy city. My college years were fun enough and I'd worked on some fantastic productions, but I'd made some pretty bad choices where men were involved. Perhaps masochism ran in the genes, given my mother's relationship with my cheating dad.

• • • • • • • • • •

BY THE TIME I returned to Starlington, it was early evening. The house seemed deserted despite a soprano belting out from the top of her lungs. Daniel Love didn't strike me as an opera buff, so I assumed it might have been his grandmother's choice. The music, however, seemed to be coming from up the stairs. And Elizabeth lived downstairs at the back of the mansion.

I'd picked up a bottle of wine along the way, with the intention of sharing a glass or two with Stephanie. I headed to the common room, where she relaxed in the evenings. The large room that faced the northern wing was deserted. Even the television, normally on all day and night, had been switched off.

Stepping into the kitchen for a glass, I was hit by the smell of disinfectant. The radio prattled on in the background while Holly moved about putting plates away.

"Hey," I said, setting my bottle down on the stainless-steel bench.

"Hey there." She stretched up and hung a pot. "How was your day off?"

"Hectic. I headed to London and caught up with a friend for lunch. The traffic was fucking awful."

"I know what you mean. I normally stay the night or catch the train."

"That's not a bad idea. I might do that next time." I reached into the cupboard for a glass. "Do you feel like some wine?"

She undid her smock apron. "Yeah. Why not? I've finished for the night. His lord is tucked away in his studio probably painting. Doesn't like to be disturbed."

"Studio?"

"It's up in the loft." She grabbed her handbag.

I raised my eyebrows. "What does he paint?"

She shrugged. "No one's allowed in there. He locks the door when he's not working. Sometimes he even has models up there."

"Oh?" That I hadn't expected. "Life models or catwalk models?"

She giggled. "Not babes. Hardly. Quite the opposite. They're generally quite large. It's often the same woman. But she hasn't been coming for a while."

She took out a packet of cigarettes from her bag and offered me one. Despite my intention of giving up that week, I capitulated and took one.

After pouring our drinks, I passed one to Holly and we stepped outside into the courtyard. With a veggie patch close by, the scent of aromatic herbs seeped into the air.

We sat at the wooden table and sipped on drinks while puffing on our cigarettes. Dusk had finally slid into night and stars sprinkled the indigo sky.

"Where's everyone tonight? I've never seen the house so empty," I asked.

"Elizabeth's gone to France, and the staff has been given a few days off."

"Oh? Stephanie too?"

She nodded. "It's just us. He didn't tell you? You could've remained in the city."

I shook my head. I thought that odd for some reason. "I didn't even know Elizabeth had gone away."

"She's often away. They have a château in the South of France. One of a few places. Charlie, that's his wife—or, I should say, dead wife—used to go there often."

"So you think she's dead?"

She stubbed her cigarette and nodded.

"Do you think he did it?" I asked.

"Maybe. They always argued. They didn't even sleep together, and anyway, she was shagging Tyson."

"Tyson?"

"He was the security guard. I fucked him once." She bit her lip and giggled. "I was smashed and he was hot. You know, in that tattooed-bad-boy way."

"What happened to him?" I asked.

"He left ages ago. I think Daniel got wind of them hooking up and gave him his marching orders." She sipped her wine. "It was a pretty intense time, to be honest. Charlie was always drinking and carrying on. A real bitch. She was awful to us. Elizabeth hated her."

"I wonder why they married."

"From what I gather, she needed the money."

"Was she from a poor family?"

"No way. Flash everything. Lord and Lady Snooty-nose." She chuckled. "I think her family threatened to—or did—cut her off. She was a wild party girl."

"So, by marrying Daniel Love, she was entitled to an inheritance?" I asked.

"Something like that. Stef overheard Elizabeth telling someone that Charlie would come into money at twenty-eight, but only if she was married and settled."

"How old was she when she disappeared?"

"Twenty-nine."

"Was Daniel short of money?"

"Are you fucking kidding? He's worth billions."

I thought of the suspected smuggling activity. "How does he make his money?"

"It's old money, of course. But who knows, maybe the stock market. He's a bit of a mystery."

That he is.

When her phone pinged, she pulled it out and scrolled over the screen. A smile lit up her face.

"Someone nice?" I asked.

"Yeah. I met him on Tinder last week. He lives in Deal." She looked up. "Do you think I should go? You know, for a booty call?"

I studied Holly, who was pretty and probably in her mid-twenties. "Up to you. Is he a good person? I mean, have you stayed with him already?"

"Yeah. He's hot. But I'm not sure if he wants a relationship."

"That's always the risk we take." I thought of all the hot guys I'd hooked up with when I was her age. Lots of actors, who were either confused about their identities and sexuality, or just plain narcissists.

She popped up. "Right. I better go and get ready, then."

Her excitement had a contagious bite. A sudden desire to feel a man again flushed through me. I hadn't been with anyone since my husband forced himself onto me. But since coming to Starlington, my heart and body had started to thaw.

Nature, with her moody albeit rejuvenating attractions, might have been responsible for that. Or was it a little less poetic... like the sexy appeal of my new boss?

An early night beckoned as I went to my room. In the morning I had bills and accounts to sort out. Whoever ran the office before me had left a mess. Despite my duties being lighter than they were at previous admin jobs, there were mounting bills. Elizabeth had asked me to run them past her first before settling any accounts, but with her away, I would have to approach Daniel Love.

It would at least give me a chance to sniff around a bit more. And he was nice to sniff.

# CHAPTER 10

AFTER A DAY OF sorting through spreadsheets and making sure wages were deposited into the right accounts, I settled in front of the television with an omelet I'd whipped up from delicious leftovers.

I hadn't seen or heard from the man of the house all day, and I wasn't even sure if he was in until I heard heavy metal music crank up. Love certainly had an eclectic taste in music.

With Jack, the chef, away, and it being Holly's night off, I was on my own. Stephanie, I'd learned, had gone for a one-week holiday to Spain with a girlfriend.

Just as I settled into a rerun of Bridget Jones, shaking my head at the lack of new romcoms, a banging came at the door.

After a few more bangs, I walked to the main entrance and opened the door.

Two policemen stood at the doorway. My heart raced. Had something happened to my mother?

"We're here to speak to Daniel Love," one of the constables said.

"One moment," I yelled over the blaring music.

I wasn't sure whether to let them in, but realized that wasn't my call to make, so I left them standing out on the portico.

My heart pounded as I ran up those forbidden stairs. With no time to hesitate, I followed the music all the way up to three flights of stairs.

I arrived at a loft and, discovering the door open, entered gingerly. The room smelled of linseed oil and paint, and easels were scattered about.

My eyes landed on one painting, which showed eyes peeping through cracks and a twisted face, as though screaming in fear. As I studied it closely, I recognized the folly as its setting, based on the spire reflecting off the pond, just as I'd remembered. This had been created by a master. Daniel Love could paint.

Screeching, dissonant guitar dominated the air, so intolerably loud I couldn't fathom how anyone could stand it. As I studied the canvas, lost to that eerie scene, a cut in the music, and the resulting sudden silence, made me flinch.

"What are you doing here?" An angry baritone vibrated through me.

I turned and saw Daniel Love and froze.

Wearing ripped jeans and a paint-splattered shirt, he looked like a different man.

After taking a deep breath, I said, "There are police downstairs. No one was around..."

He raked his fingers through his hair. "You didn't let them in?"

"No. I left them standing outside."

"Tell them I'm not here."

"But they heard the music." I splayed my hands.

"Just make something up." He turned away from me and fluttered his hand for me to leave.

I could tell my presence had ruffled him by the way his eyes darted.

I ran back down, then taking a steadying breath, confronted the police. "I'm sorry. I can't find him. He must have gone out."

"Your name?" the policeman asked.

Just as I was about to speak, Daniel Love joined me. Regarding him, I said, "Oh, you've returned."

"What do you want?" he asked the policeman.

As I walked off, I heard Daniel say, "You better come in."

Ten minutes later, a knock came to my door. I'd removed my wig, so I quickly grabbed a towel, and with trembling fingers, wrapped it around my head.

I opened the door to find Daniel before me.

"Can I come in for a moment?" he asked.

I stepped out of the way and did a quick scan of my room to ensure there was no underwear strewn about.

He walked over to the French door and stared out into the black night. "I have to go first thing in the morning."

"I see."

"I need you to do a few things for me. Do you mind helping me now?" His voice cracked.

"Yes. Of course."

"I know it's late." He turned to me, looking at my toweled head.

"That's okay. I'm here to help. I'm a late person anyway." I gave him a glimmer of a smile.

"Good."

I noticed his hands trembling. "Are you okay, Mr. Love?"

His eyes lifted slowly from the floor and settled on my face. He looked torn from so much conflict and pain. I could only assume they'd found his wife's body.

"Call me Daniel." He lingered awkwardly. "I need a stiff drink. Can I offer you something?"

I released a tight breath and nodded.

"Follow me into the office, if you wouldn't mind. I'll give you a few minutes to dry your hair."

"That would be great. I'll be there in a moment."

He nodded and left.

I raced into the bathroom and wet my wig a little, castigating myself for not cutting and dying my wavy red hair. Turning it into a black bob was never going to be easy. This was getting tricky.

Daniel was on his phone when I entered. I noticed him wiping his eyes. He'd been crying.

He poured whisky into two glasses, then passed one over to me.

"Thanks."

He turned his back, grabbed a tissue, wiped his nose, and then faced me again. My heart went out to him. I sensed a battle raging within, considering his cool exterior.

"My grandmother had a fall." He exhaled. "She's dead." He looked down at his drink.

My mouth opened. I was expecting something else. Not that. Elizabeth struck me as someone strong and vital. "Oh, I'm so sorry. That's awful."

He gulped his drink down. "I have to go to Antibes first thing in the morning. Can you arrange everything for me? I know it's ten o'clock. But I'm . . ." He rubbed his jaw. The poor man could barely talk.

"Don't you worry about a thing."

He rummaged through the drawer in my desk. "Did my grandmother show you my contacts?"

I turned on the computer and opened up a file. "Here it is." I scanned the list. "Do you want me to arrange for a driver? Or I can drive you if you'd like?"

He shook his head. "The drivers' names are listed there."

I found the list. "Okay. So will I book a ticket to Paris?"

He shook his head. "I've got a private jet."

I settled on a folder. "Okay. Here it is. I'll call the pilot and set that up. For the morning?"

He ran his hands over his hair and nodded. His eyes looked glazed with a film of moisture.

"You were close?" I asked softly.

He nodded, biting his lip.

I could see he needed to be alone.

"Leave it to me." I paused to think. "Would you like me to text you the details?"

He nodded. "You've got my details there." He rose and headed to the door, then stopped and turned. "Uh . . . can you inform the staff?"

"Leave it to me," I repeated.

"The family's solicitor is there among your contacts. Please call him first thing so that he can take care of all the necessary arrangements. He was close to my grandmother." His voice thickened again.

I followed him to the door. "Whatever you need. If you need to talk, call me at any hour. I'm here. I'll make the flight arrangements now."

He continued to stare at me as though in a trance.

Weirdly, a charge of electricity ran through my body. It felt as though we'd known each other forever. I felt his need and aloneness, as though we were connected on a deeper level. I wanted to hold him as a mother would. I could see he was bereft. But he was also reserved, as though the words he wanted to speak were blocked.

• • • • • • • • • •

THE NEXT MORNING, I was in my office, about to make a call, when Daniel entered.

"I'm off now. I appreciate you helping me with such short notice." He passed me his card. "Here's my private number. Please call me if you need anything. I imagine the funeral will take place by the end of the week."

The dark rings around his eyes suggested he'd been awake all night.

I nodded. "No problem. I'll only call if something urgent comes up. Leave everything to me."

He hovered again. What was he trying to say? "Okay, then."

I went to the kitchen, where I'd already spoken to Jack and Holly about Elizabeth, and like me, they were shocked.

I found the gardener, Randall, sharing a cup of tea with Jack. They turned, nodding when they saw me.

"I'm sure the lord's gutted. He was really close to his grandmother. She was all he had," Randall said.

"He didn't have any other family?" I asked.

He shook his head. "All dead."

"Is he a lord?" I had to ask.

"Not officially. But he's the lord of the manor." He shrugged. "How did she die?"

"Apparently she had a fall," I replied. "She was at their château on the Riviera, I believe."

"That's where Charlotte disappeared," Holly said, leaning against the counter, sipping tea.

"And now Elizabeth," I said.

"Weird, eh . . ." he said.

My brow furrowed. "You think there's more to it?" Now, that I couldn't believe, having seen Daniel and how pale and bereft he looked straight after hearing about her passing. No actor could paint that shattered expression.

He shrugged. "Can't say. They reckon he did away with his wife."

"He doesn't strike me as someone who'd do that," I said.

"Well, she was a loose one, that one. A spoilt brat. And she was fucking the security guard." He smiled apologetically. "Sorry for being coarse."

"I'm a grown-up." I raised a brow. "She doesn't sound like a good person."

"No. She was a bitch," Jack said, stirring a pot.

Holly nodded. "She was bossy, and Elizabeth and her didn't get on."

"Oh well. They're all gone now," Randall said, taking a breath. "I liked Elizabeth. She was a keen botanist. Always talked to me about flowers. She had a genuine interest in the garden. I'll miss her."

Although I hardly knew her, mainly because she kept things close to her chest, like her grandson, Elizabeth had treated me respectfully.

As I left to make some more calls, I thought of Detective Somers. I imagined she'd hear about it somehow.

# CHAPTER 11

ELIZABETH LOVE'S FUNERAL TOOK place in a bluestone Gothic church, the interior in contrast to its dark, gloomy shell, beamed with colored rays from the stained-glass windows.

It was a big turnout. Women dressed in black, dripping in designer from head to foot, paid their respects to Daniel, who cut a striking figure in a black, beautifully tailored suit. And, despite my being there as part of the staff entourage, he still found the time to acknowledge me with a nod.

After the service, the mourners arrived at Starlington for refreshments. Having arranged catering and staff, I had little else to do, and keen for a walk on the beach, I headed outside.

Daniel sat on a marble bench and smoked while Camilla whispered in his ear and giggled. Remaining stony-faced, he didn't seem to share in her mirth, which I thought inappropriate for such a grim occasion.

As I walked past, he cast me one of his lingering gazes.

"You're off?" he asked me, turning away from pouting Camilla.

"I'm just going for a walk," I said. "Everything's in full swing."

He nodded. "I'm grateful for your help today."

Camilla looked up at me with a cool smirk, bordering on derisive.

I waved and left them to it, feeling his gaze even with my back turned. After a few steps, I peered over my shoulder.

While Daniel's eyes remained fixed on me, Camilla continued to chatter close, almost nibbling his ear. Although difficult to comprehend how she could be so blind to his blatant indifference, I couldn't blame her persistence. He'd never looked more handsome—especially in that fitted jacket worn over a white shirt that highlighted his swarthy complexion.

Most people looked their worst when sad. Not Daniel Love. He became more alluring. Magnetic.

I moved off swiftly, my body burning. He'd started to spellbind me. I even wondered if there was some kind of magic around that estate, especially in that thick wood with its glowing variegated greens that flickered playfully in the late afternoon sun.

As I ambled along, beams of light penetrated through the tall trees, reminding me of spotlights on stage.

I exited the wood and walked to the edge of the earth, for that was where the land ended and the sea began, at the bottom of an unforgiving, vertiginous precipice.

As I closed my eyes, the soaring wind felt like a cold, silk scarf dragging along my skin. Prickling my flesh, the salty spray felt addictively invigorating.

Descending rocky steps to the bay, I tasted the salt on my lips.

Being surrounded by nothing but water beat going to meditation classes, which, with my busy mind, I sucked at. By the sea, however, I'd found stillness and even the odd glimpse of my soul.

I smiled at the irony. Here I was pretending to be someone else, only to find my true self in the process.

I'd also forgotten how it felt to breathe easily and not jump at shadows. And when Daniel Love wasn't intruding my thoughts, I slept like a baby, lullabied by a medley of the sea's rumble and the wind's howl.

After removing my sandals, I tiptoed over the pebbly ground to the water's edge where a frothy wave splashed over my feet and sent a shiver up my legs.

With the sun beating down on me, I unbuttoned my shirt and stripped down to my camisole, indulging in its caressing warmth. I tied my shirt around my waist.

Partly submerged rocks reminded me of crouching monsters as the waves crashed against them.

Looking up at the cloudless sky, I watched in wonder as a gliding cormorant cut his journey by perching at the peak of the wind-chiseled monolith.

"How's the water?"

I turned and Daniel stood before me.

It took me a moment to speak. "It's nice and cold as always." I shaded my eyes. "You're not with your guests?"

"I sent them home."

"Oh. I see."

"It was only an afternoon affair. Out of respect for my grandmother." He picked up a pebble and skimmed it along the water.

"You were obviously very close."

"Yes. She was the only one," he said quietly, as if to himself.

I fell into his dark, complex eyes. And despite his natural remoteness, I thought I might have gotten a rare glimpse of his soul too.

Shifting my focus away from him in order to think, I stared up at the sky, where a bird launching off the cliff dived into the sea.

Watching the spectacle, Daniel said, "Gannets are impressive for their nose-dives from high altitudes. The speed at which they plummet is remarkable."

"Do they survive it? He's been under for a while."

His rare smile revealed the hint of a boy.

"They can remain submerged for a mile or so. They're extraordinary creatures. The puffins are a fun lot too."

"You like birds?" I asked.

"Of course. Who doesn't?"

I smiled at his surprised frown. "Living in the city makes one ignorant of nature. However, it also makes it awe-inspiring when visiting places of natural beauty like this."

He trapped my eyes again. Remembering I was in my camisole, I crossed my arms to hide my erect nipples.

"Are you cold?" he asked.

"I just realized I'm underdressed." My nonchalant chuckle belied sudden shyness.

"People often wear less on the beach," he said with the hint of a smile.

While Daniel removed a pack of cigarettes from his pocket, I untied my shirt and shrugged into it.

He offered me one and I accepted.

He pointed. "When I was a boy, I used to think those sea stumps were monsters. Especially at night. Sometimes they even looked like they were moving."

"They have an imposing presence," I replied, dizzy from the nicotine—or was that him?

He pointed at another large rock. "That looks just like a lion. But only in the afternoon light."

I smiled. "I can see that."

With his eyes softening into a melty-chocolate color, Daniel Love was, by far, the most beautiful man I'd ever laid eyes on, but I told myself he was way out of my league. And eight years younger. But worst of all, I was meant to be spying on him.

I'd even decided to tell the detective that I wanted out. Even willing to lose my job. Having gained some of his trust, I hated the idea of him finding out.

I was profoundly conflicted, however, because I loved being there. And what of Scarlet Black? I preferred her to Ainsley Alcott, whom I'd left behind in the suburbs, crouching in a corner, dreading her ex.

"Let me show you something," he said, removing his shiny black leather shoes and socks and rolling his pants up to his knees. The diamond cufflinks sparkling in the sun seemed as incongruous as someone wearing a ball gown with flip flops.

"We'll have to walk through the shallows to get there," he said regarding my naked feet.

"My feet are acclimatized now. It's actually not too bad."

We moved along the shallows to a rocky wall, where a rising tide would have swallowed us up.

"The tide's moving out," he said, as if reading my fear.

"That's comforting to know."

"You're not into adventure?" There was a twitch of a smile, very slight, but enough for me to wonder if he meant something more than exploring nature.

"I'm not much of a risk-taker these days."

His unblinking stare made my face scorch. "You've had a few misadventures in the past?"

"Nothing so exciting as misadventure."

"I wouldn't describe misfortune as exciting," he responded.

"Not at the time, for sure. I meant with the distance of time. Once the mess is cleaned up." I chuckled. "What I'm trying to say is: A little misadventure makes one's life look less dull."

"Maybe in the telling, but in the experience, give me a boring history anytime." His fleshy mouth lifted at one end.

Creeping along to avoid landing on reef, I said, "Something tells me you haven't had a boring history."

We arrived at a secluded bay area and stepped onto the pebbly beach, which, once my bare feet had adjusted, offered a pleasant massage.

"Why would you think that?"

I shrugged. "Your art."

"What did you see?" He became serious again, making me regret mentioning it.

"I saw accomplished work that had a dark, perhaps Gothic, edge."

His brow puckered as though I'd thrown him a puzzle.

"Do you exhibit?" I asked.

"I don't show my work."

"Not even your grandmother?"

He shook his head. "I'd show her the odd sketch to appease her curiosity."

"I hope you don't mind me mentioning Elizabeth. I imagine her passing is still painful."

He looked out to sea and nodded slowly.

"I liked her. She didn't suffer fools. A strong woman, I believe."

"She had to be." He turned to face me again. "Women generally are stronger than men."

"And men are generally physically stronger. So I guess there's that yin and yang fit."

"That's only if the fit is right." His subtle eyebrow lift made me want to smile, but I controlled that urge. In ordinary circumstances, I might have even read that as an innuendo. However, something told me Daniel Love didn't do ordinary. Ever.

He gestured. "Come. I want to show you something."

I followed him around another rock wall, and hidden behind it was what looked like a cave.

As we stepped into the damp rocky chamber, an odor of rotting seaweed raced up my nose. My teeth chattered. "This is kind of creepy."

"It frightens you?" His voice echoed.

Crossing my arms, I nodded. "It feels like another world. Almost prehistoric."

"That it is. Imagine its history? All the creatures that have lived in here. And most of the time, it's submerged. I always like to visit when the tide allows."

I peered at the rippling teal water, calm and glistening under the sun's beams. "You're sure a sudden wave's not about to take us out?"

"I know this place very well. As a boy, this was my sanctuary. I came close once. Narrowly escaped being smashed against rocks."

"That sounds scary."

He held out his hand, which touched mine, and a spark shot up my arm. "Let's step outside. I can see you're cold."

He pointed at the sea stump, which was more exposed than before. "See, the tide's ebbing." He turned, and squinting in the sun, wore the makings of a smile, which was like seeing the blue sky after a long period of overcast weather.

"I can imagine many have drowned by not timing it right."

"Oh, there's been all kinds of tragedies here. The sea's merciless."

I thought of his wife and how she may have drowned—at least, I hoped. I found it increasingly difficult to believe him a wife killer.

His gaze lingered on my face, then moved to my hair, making my palms sweat.

"Tell me, if you don't mind me asking, what's beneath that wig?"

I swallowed tightly. "I have hair."

He nodded slowly while continuing to gaze at me.

By this point, sweat dripped down my arms. I craved a dip in the ocean to cool down.

"I know it's none of my business, but I'm curious to know what the real Scarlet Black looks like." He tilted his handsome head.

A nervous chuckle scraped my throat as I removed my wig, tugged the hairnet off, and unraveled my long, wavy mane. The soft breeze came as a relief as I rubbed my head to loosen my hair.

His scrutinizing stare had me close to hyperventilating. "Why would you want to hide such beautiful hair?"

I smoothed my hair down. "I . . ." Biting my lip, I searched like mad for a plausible lie. Where was that actress when I needed her?

He was too perceptive for bullshit, so I opted for honesty—not to revealing I was a spy, however. How could I ever confess to that?

"Okay. Look . . ."

He touched my hand again and the scorch this time went all the way to my core. "Save it. I can see I've put you on the spot. As someone who guards his privacy as a lone wolf would their offspring, I'm not going to force it out of you." He cocked his head. "Let's get back. I haven't eaten properly for a week and my appetite's returned."

By this stage, my armpits were soaking. I picked up my wig and wavered. Was I to wear it? I went to tie my hair up when he shook his head.

"No. Leave it off."

That sounded more like a plea than a demand. Again, I wondered if I reminded him of someone because he kept staring at me.

"But the staff," I argued.

"I've sent them away for the night. No one's in the house. I've asked for complete privacy."

"Not even Holly?" I asked.

"She's been sacked."

My head jerked. "You're kidding?"

"I'm letting everyone go—except Jack in the kitchen and Randall, the gardener."

My jaw dropped. "Even Stephanie?"

He nodded. "They were here for my grandmother's sake. I want an empty house."

"Oh." My heart sank. That was the end of my job.

"I'd like you to stay, though," he said.

My brows collided. "Okay. Sure. I mean . . . I'd like to stay. I love it here, and the job . . ."

"I'll employ help. But they won't live at Starlington. That's a past tradition."

"It's a very big house," I said.

"We've always had a lot of staff. There was too much spying and gossip for my liking."

I felt like a traitor, especially since he'd taken me into his confidence. Why had he asked me to stay? Why hadn't he further questioned my hiding under a wig?

"There's a cottage you can use."

I stopped walking. "Oh . . . I'm more than happy to pay rent."

"That won't be necessary."

"Is that the folly by the pond?" I asked, terrified at the prospect of living in such a dark, gloomy place.

He stopped walking. "No. That's out of bounds."

"Of course, you've said that before. Sorry to bring it up."

He kept moving along swiftly, despite his bare feet. I could tell he was a creature of the sea by how easily he strode on that pebbly terrain.

# CHAPTER 12

*Daniel*

WHO WAS THIS WOMAN? I'd sensed from the word go that she was holding something back, but a wig?

I was meant to let her go.

I never expected to ask her to stay on.

But after Scarlet removed her wig, I made that snap, if not irrational, decision.

With that full figure and gorgeous face, Scarlet was the most beautiful woman I'd seen in a long time.

She was so sexy I felt my dick stir for the first time in ages. Seduction was the last thing on my mind, but I also didn't want her leaving. Not now. I had to know everything about her first.

It felt strange stepping into that empty house. For the first time ever, it was just me and those endless rooms filled with memories and history. And while I missed my grandmother as I would an arm, I welcomed the space.

Asking Stephanie to leave hadn't come easy. To soften the blow, I scribbled a check which was equivalent to an annual salary. Despite her being with the family for a long time, I needed a fresh start.

Since Charlie's disappearance, the gossip and those furtive glances from both Holly and Stephanie had gotten on my nerves.

One thing I knew for certain: I would never move from Starlington.

We stood in the front room bathed in the late afternoon sun, resembling any old day. Only my darling grandmother was no longer there.

"This is such a beautiful room," Scarlet said.

In the sunlight, with that thick red hair, she looked ravishing especially with those large, limpid green eyes sparkling with inquisitiveness, and her abundant curves reminding me I was a man.

She sat down in a green velvet armchair, and with her lustrous red hair, I envisioned a stunning painting that I would have paid a fortune to possess.

I lifted the bottle of whisky. "Can I offer you one?" She nodded and I poured two shots.

I passed her the crystal glass. "I need to eat."

She took a sip and rose. "Let me help, since the staff is away. I can set the table."

I gestured for her to remain seated. "No. I don't want to put you to work. We can eat in the kitchen. I'll just go and get changed, then grab some wine from the cellar."

• • • ● • ● • • •

AFTER EATING MORE THAN I'd eaten for a long time, I suggested we move into the sitting room—one of my favorite rooms in the house, situated in the back, overlooking the garden and the pool. The yellow room opened out onto a large courtyard that offered a great view of the sky.

"This is a lovely space," she said, following me out to the courtyard.

"Can I offer you one?" I held open my gold cigarette case, the same one my grandmother owned. She'd given it to me when she quit smoking. It had been a gift from my grandfather with the cold inscription: To Elizabeth from Ben. No testament of love, a line from a poem, or even an "x."

Scarlet took one. "I'm trying to kick the habit. But it's not a good time to give up."

I flicked open my lighter and lit her cigarette, which trembled in her lips, drawing my attention to them. "Are you stressed?" I had to ask. Although I didn't make a habit of prying, I could see I'd unnerved her.

"I just don't understand why you've asked me to stay."

"You interest me." I tilted my head. "Tell me, who is Scarlet Black?"

She sucked on her cigarette as a person condemned. A sure sign of someone trapped in secrets. I should know, I'd made a habit of collecting them.

"She's Ainsley Alcott," she said.

I puffed on my cigarette. "You've saved me hiring a PI."

Her brows gathered sharply. "You were going to have me investigated?"

"I was just about to. But when I got that call about my grandmother, I got distracted."

She sat down and stubbed out her cigarette. Under the lamp, with that fiery red hair, her milky complexion, and those expressive eyes, Scarlet would have looked astoundingly beautiful in a green gown.

"Why?" she asked.

"When you tripped and I broke your fall in the wood, your wig shifted. I naturally became curious."

She bit into a nail.

I joined her at the table. "Tell me about Ainsley."

"She's a forty-year-old woman, who, up to a month ago, was living in a council house with her divorced mother." She stared up at me, her shining eyes wide. "I'm an unemployed actress. I studied theatre and literature, majoring in French literature." She pulled a shy smile.

"Ah . . . let me guess, Stendhal?"

"One can't enter that world and not read Stendhal." A faint smile touched her lips. "It was probably a giveaway."

I shook my head. "Not really. If the wig hadn't slipped, I wouldn't have thought anything of it."

She nodded slowly and looked down at her fingers. "I suppose I should go and pack my things."

"No. I've heard worse. But why the change?"

"You really want to know?" she asked.

I nodded.

"I'm running away from my ex, who's a cop. He keeps stalking me. I had to get away, so I arranged to have my identity changed. I paid some underground crew for a new passport, and they whipped up a past."

"Where is he now?"

"He's still harassing my mother. I've got restraining orders on him, but they don't do anything."

"Was he physically violent?" I asked, as my jaw tightened. This subject sat uncomfortably with me, knotting my stomach.

She nodded, biting into her fingernail again. "Controlling. Violent. An absolute bastard."

"Then you'll have to stay on. That's if you wish to take up my offer of the cottage."

"I would love that." Her voice broke and she looked up at me like a lost child, her large eyes pooling with tears. "I'm sorry. I hope you aren't angry."

I took out a hankie from my pocket. "Here."

"As soon as I heard of this position, I jumped at the chance for a clean break," she said, wiping her nose.

"That makes sense."

We remained silent. I kept close, drawing in her rose fragrance, which seemed to conjure up warm memories. It was my mother's favorite scent.

Fake identity or not, I wanted her to stay.

"Will you need me to work in the office?" she asked.

I shook my head.

"Oh?" A line formed between her brows. "What will my duties be, then?"

"I want you to model for me."

Her shocked frown made me smile. "Hey, nothing untoward. I mean no nudity or anything sleazy."

"Okay." She kept looking at me puzzled.

"You seem surprised," I said.

"I don't understand why you'd want me as a model when there are so many others who are younger and skinnier."

I shook my head. "I don't want them skinnier. You're perfect for what I want."

"You want to paint me?" She looked bewildered as though I'd asked something preposterous, like asking her to drape herself in a swastika and enter a synagogue.

"Yes. Drawings too." I felt a bubble of excitement surge through me. Scarlet was the first woman in years whom I wanted to paint.

"I did some life drawing modelling when I was at college. But I take it I'll be clothed?"

"Yes. But in costume."

Her face lit up. "Oh really?"

"We'll start tomorrow. Late morning. The light's good then. And then late at night too."

"Late at night?" she asked.

"I prefer the mood," I said.

She rose. "Well, then. I best get my beauty sleep. That morning light can be a bit brutal."

I smiled at her animated expression. "After breakfast, then—say, eleven?"

"Yes." She hovered. "Who'll be looking after you? I mean, aren't you used to having food prepared?"

"Jack will be here. I'll hire a maid. Can you do that for me? I want someone older, who lives in another village. Away from here."

"Sure," she said.

"Tomorrow, then," I said.

# CHAPTER 13

## *Scarlet*

THERE WAS SOMETHING BROKEN in Daniel. The way he'd look past my face, as though lost at sea. His long pauses. The furtive, stolen glances that would burn a hole in my skin. I always sensed his gaze, even with my back turned.

But that was me too. A tangled mass of knots, like a piece of macramé created by someone on acid.

I no longer recognized my former self. Although I wouldn't have described myself as a people person, I could still hold my own in a conversation. But around Daniel, I'd turned into a brainless mouse. Despite that, he felt strangely familiar to me. I couldn't understand that at all. Perhaps I was being swept away by the romance of that forest and our long walks along the cliffs, by our companionable silence and his occasional undressing gazes that made my heart pound.

What the hell did he see in me?

The fact he'd taken me into his confidence—for a man as private as Daniel—was huge. I should have confessed to my assignment. Instead, I'd crawled into a corner and buried my head. I wasn't ready to be tossed away—or, more significantly, to wear his justified contempt and hatred.

And then there was Detective Somers, who kept leaving messages.

• • • • • • • • •

THE FOLLOWING MORNING, I rose early and texted the detective. Within a minute or so, my phone rang. I swallowed tightly and took the call.

"You've been hard to catch this past fortnight," she said.

I walked to the window and stared at a rainy morning, which made the purple flowers glisten brightly. The only nice thing about a grey day was how it intensified colors.

"A lot's been happening. It's been difficult to find the time."

"I've heard about the death of his grandmother."

"He's discovered I'm not Scarlet Black." My voice trembled.

"That's not good."

"My wig shifted. He doesn't know I've been planted here." I puffed out a breath. "About that..."

"You need to stay the course. Information has come to light about the night his wife went missing. We're about to bring him in for more questioning. I need you to be there when that happens to see how he reacts to being summoned."

"You're coming here?" I asked, alarmed at the thought of her visiting Starlington, the incongruity of her presence akin to an earthmover in a manicured garden.

"No. See if he looks ruffled. We're still receiving signals from there. Can you get to his computer?"

My head started to spin. "I want out."

"Now's not the time. Just see what you can see. So far, you haven't given us much."

"I've earned my keep as a hardworking administrator." I squeezed my phone. "There's nothing worth relaying. That's why I want out."

"Your mother's getting round-the-clock surveillance. That will stop."

My face pinched. "You should do your job and get my fucking ex charged."

"He covers his tracks. We've got nothing on him."

I released a frustrated breath. "So, you're saying I scratch your back and you'll scratch mine?"

"Something like that."

I shook my head at how fucked up everything had suddenly become. "I'll see what I can do," I said with resignation. My mother needed protection from that asshole, who I could see pushing his way in and torturing my poor mother for my whereabouts. "I'm coming to London at the end of the week. We can catch up then."

"Let's do that. And Ainsley..."

"Mm..."

"Don't let his movie-star looks cloud your judgment. Try to see him as a potential murderer."

"I'm not a fucking teenager." I felt like smashing something. The fire in my belly bubbled away from frustration.

She chuckled. "No. But you're a woman."

On that note, I closed the call. She had that right. I am a woman. A woman who hadn't experienced the tender touch of a man for years, if ever.

After I called an agency to arrange for a new maid, I went to the kitchen, where Jack stood by the bench chopping onions.

He looked up and his head jerked back. "What have you done with your hair? Or, I should ask why the wig?"

I nearly laughed. "I felt like a change."

"It suits you. I prefer it."

Did my real hair really look like a wig?

"I see you're still employed," he said. "We're the last ones standing."

Scones sat on the counter, and the freshly baked aroma made my stomach rumble.

I grabbed a cup and went to the espresso machine. "Would you like a coffee?"

"No, thanks." He wiped his hands. "Hey, a tearful Holly rang me. She's really upset."

"I bet it came as a blow," I said.

"Who's going to serve and clean?" he asked.

"I've just been in touch with an agency."

"Do you know why?"

I shrugged. "He just wants a fresh start."

"I should feel so lucky, although he's asked me to find another place to live."

"I guess he wants privacy." I hoped Jack wouldn't ask about my new arrangement, which I was still processing.

"I bet he does."

I poured my coffee, but unable to let that comment go, I had to ask, "What do you mean by that."

"After what's happened with his wife. I mean, you know they didn't get on. And he's a very mysterious fellow. Always keeps to himself."

"So do you think he did it?"

He shrugged. "He's always been kind and generous. A little gruff at times for my liking, but you know, he treats the staff well—or did, I should say. But him and Charlie . . . that was something else. She'd smash things. He'd raise his voice."

"From what I've heard, she sounded difficult and spoiled."

"Oh, she was that all right. Rich and snooty. A looker, though."

I'd seen photos. With her large blue eyes and thick blonde hair, Charlotte was beautiful in a manicured way. Her smile, however, never made it to her eyes. She didn't strike me as someone Daniel would be drawn to, particularly after witnessing his coldness toward Camilla, who bore a resemblance to his wife.

I carried my coffee and scone to my about-to-be-former office. Just as I sat down, a knock came to the door and Daniel stepped in.

"Good morning," I said.

He nodded, and as always, he looked as though he'd been up all night with those perpetual dark rings under his eyes.

Dressed in a pale-blue shirt over cream chinos, he wore his clothes with effortless elegance. I could imagine him in baggy, non-descript coveralls and still making it to the cover of Vogue.

"I'm just finishing off my tasks. I had to tally up the wages."

"There's no need for that anymore. I'm outsourcing it to my accountant."

I nodded slowly. I was mystified and somewhat flummoxed over my new role as his model.

"The new maid should be here late this afternoon. She's a forty-year-old woman from Ripley."

"There's a non-disclosure agreement in among your files. Print it up and have her sign it. That will be the last of your administrative tasks." He looked me up and down. "Are you good to start?" He glanced down at his Rolex. "Let's say, in an hour?"

"Yes. Sure." I paused to gather my thoughts. "How will we do this? Will I model all day?"

He shook his head. "No. The occasional morning. Just so I can get used to sketching you. But mainly late at night."

"How late?" I asked.

"From around nine to midnight." His eyes traveled over my body, making my temperature rise.

"I'll be sure to drink lots of coffee," I joked.

His tanned brow lowered. "Is that too late for you?"

I shook my head. "I tend to stay up late reading most nights."

"Some nights you won't be required, depending on my mood. If I'm in the zone, then I'll call on you. Even if it's a Sunday. Art doesn't do nine-to-five."

"I've worked in theatre. I totally get that."

"Good." His attention burned a hole in my face. I could only assume, that as an artist, he was familiarizing himself with my features.

"Can I ask something?" I fumbled about with a pen. "Will the standing arrangement of my employment remain?"

"Whatever you're being paid now, I'll double it."

My eyebrows crashed. "Really? I mean, that seems very generous."

"I can afford it." He turned to leave.

"Will I come up to your studio in an hour?" I asked.

He shook his head. ""We'll work outside—in the back around the rose garden near the pool. I like the light there."

"Should I wear anything specific?"

"No."

As he left with that agile but measured stride, the thought of six-thousand pounds a month brightened my day. I'd almost paid off my credit cards. Life was smiling on me suddenly.

For that kind of wage, I would pose with one leg in the air, or even in the nude.

# CHAPTER 14

MY NEW SPACIOUS, COMFORTABLE cottage came with breathtaking views of undulating, iridescent green meadows from the bedroom, and from the living room, I had a view of the pond and folly, which at night, with those sharp black spires, reminded me of something out of a Grimm fairy tale.

It was late afternoon and I needed to fill the kitchen cupboards with more than just tomato ketchup and condiments, leftovers from when Stephanie lived there, so I decided to head for the village to shop.

After parking my car, I walked to the main street toward the general store.

Ambling along the cobbled path, I peered through a shop window at antique clocks and all kinds of attractive knickknacks. The bottle-green shopfront was as old as the antiques on sale. For someone who had a thing for the past, the historic atmosphere of that sleepy fishing village felt as cozy as a pair of hand-knitted socks.

After buying enough supplies to stock my fridge and cupboards with staples and snacks, I'd promised myself a drink at the local pub before heading back to Starlington.

It had been an interesting first day in my new role as a model. Daniel hardly spoke as he sketched my face for two hours.

But it was nice anyway. Just being out there in that stunning perfumed garden left me feeling lightheaded. Only I imagined it wasn't the flowers to blame. Daniel Love had a drugging effect, especially as I watched him with that concentrated expression he wore while drawing. He used his left hand, which, as a left-hander, I appreciated—one of those silly things that I imagined had something to do with us being in the minority.

Sitting outside by a pretty duck pond, I sipped on my beer and pulled out a pack of cigarettes. Refusing to allow guilt to rob me of pleasure, I quashed my inner nag.

As I indulged in the late afternoon sun's radiance, I heard my name from behind.

I turned and found Stephanie and Randall smiling at me.

I just wanted to scrunch up into a tiny ball and roll away, but instead, I channeled my sunniest smile and said, "Hey, there."

Stephanie shook her head. "What's with the hair?"

I touched it and grinned sheepishly. "I decided on a change. I've got this thing for wigs."

Her eyebrows drew in. She wasn't buying it. "It suits you." She turned to Randall, who kept gawking at me. I sensed his attraction. He always went out of his way to chat with me.

"So has he given you your marching orders?" Stephanie asked, taking a seat.

"Nope. But I'm not required in the office."

She looked at Randall, then back at me. "Really?"

I nodded. "He wants me to model for him."

Stephanie's mouth fell open. "You're kidding. Seriously? And you're going to do it? Is that why you've changed your hair?"

"Uh-huh. We had our first session today. Just drawings of my face. I think I remind him of someone."

"With that hair, you're a young version of Georgina," Randall said, looking from me to Stephanie, who nodded in agreement.

A duck waddled our way and I tossed it one of my crisps.

Now, that really piqued my interest. Did that explain his lingering gazes? "Who's Georgina?"

"Georgina Preston. She used to visit often. Rumor had it she broke his heart." Stephanie munched on a crisp. "Elizabeth hated her, so she'd arrive late at night, sometimes as late as midnight, and she'd sneak out in the morning."

"Was this while he was married?"

"No way. But she still visited at times, even recently, though she didn't stay. They've had a falling out, I think."

"So was Georgina his lover as well as his model?" Feeling giddy, I was suddenly deluged by curiosity.

"She was. But she was old enough to be his mother," Randall said.

"How much older?" I asked, taking a sip of my beer.

"Fifteen, eighteen years older, I think. Rumor has it . . ."—Stephanie leaned in close—"that he got with her when he was a teenager. She was married. She still is, I think."

"Right. And I look like her?"

"You're a prettier version," Randall said with a smile. I side-glanced Stephanie and noticed her face turning stony.

"Did Charlotte know about her?" I asked Stephanie, ignoring her sudden coolness.

"She did. They hated each other."

"Is that why Daniel's had a falling out with this Georgina?"

She shrugged. "Not sure. He's changed a lot after he returned from France, and after Charlie disappeared."

Randall nodded in agreement. "He's definitely changed. Sacking Stephanie was a low act."

I touched Stephanie's hand. "Are you going to be okay?" I didn't have the heart to tell her I'd moved into the cottage, but Randall would tell her, no doubt.

"I'm staying with my sister for now." She looked at Randall. I could see they were together, even though I didn't like the way Randall kept ogling.

"Is there anything I can do?" I asked.

"No. It's all good. It came as a shock, but at least I can focus on my online business now. And he was pretty generous with my redundancy package."

"Well, that's good. If you need a hand with anything, let me know," I said.

She rose and looked at Randall, who continued gawking at me and tapped his arm.

"We'll stay in touch," I said, giving her a hug. Her body seemed rigid.

I hated how suddenly I'd become the enemy through no fault of my own.

• • • • • • • • • •

I TOOK TENTATIVE STEPS up a windy, wrought iron staircase to Daniel's studio. Ethereal piano music, a pleasant change from heavy metal, became louder the closer I got.

Despite the open door, I knocked before entering.

A fire raged in a big open fireplace flanked by carved goddesses. The high domed ceiling and encircling windows made the room appear larger than it actually was.

Daniel stepped out from behind his easel and instantly took my breath away. His white, paint-splattered shirt with the buttons half undone exposed part of his manly chest. Barefooted in torn jeans, he could have been a model. But he was too intense for that.

He pointed to a rack of gowns. "I'd like you in green."

My jaw dropped at the labels: Oscar de la Renta, Givenchy, Dior.

"These are exquisite," I said, sliding my hand down a slinky gown.

He stood so close; I could smell his shampoo. And my nipples hardened. I needed to get a grip. I'd never been affected like this before. If only I could shut down my feminine instincts. All I needed was a blindfold and a nose plug. Ridiculous, really.

He selected a green gown with a low-cut back, handed it to me, and pointed to an ornate Art Nouveau screen.

"You can get changed there."

Treating it as a precious thing, I held the green gown that I would have joined a peace mission in the Gaza Strip to wear.

Then reality hit me: With those spaghetti straps, my bra straps would show. Not nice.

"I might need to go and get something to wear underneath."

He shook his head. "Not necessary. Just the gown."

"Excuse me?"

"Just the gown. Nothing else." He picked up a palette and mixed paints with a metal implement.

The dress was a twelve. My size. Coincidence?

I'd paraded in much less, and I'd also modelled nude in my younger days. But I wasn't a forty-year-old woman with large tits and a big ass. At least my waist was still indented. That was a small mercy.

I changed into the slinky dress and studied my reflection in a cheval mirror. The back was cut to just above my butt and the skirt cascaded into a tulip shape. The silk against my naked flesh felt as soft as baby's skin.

I removed my sneakers and stepped away from the screen. "Where would you like me?"

He studied me so intently, my face burned. I'd never blushed so much in my life.

He pointed to a gold brocade armchair.

"I'd like you there," he said.

I sat down and saw myself in one of the many mirrors. The rich bottle-green fabric against the golden satin upholstery made for a luscious composition.

Daniel moved a couple of lamps close to me, pausing every now and then to study the effect.

"Where do you want my feet?" I asked. As they were bare, I tucked them under the draping silk.

Approaching me again, he stood so close I could see his nipple through his half-unbuttoned shirt, and my skin puckered—not because of the room's temperature. I invited mundane thoughts, like what I was going to have for breakfast. Anything but feeling a man inside of me.

As his gaze toured up and down my body, it was like his eyes had turned into fingers gliding over my prickling skin.

He lifted my dress so that my feet and calves were exposed. Lambasting myself for not shaving my legs, I prayed he wouldn't notice dark regrowth.

Lost in his own world, I left him to arrange my dress. My breath hitched when his hand reached over to my strap and slunk it off my shoulder, leaving a tingle in its wake.

I swallowed tightly as I crossed my arms to hide my out-of-control nipples.

"Relax your arms," he commanded. His brow creased and in serious mode. His mode. That fleshy mouth rarely curled.

I looked outside the window at the mesmerizing view of the starlit night, to steady my breath.

"Try to relax a little more. You're an actress."

I'd never played this kind of role, where sexual tension was so thick, I needed a shower.

He went over to a gold filigree box and removed a diamond necklace.

Dangling from his large hand, the sparkling jewels danced in the light as he handed it to me.

"Oh . . . how beautiful," I said, ogling the dazzling necklace.

He studied me. "Yes."

Did he mean the necklace? His eyes burned into mine when he spoke.

He clasped it on and the touch of his fingers on my neck shot a sizzling thrill through me.

"Can you tie your hair up?" he asked.

"Of course. Only I don't have a clip."

He passed me a box and flipped it open. An emerald-rhinestone-encrusted slide caught my eye and I selected it.

"Good choice," he said.

I twirled my hair into a topknot and clipped it in place with strands cascading over my shoulder. I peered up at him for his approval and he nodded.

I prayed my clammy armpits wouldn't stain the Givenchy. I'd never worn designer anything in my life. But the way that dress caressed my skin was almost as sexy as a man's touch.

"Relax." He studied me closely and then his eyes returned to my face. "Am I making you nervous?"

I released a trapped breath. "A little. But I'll be fine." I pulled a smile and told myself to get a grip. I'd been on stage with less clothes. I'd been on stage with less clothes, but never around an eccentric, tall, dark, and handsome recluse.

"Mold your body into the chair," he instructed.

I summoned the image of a languid model, imagining myself in a late nineteenth-century Parisian studio, and shifted into position. He adjusted my dress again exposing my calf. This time, I lowered my strap.

A glimmer of a smile came and went, as though he acknowledged my fear of his closeness. "That's perfect. Stay just as you are." He squinted his eyes, studying me again.

We remained in silence as he concentrated on his work. He'd paused at times and held up his finger to size me up.

After two hours, with barely a word spoken, he said, "That will be all for now. You can change."

I unclipped the glittering necklace and placed it back in the filigree container. Covered in red velvet, that box contained all kinds of eye-popping pieces. "How exquisite," I uttered, staring wide-eyed at jewelry encrusted in rubies, sapphires, and diamonds.

"They belonged to my mother," he said, before returning his attention to his work.

I changed back into my leggings and sweater, and when I stepped away from the screen, he asked, "Can I offer you a drink?"

I smiled. "Sure. If you're having one."

He ambled leisurely to a cluttered shelf of statuettes, vases and curios and lifted a crystal decanter. "It will have to be neat, I'm afraid."

"Fine." My nerves were so jaded, I would have drunk meths.

He poured our drinks, then offered me a cigarette. After lighting it, he opened bevelled-glass double doors and stepped onto a wrought-iron-fenced balcony.

"Do you paint every night?" I asked, joining him.

"It depends on my mood. Sometimes, especially when I can't sleep, I'll sketch." His mouth lifted at one end. "For me, emotion dictates creative output."

"Aren't the two inseparable?"

He shrugged. "Depends. When I studied art, we'd spend hours drawing bowls of fruit, hands and feet, that kind of thing. It was purely technical and required little or no feeling."

I nodded slowly. "An artist must practice. One can't create a masterpiece without skill."

He drew on his cigarette while staring up at the sky. "I don't know about that. Skill can be a ball and chain. Picasso spent half his life learning his craft only to spend the other half unlearning it so he could draw like a child."

I dragged on my cigarette while reflecting on his comment. "I believe our inner child lives within our deep spirit. The more complicated and convoluted our lives become, the more hidden it becomes. Art, I think, opens up a conduit for us to find our inner child, or free spirit, if you like."

After a period of silence, he asked, "And how close are you to your inner child?"

"She's buried deep." I shrugged. "I don't get much access to her these days. I haven't been creative for a long time."

His brows gathered as he studied me closely. "You're not drawn to perform anymore?"

I shook my head. "I audition every now and then for TV shows, but not much happens. I've moved on. I'd like to write. One day. I've become a little unanchored."

"From the little you've told me, being in an abusive marriage wouldn't have helped." His mouth lifted at one end. "If I didn't paint, I think I'd lose my mind."

His sober tone belied the magnitude of that statement.

I finished my drink and went back inside.

"Another?" he asked, then stepped back inside too and poured himself half a glass.

"Um . . . perhaps I should go." I wanted another drink. That room had mesmerized me. Or was it the beautiful, enigmatic man before me?

"Stay." His deep resonant command almost pushed me back down onto the armchair. "Have another." He gestured for my glass, and I passed it to him.

"Why not." I smiled.

"So Scarlet, or would you prefer Ainsley?" he asked, passing me my drink.

"Scarlet feels right. I want to bury Ainsley. Along with the last five years." I chuckled grimly.

He held my gaze for a moment, as though trying to read into my words. I could almost see the questions forming. "It suits you," he said at last. You strike me as more of a Scarlet than an Ainsley."

He had that right. I no longer related to that former shadow of me.

I looked over at the easel where he'd been working. "Do you mind if I see what you're working on?"

"I prefer to keep my art private. For my eyes only."

"But that seems so unfair."

"Unfair to whom?" he asked, tilting his head.

"But don't you want to share it? Art offers a deep philosophical, and at times emotional, dialogue between the creator and their audience."

"I'm happy to share money, food, drinks, and cigarettes, but not my emotions—or my art, for that matter. That's private. In any case, why should I make a public display of my neurosis?"

"Neurosis?" I frowned. "I'd hardly consider you neurotic."

"You don't know me."

I couldn't deny that.

"But that's the thing," I argued. "By not expressing one's emotions, one becomes neurotic."

He shook his head. "I disagree. Over-sharing has become fashionable. It's turned some of us into reluctant counsellors."

I shrugged. "But humans have always discussed their feelings. That's what makes us heal."

"I understand that having a shoulder to cry on occasionally is something real and necessary, but one should use that sparingly."

"But if we bottle our feelings, deep scars start to fester."

"I don't bottle my feelings. I just don't share them." His mouth curled slightly as he lounged back in a burgundy velvet armchair, under the glow of a leadlight lamp. I would have loved a photo. If anyone deserved a portrait it was Daniel Love.

"I suppose creating art in itself is a form of therapy," I said.

He nodded wistfully. "Sometimes it is. Sometimes it frustrates the hell out of me. And sometimes it alarms me."

"It alarms you?" I asked.

"Tell me, what have you heard about me?" he asked.

That jarred me. I was still lost at sea from his last comment. "Um . . . that you're a fair but mysterious man. That . . ." I considered my words carefully.

"That I murdered my wife?" he asked.

"Did you?" I asked.

He poured himself another drink and took a sip. "What do you think? Do you think I'm capable of murder?"

I stared at the window to hide my face so that he wouldn't uncover my secret. "No."

"But everyone's capable of murder," he said.

Funny, that was exactly what the detective had said.

"I don't believe you did it." I turned to look at him in the eyes. "However, you don't strike me as a grieving widower."

"I am in mourning. For my grandmother."

"And your wife? You're not sad about her absence?"

He shook his head. "I'm sad that she's probably lying at the bottom of the ocean. But I don't miss her."

"You're convinced she drowned, then?" I asked carefully while a cold finger touched my soul. He seemed so unaffected by that grim statement.

"I don't know what happened."

"Why did you marry her, if you don't mind me asking?"

"She faked a pregnancy." He turned away. "I'm tired. Let's leave it there for tonight."

He followed me to the door. "Tomorrow night, same time."

Still processing his last comment, it took me a moment to answer. "Um... you won't be needing me in the morning?"

"No. I have to go to London. I'll be back later."

Was that a glint of vulnerability in his eyes?

Daniel Love confused me. He was like a seething volcano, about to erupt at any moment, but his reserved, bordering on proud, nature acted like a stopper.

I walked away with his scent rushing through me, as though injected into me, and his stormy eyes burning before me, my heart pounding like I'd collided with a life-changing force—or a force of nature.

# CHAPTER 15

*Daniel*

I ENTERED THE GLASS building, finding sharp edges everywhere and nowhere to hide. People's amplified voices and footsteps collided against the faux-marble surface, while cheap perfume, plastic, and aftershave—a nauseating cocktail—thickened the air. I wanted to run away. But I had to be there.

I rode the dizzying escalator up to the elevators and hesitated before a glass chamber—an acrophobic's nightmare. While I could manage teetering over the edge of a precipitous cliff with the calmness of a monk, my blood pressure rose as soon as I stepped into that capsule.

I arrived at the tenth floor and announced my arrival. Within a few moments, the detective lumbered over and beckoned for me to follow her.

"I thought we'd have to come and bring you in ourselves," she said.

"I'm not accused of anything." I held her steely stare. "I've been occupied. I'm here now." I took a seat in the bland, windowless room that threatened to choke me.

I'd been there before. Too many times. And in my nightmares too. Always the same questions designed to trip me up. Poker, my game of choice, had trained me well. Show nothing, and the game's yours to manipulate.

She turned on her recording device and opened her file.

"It's been brought to my attention by one of your former staff members that the day before you left for Antibes with Charlotte, she overheard a heated discussion between you and your wife."

"And?" I asked, leaning back on my chair.

"I'm told you asked for a divorce. Your wife responded, and I quote, 'Bring it on. I'll take everything.'"

"So?" I shrugged. "Isn't that a standard disgruntled partner's response?"

"Tell me about your marriage."

I took a deep breath. "We were married two and a half years ago. You know all of this."

"Why did you marry her? Did you love her?"

"Probably not." I looked up and her eyes widened slightly. "Not all marriages are based on love."

"So you married her because of her breeding?"

"I'm not a snob, or a social climber. I don't need to be." I raised an eyebrow. "I married her because she told me she was pregnant."

Her eyebrows gathered. "You never mentioned that before."

"You didn't ask." I sat back again and stretched my legs. The chair was hard and cold. For someone accustomed to the finer things in life, that dank room and its grey neutrality robbed me of air.

"You must have carried a lot of resentment for being lied to."

I nodded. "I'm only human. Most people would."

"Why didn't you divorce her when you discovered she'd faked her pregnancy?"

"Because I'd only just discovered that recently." I shifted again. And of course, she noticed.

"When and how did you discover that?" she asked.

"When I got back from Antibes, her psychologist called me about her missed appointments. And when I mentioned that Charlie was missing and she'd spiraled after the miscarriage, he asked to see me, and revealed she was never pregnant."

"Missed appointments?" she asked.

"Charlie had a split personality disorder."

"So that's why she was seeing a psychologist?"

"Yes. Mainly for an eating disorder. She'd been bulimic since she was a teenager. You might need to get that information from her family. She didn't really share those deeper issues."

She frowned. "You weren't close?"

I shook my head.

She kept eyeballing me. Looking for something. I'd had that before. Somehow, they thought they could understand me by staring, get to know me. Fat chance of that. I didn't even know me.

"Split personality? In what way?" she asked.

"There was shallow Charlotte—society girl, hooked on social media, shopaholic. And then there was angry, petulant Charlie, who drank too much and fucked around."

"So she was conducting extra marital affairs?" she asked.

"I'm not sure if it was with the same men."

"Did you catch her?"

"No. But she'd stay away for weekends in London, where she was spotted. She didn't even hide it. I'm told she had a thing for guys born on the wrong side of town."

"Did you have a sexual relationship with her?"

"Occasionally," I lied.

Why should I talk about my sex life with this smelly detective? I wasn't about to admit that after learning of Charlie's rampant cheating, my dick barely moved around her.

"Your staff member told me that Charlotte was having an affair with your security guard, Tyson Drill."

I nodded. "That's old news."

"And it didn't make you angry?"

"Sure. That's why I demanded a divorce."

"What was her excuse for staying in the marriage?"

"She wanted to patch things up. It was more a charade—a front to keep her family happy."

"Why did she have to do that?"

"She would come into her own wealth at twenty-eight on the proviso that she was in a stable marriage."

"She was twenty-nine when she disappeared."

I nodded.

She looked at me square in the face and frowned. "What I don't understand is why she wanted to remain in what is sounding like a loveless marriage."

"For the comforts. I'm a very rich man."

"Yes, but she came into her own wealth."

"A meager ten million."

"Meager?"

I grinned at her mocking scowl. "That wouldn't last her a year."

"Then, you had a lot to lose from a divorce. Financially."

"I didn't care about that. I wanted out."

"So why didn't you leave her?"

Great question.

"Out of respect for my grandmother. She made me promise her I'd stay the course for at least five years. Put on a public front to keep the media off our backs."

"That's right, your father murdered your mother. Could she have been worried about the media speculation surrounding that tragic history resurfacing? Wife-bashing is known to be passed down in the genes."

Blood rage pushed me off my chair. "What the fuck's that got to do with it? I don't like your fucking tone. I'm leaving now. Next time, call my lawyer."

I stormed out, disturbed beyond reason.

Just as I left that ugly building and stood on the pavement, looking for the nearest bar, I received a call from a PI I'd recently hired.

"Have you got time to drop in?" he asked.

I took a deep breath. "Sure. I'll be there in half an hour."

• • • • • • • • • •

I SAT IN THE cluttered, cracked-wall office, imagining I was in a scene of a Humphrey Bogart movie. Clutching a paper cup, I sipped on lukewarm coffee while peering at the bottle of cheap scotch on the dusty shelf. Reading my mind, the middle-aged PI rose from his desk and grabbed hold of the bottle.

"Can I offer you a hit?" he asked.

In response to my nod, he poured some into a glass and handed it to me.

My spirit had yet to thaw after that grisly detective's cheap shots.

"What have you got for me?" The scotch scraped my throat like a razorblade. I made a mental note to gift him some quality single malt next time.

"Her name's Ainsley Alcott. She recently moved back to her mother's in West Ham. A rundown two-story home. Her father was a petty thief, a conman, and a gambler." He looked up from his notes. "Your regular good guy." His irony-infested chuckle grated.

"What else?"

"She trained as an actress. Performed in amateur theatre before taking on bit parts on stage and television. All the details are in this file." He pushed the manila folder toward me. "She did well at college. Passed with distinction in literature. She seems like a bright woman who married an asshole cop."

I sat up. Now we were getting to the important details. "What's his story?"

"He's stalking her. I imagine that's why she changed her identity. She wouldn't be the first." He paused and looked up at me over his glasses.

"What else have you got on him?" I asked.

"He's a detective on the take, or so rumor has it. He's best buddies with the chief. His old man was also a cop and a wife beater." He snorted. "And it seems this dick is following in dad's shoes." He shook his head. "Don't they all?"

I thought of my meeting with Detective Somers and her gut-curdling theory that violent genes were passed down from parent to child.

"That's a simplistic view." I took the folder and rose. "Keep digging."

He stared at me for a moment and nodded. "Will do."

There was nothing new in what I'd learned, just a little added detail to what Scarlet had already revealed.

As I walked to my car, I heard my name and when I turned, I saw a familiar smiling face. "Jerry."

He hugged me.

We went to art college together. A good friend. One of very few.

"I've been calling you," he said. "How have you been?"

"I've been better."

His eyes reflected sympathy. "What are you doing now? Let's grab a drink somewhere."

I stared down at my watch. Despite wanting to leave the city, I nodded. "Sure. Why not?"

We entered a bar tucked away in a laneway just off Trafalgar Square, ordered a couple of beers, and sat in a quiet corner.

"Any news of Charlie?" he asked.

I shook my head.

"What happened? I mean, I've read the reports." He smiled apologetically. "You must be sick of that question."

He got that right. "She was seriously drunk."

"That's unsurprising for Charlie." Jerry knew my wife well enough. She hated him because he wasn't from money. And he could never understand why I married her—apart from that small detail of her faking her pregnancy. As the only person I could openly talk to, Jerry had always been there for me, even after college.

I owed him my life.

"You haven't been returning my calls. I haven't spoken to you in six months," he said.

"I'm sorry." I rubbed my neck. "I've been living in a cave. You know me."

"I do. That's why you should talk to me. Remember last time?"

How could I forget?

"My grandmother died."

His face pinched. "Why didn't you tell me? I would've gone to the funeral."

"I'm sorry." I stared down at my drink. "I couldn't speak for days after she died. She was all I had."

"You've got me." He touched my hand and a lump formed in my throat.

"Thanks. And look, not even Georgie knew about it."

"Oh, really? You didn't tell her?" His eyebrows flung up.

"We're not as close as we used to be."

"You're not sleeping together, you mean?"

"That ended ages ago. I didn't cheat on Charlie."

"Nobody would have blamed you if you had," he said.

"Despite my cynical views on marriage, I believe in upholding my end of the bargain."

"You're loyal to a fault," he said, toying with his glass.

"Loyalty civilizes us. Without it, we end up like savages."

He smiled. "It's good to see you." He looked out the window at a pretty woman walking by. "So back to the yacht incident. Why were you both even there? I thought you'd decided to live separate lives."

I puffed out a breath. "Charlie followed me to Antibes. I wanted to be alone. She was really out of control. Her coke habit had gotten worse. I begged her for a divorce, but she wanted to patch things up, so she followed me to France. Once we were there, Charlie suggested we spend a week on the yacht. I really didn't feel like it. But she begged me."

I pictured her pinning me in the bedroom and running her hand over my dick, suggesting we have a dirty weekend. By that stage in our relationship, she repelled me. But I went along with it, hoping we could broker a fair split away from drugs. She was impossible when hammered on alcohol, and coke made her aggressive and nasty.

"The conditions were perfect, so I agreed."

"Were you able to move on after that drug lord?"

I nearly laughed at his description of Charlotte hooking up with her dealer. "She insisted she'd left him and that she wanted to make the marriage work. I just wanted a divorce."

"I'm not surprised. I would have fucked her off ages ago. But she had that miscarriage. You're a good guy."

"She faked it," I said soberly.

His eyes widened. "You're fucking kidding me? Hell, man."

I shrugged. I'd had enough of feeling bitter.

"So what happened that night?"

"I just don't fucking remember." I looked down at my fingers. That was the first time I'd shared that. I hadn't even told my grandmother, for fear that she'd think I'd become my father. "I must have gotten seriously drunk, which doesn't make sense."

"Did you hit the bottle?" he asked.

"No more than I normally drink." I released a tight breath. Opening up about that weekend was like piercing a festering boil.

After a long pause, he asked, "Are there cameras on the yacht?"

"They weren't working."

"Did someone tamper with them?" He frowned.

"Great question. That's why the cops are up my ass."

"So they're looking at this as premeditated?"

"It's a nightmare." I ran my fingers through my hair.

He shook his head. "I've never seen you drunk. You hold your liquor better than anyone else I know. You've got the liver of a Welshman."

I sniffed.

"So you don't remember passing out?" he asked.

"Nope. All I remember was that it was late evening, I'd had a few drinks, and next thing I knew, it was morning and I was in bed."

"Do the cops know that?"

Biting my cheek, I shook my head.

"I'm here for you. You know that, don't you?"

"I know." I smiled tightly. "How's Archie?" I asked after Jerry's five-year-old autistic son.

"He's doing well." He shook his head, wearing a look of relief. "I can't thank you enough."

"How's the new school?" I'd enrolled the boy in junior and senior schooling and paid for it.

"Oh man, it's a huge help. A game changer. You got all my emails and love letters?" he asked with a cheesy smile.

"I did. It's the least I can do. And I'm fucking rich. If I can't use my money to help friends then what's the point?" I opened out my hands. "So what are you working on?"

"I've just scored a commission for a mural close to home. At a rundown, drug-riddled public estate housing that society's forgotten." He sniffed. "Although the place should be condemned, it offers an interesting challenge. All those grey walls lend themselves to color. And it's a year-long commission."

"That's brilliant news."

"I'm also seeing a new girl," he said.

"Girl?"

"She's my age." He chuckled. "Melanie's great. And she's amazing with Archie."

"That's nice," I said, feeling the first bit of warmth that day.

"What about you? What was her name? She was all over you like a rash at your thirtieth. They all are." He grinned.

"Camilla. I'm not that desperate, to be honest."

"She's gorgeous."

"As is, or was, Charlie." A heavy weight fell on my shoulders again. My stomach twisted in knots at just the mention of my wife.

"But what's wrong with a little taste?" He raised his eyebrows.

"My libido's not that hungry." An image of Scarlet in the green gown came to mind and sent blood charging to my dick.

"I need to get back. I'm working with a model at the moment."

"Oh?" His eyes sparked up. "How's that going?"

"We've only just started, but I'm inspired."

"When are you going to exhibit?"

"Never."

"You won't even let me have a peek?" He tilted his head with a teasing smile.

"Maybe one day."

"Money has robbed the world of a brilliant artist. See, if you were struggling like me you'd have to show."

"I paint because my soul demands it," I said. "Not for money and certainly not for impossible-to-please critics or public adulation."

"Where were you when they were handing out that narcissism gene?"

"Admiring my reflection," I quipped.

He laughed. "But jokes aside, I admire your lack of ego."

"I'm far from perfect. And I do have an ego. It's just that pride takes the center stage with me."

"But aren't they related? Ego and pride."

"They can be. It's getting the right balance of both. A self-bloated person acts without thinking. Egomaniacs see themselves as infallible. Pride, on the other hand, makes one consider each step carefully, to avoid looking like a clown."

"But that's it. You're just scared of being judged, Daniel. You always have been."

"It's not fear. I just don't crave the attention." I stared down at my naked fingers. I'd removed my wedding ring. That slovenly cop had noticed. Although she might have forgotten to comb her hair, she was still eagle-eyed.

"Art doesn't have to be judged," he pressed.

"That's the idealist talking again." I grinned at my friend's romantic take on life. "Art is currency, which means it's up for evaluation."

"Just because you don't sell doesn't mean you can't show," he argued.

I swallowed the last of my beer and rose. "As much as we could keep going on this subject, I really must go."

Jerry followed me out and gave me a hug. "It's great to see you. I'm hosting a dinner party soon. You'll have to come."

"I'd like that." I smiled and headed back to my car.

# CHAPTER 16

## *Scarlet*

I CLOSED THE CALL and sighed with frustration. Detective Somers had again grilled me about Daniel. How was I to pick his brain with that closed, hard-to-navigate manner of his? Again, I asked to be removed from our arrangement, but she reminded me of my ex and how he'd been spotted loitering around my mother's house.

Deciding on a walk, I took the path to the wood. Breathing in moist earthy scents, I let go of my nagging issues.

Randall walked toward me carrying a fishing rod. It was the first time I'd seen him since that afternoon at the pub.

"Hey there," he said with a bright smile.

"You're off fishing, I see."

"I like to every now and then."

I pointed at his six pack. "Looks like you're making a night of it."

"There's a moon and it's sure to be a nice night. Want to come along?"

I shook my head. "Thanks. I've got a few things I need to do."

Like model for my alluring but strange boss in a designer gown and a diamond necklace that cost enough to feed half of the world's needy.

Sounds of rustling made me look over my shoulder.

He smiled. "Probably a fox. Wiching Wood's full of them."

"I didn't realize it was called that," I said.

"This wood is rich in folklore. Witches still perform rituals here. They summon up the dead and perform all kinds of magic."

"That's fascinating and scary at the same time," I said.

"So how are you settling into the cottage?" he asked.

"It's comfy." I kept it brief, in consideration of its former occupant. "How's Stephanie?"

"I haven't seen her." He shrugged.

"Oh... I thought you might've been dating."

"It didn't really work. We're different in many ways." He tilted his head. "Does that mean you'll have a drink sometime?"

Randall had the chiseled, healthy features of someone who worked the land. He had a strong body, and his face, although weathered, had a handsome appeal, especially his nice, smiling blue eyes.

"Let's do that," I said.

"How's tomorrow sound?"

I wondered about my arrangement with Daniel. "Let me get back to you."

"Okay, then I might drop in tomorrow to get your answer."

"Sure." I returned a smile.

"Better move on. The witching hour's arriving." He grinned. "You don't want to be in here when the dark sets in."

I frowned. "Why?"

"Strange things happen. Voices are heard. The locals have sworn it's haunted with ghosts."

A shiver ran through me. "I heard the folly is haunted."

"Oh, that's for sure. Love Senior murdered his wife there. No one is allowed to talk about it. The last person who did was given his marching orders."

"Daniel's father?" That explained his dark moods.

"That's right—although it didn't come from me."

"When?" I asked.

"I believe Daniel was only a teenager. Apparently, his father had a thing for young maids." He arched an eyebrow. "He was bonking one of them and the wife found them. A fight broke out and she fell to the ground, hit her head, and died."

"Oh my God, that's terrible," I said.

"Don't say a word, whatever you do."

I nodded. "Sure. I'll remain tight-lipped."

Despite itching curiosity to learn what happened to Daniel's father, I took my leave and drifted off, disturbed by what I'd heard. Daniel's missing wife popped into my thoughts. Had history repeated itself?

His own brutal family history helped explain that dark glint in his eyes after I spoke of my violent husband.

With a medley of dramatic scenarios playing in my head, I entered my cottage, where I noticed a message on my phone. It was from Daniel, and my heart skipped a beat.

The message read: Same time. Upstairs, tonight. Daniel.

Two hours later, I was behind the screen removing all my underwear and slipping into the slinky green gown.

Crossing my arms, I stepped out. "Will you want my hair up or down?"

"Leave it down," he said, studying my face closely, making my cheeks flush.

Would these visceral reactions ever stop?

Remaining silent, he turned on the gas log fire. He seemed withdrawn. More so than usual.

Always sensitive to his mood, I remained respectfully quiet. Our dynamic revolved around him leading the conversation. And now, knowing what I'd just learned of his tragic history, Daniel's remoteness made sense.

He passed me the diamond necklace. I was dying to know why he'd chosen a socialite theme. At least I wasn't posing nude, even if there was little between that fine silk and my skin.

Like before, he wore the same white, paint-splattered shirt hanging loose over ripped, faded jeans and bare feet.

I lowered my strap. The thought of his hands on my skin made me jumpy. My flesh was prickly enough from his penetrating gaze roaming over my face and body.

He shook his head. "No. Leave it up."

"Oh? You're doing a new painting?"

He nodded without moving his eyes from his easel. His mood had become too dark for me to navigate. Or was that just an artist at work in deep concentration?

One silent hour into the session, he moved away from his easel and said, "That will be all."

"Um . . . will you be needing me tomorrow evening—with it being Saturday?' I asked.

He looked at me and held my gaze for what seemed a lifetime. He was so handsome I had to look away. His beauty blinded me like the sun, even though he was more like the moon.

"I'm not sure."

"It's just that Randall suggested we have a drink."

"The gardener?" His eyebrows drew in. "You're going out with him?"

I bit my lip. An urge to giggle gripped me, but I composed myself. At least his expression had shifted from brooding tautness to one of surprise. "Not a date, as such. Just a few drinks."

He studied me further, as though trying to understand me. I sure as hell was trying to understand him. Was he interested in me? Or was it something else?

"If you prefer, I can stay and model."

He shook his head. "No. It's a weekend. I forgot what day it was."

"Okay, then."

He turned away without another word.

After I changed, I passed him the diamond necklace and our fingers brushed. I wondered if the electricity had reached him too because I walked away with the thrill of that touch searing through me.

• • • • ● • ● • • •

HAVING ARRANGED TO MEET Randall at the Black Swan, the pub I'd visited with Stephanie, I found him at the bar sharing a laugh with the barmaid. I could tell by that cheeky sparkle in his eyes he was chatting her up. Something told me that Randall was the village Lothario.

A good enough reason to keep this platonic. I wasn't in the mood to set tongues wagging. Gossip travelled fast in those tight-knit communities.

"Hey," I said, catching his attention.

He turned and smiled. "Oh, there you are, I thought you were going to stand me up."

"Sorry. My Uber had trouble finding me."

"You're looking lovely, as usual," he said, his gaze traveling up and down my body. "So, what can I get you?"

"Just a beer." I smiled.

He regarded the blonde barmaid. "My kind of date." She giggled back.

At least he had her to fall back on, I told myself. I hated the expectation that came with dating since I was only there to find out all I could about Daniel.

# CHAPTER 17

FEELING TIPSY, I STEPPED out onto the street with Randall, who was trying to convince me to stay. I knew if I did, I'd get drunker. With a tendency to act impulsively when over the limit, I turned him down gently. The last thing I needed was that bad choice leading to teeth-clenching regret the morning after. Not that Randall was a bad person, but he wasn't my type, despite his attractive face and strong body.

I'd learned the hard way. All those random hook-ups from my wild, younger days. The last one I ended up marrying and now I was in hiding.

Glancing down at my watch, I noticed it was ten o'clock. As I looked for a cab, I noticed Daniel stepping out of a bookshop.

Persistent Randall remained close. "We could go dancing, if you'd like. The night's still young."

"I'm not really in the mood." I watched Daniel heading in our direction.

"Oh, look at that," Randall said. "It's the boss. I never see him down this way, especially at this hour."

That took me aback. "And he's visiting a bookshop. At this hour?"

"That's Crowley's shop, which I'm told Mr. Love pays for."

"Really?"

Randall smiled at my shocked expression. "He's close to Crowley's grandmother, Oleander Sage. She was in thick with Daniel's mother."

"How odd that the bookshop's still open at this hour."

"It's an odd bookshop in general. You won't find P.D. James or John Grisham in there." He laughed.

"Oh, more literature, I suppose." That had me admiring Daniel Love a little more for spending his Saturday night around books.

"Maybe not. The shop's called Esoterica and sells nothing but hocus-pocus stuff."

"Oh, it's a mystical bookshop."

"Yep. A place for weirdos to hang out." He chuckled.

"It seems to suit this place," I said, watching Daniel heading our way with that elegant, assured stride.

My heart picked up its pace the closer he got. Curious as to whether he'd acknowledge me, I stared straight at him.

He couldn't exactly not see me since his eyes found mine and remained staring. He had this uncanny ability to make my face burn. I turned to Randall. "I'm sorry. But I really do want to go home."

He shrugged. "Oh well. I might stay around for a while."

"Why don't you do that?" I tipped my head. "I can get back easily enough."

Daniel stopped walking, and I looked up at him. He seemed to tower over me. Or was it that his magnetic presence added inches?

"Good evening," I said with a surprised smile.

He regarded Randall and nodded.

"Mr. Love. It's unusual to see you out."

"I felt like a walk," he said, returning his attention to me.

I turned to Randall. "I'm off, then. Thanks for the drink."

Randall saluted us both and shuffled back in. Knowing he had the barmaid to chat up made me feel better about ending the night early.

We shared little in common, other than working for an intriguing man. And between flirtatious Randall's innuendos, I was able to learn more about Daniel's father, who died of a heart attack. The fact he was found half-naked in Wiching Wood generated all kinds of salacious speculation, orchestrating an avalanche of conspiracies since he died just before his murder trial.

Was it a vendetta? Or had he just fucked his brains out at a cost to his ticker? That was one discussion I would have loved to have continued, but then Randall looked into my eyes and asked about my romantic history. The night spiraled down from there.

Daniel cut a handsome figure in his casual but classy look, dressed in fitted slacks and a blue blazer.

"You're heading back?" he asked.

"I thought I might, but then I noticed that bookshop." I couldn't resist. I needed to know more about the black shopfront, seeing that Daniel was its benefactor.

"It's not a normal bookstore, as such."

"Oh really?" I feigned surprise.

"It sells tarot cards and esoteric books," he said.

"I wouldn't have thought of you as someone into the occult."

His lips twitched into a hint of a smile. "Crowley's a friend. I pop in occasionally to see him."

"Is there a connection to Aleister?" I asked referring to the famous occultist.

"I can't say. It's possible his mother had Aleister Crowley in mind. I've never asked. But he's nothing like that. If anything, Crowley's just an ordinary person carving a living out of a family business." He studied me for a moment. "In any case, like you, I'm not into astrology and the mystic arts."

"You remembered?" I asked.

"I remember everything about you, Scarlet." His head tilted.

Now, that made my knees weaken. Lost for a response, I uttered, "I'm far from interesting."

"That's where you're wrong." He held my gaze. "You're also a good art subject."

"While I appreciate your compliment, I don't understand why that would be."

"You've got an expressive face."

I nodded slowly. "It's lucky I chose to act, then, even if it hasn't exactly paid my bills." I chuckled.

"Did you say you were heading home, or would you like a quiet drink somewhere?" he asked.

And there we remained on the pavement, in our own bubble. People drifted by and some even turned to look. I snapped out of his gaze after realizing I'd fallen into a trance again.

"I'd like to, only I don't think we should go in there." I pointed at the pub. "Randall might get offended." I looked up at him with a faint grin. "He wanted me to stay." It felt weird sharing that detail—as if talking of something as mundane as dating the gardener broke this strange spell between us.

"I know a nice quiet place. It's not far. Interested?" he asked.

"That would be lovely." I smiled.

We walked along a lamplit laneway and came to a discreet bar. He held the door open for me and we stepped into the moody setting, a sharp contrast to the rowdy pub earlier.

The patrons turned and stared before going back to their conversations.

"You seem to attract attention," I said, following him to a quiet corner.

"Maybe it's you they're looking at?" His lips curled into the makings of a smile. "What can I get you?"

"A G and T would be nice," I said.

I watched him move to the bar with that smooth, confident walk. From a distance, Daniel Love had a proud, bordering on supercilious, demeanor, but it was a front. I sensed there was a complex, fragile man beneath, and although he was miles out of my league, I savored every compelling moment we spent together.

He returned with our drinks and sat opposite me with a lamp between us. The warm light on his face made him the perfect subject for art. With that sculptured jaw, dimpled chin, and eyes that switched from intense to seductive, Daniel Love would have had film makers eating nothing but kale for a year to sign him.

"So how was your drink with the gardener?" He wore a slight grin.

I cocked my head. "Are you being a snob?"

"Why would you think that?" His perfect brow wrinkled. "Randall's not a bad guy. He's just a hopeless womanizer."

"He was respectful." I stared down at my hands.

"I wouldn't have thought him your type."

"How would you know what my type is?"

"I don't. But one gets a feeling about people," he replied.

"And you're feeling about me is?"

"That you're an intelligent, beautiful woman who's a little damaged."

My face pinched. "Why would you think that?"

"Which part? Your being beautiful or damaged?"

"Both. I'm far from beautiful. But why do you think I'm damaged?"

"You're very beautiful. You just don't see it, which in many ways enhances your beauty. Vanity makes a person ugly."

I smiled tightly. Compliments were rare in my world. I was ill-practiced at receiving them. "How is it you see me as damaged?"

"You're always looking over your shoulder. You're jumpy." His eyebrow rose slightly. "I also recognize that remote look you often get."

"When I'm posing?"

He shook his head. "No. I've seen it from a distance."

"And you recognize it how?" I asked.

He ran his finger over the rim of his glass. "Because that's me sometimes."

His eyes fell into mine and my heart missed a beat.

"Is that why you wished to paint me?"

"That's just an indulgence." He jiggled the ice in his glass.

"But why the gown? The necklace?"

"Why not? Artists are entitled to their fetishes." His lips tugged at one end.

"I'd hardly call being dressed in designer with an expensive diamond necklace a fetish," I said.

"Let's just say, I have a thing for women in slinky gowns." His perfect eyebrow lifted as a hint of flirtatiousness flickered in his eyes.

I gulped down my drink. The air between us seemed to thicken. "I'd love to see your work. For all I know, you might be painting me to look like a cow."

"If I wanted to paint a cow, I'd go out to the fields and find one."

I laughed. "What I meant is that I'm hardly young and slim."

"You're a woman. In the true sense of the word." His eyebrow rose slightly. "You're real, and that makes for a great subject."

I sipped on my drink trying to find the right words. We normally fell into easy conversation about anything but him, but this was the closest to an intimate conversation we'd shared.

"I'm not scouting for compliments, but your interest in me as your art subject borders on surreal for an ordinary woman like me."

"Scarlet, you're far from ordinary."

I nearly melted in my seat as his eyes ploughed into mine.

"Do you often come out alone on a Saturday night?" I asked, trying not to guzzle my drink after that comment. "I mean, do you catch up with friends?"

"No." He swallowed his drink. He looked over at the waiter and lifted his chin. Daniel pointed at my glass. "Another?"

Having drained my glass, I nodded. How could one remain sober around this handsome and intense man?

After the waiter had replenished our drinks, I couldn't help but dig deeper, especially with the assistance of tongue-loosening liquor.

"If you don't mind me saying, you're a very unusual man." I toyed with my glass. "You're super rich, extremely talented, and ridiculously handsome, and here you are sharing a drink with an older woman brought up on the wrong side of town."

"I'm not a snob, Scarlet." His sculpted lips lifted at one end. "Apart from being super rich, I don't ascribe to those other attributes. Beauty is subjective, and age is meaningless. I've met twenty-five-year-olds who could be sixty and refreshingly child-like fifty-year-olds."

"Are you in touch with your inner child?" I asked.

His face cooled. "I'm no longer that boy. I had that stolen from me."

A cold finger slithered down my spine. His darkness had returned, and although questions came flooding in, I remained silent.

"And what about you, Scarlet? I recall we touched on this subject once before. Where's your inner child?"

I studied him for signs of that earlier darkness but was met by a hint of warmth. Strange man. Perhaps he suffered a split personality.

"I'd like to think she's there somewhere." I smiled tightly. "Life's gotten in the way, and that dreamy child who couldn't wait to grow up is now a memory."

He sniffed. "I also wanted to get to that age where I could make my own decisions. But once I became a teenager, the fun stopped."

I nodded pensively. "But still, you must have had adventures during your late teens? Late nights getting up to no good?"

He shook his head. "I missed out on that chapter, I'm afraid. Someone tore those pages from my adventure manual for young men." A rare smile grew, and an echo of the boy touched his face. "And what about you? I imagine working in theatre must have exposed you to interesting people and experiences."

"Uh-huh. Lots of parties. Every night during a season. Same with television. Actors can be shameless reprobates."

He raised his eyebrows. "You saw yourself as a shameless reprobate?"

I giggled. "No. Not at all. But they're fun to observe, especially at parties."

"But you wouldn't want to marry one," he said.

"Oh God, no." I took a moment. "I married a boring brute instead." I sniffed.

"You sound like you're full of regret."

I nodded. "Oh yeah. But I try not to think about it. It's such a wasted emotion, regret. What can one do about it?"

"Regret is a part of being human though—those past choices we wished we'd never made."

I wanted to ask about his marriage but decided to remain with the relaxed version of Daniel for a while longer. Having developed a growing awareness of his triggers, I opted to go with the philosophical flow instead.

"I get that. But it's also like a game of chess. One wrong move—or decision, if you like—can take us to a place filled with surprises."

He nodded slowly. "You wouldn't be here had you not been running away from your ex, whom I'm sure you regret marrying."

"Oh yeah." I rolled my eyes. "You got that right. And I do love Starlington. It's given me a new lease on life, being surrounded by so much natural splendor."

"I'm glad you're enjoying it. I know I couldn't live anywhere else."

And so the night continued like that. Nothing too intrusive. We shared another drink, and I kept away from heavy questions.

# CHAPTER 18

THE IMPOSING MANSION APPEARED animated draped under a lunar shadow, especially with the beaming ground lamps revealing its weathered and chiseled detail, like an old person's face under sunlight.

Cool, damp air slapped my face as soon as I stepped out of the car. Daniel held the door open for me, the novelty of that chivalrous act not lost on me. I couldn't recall a man ever doing that.

As I breathed in a medley of flower, herbs, and earth, like I would an exquisite perfume, indecision rooted me to the spot. Should I hurry back to my cottage or wait there?

It was midnight, and although I'd been drinking, I felt wide awake. Daniel removed his gold case from his blazer and offered me a cigarette.

We stepped onto the bluestone path leading to the house and paused to smoke.

"It's been an interesting night," I said.

He turned and looked into my eyes. "It has. You have this way of making me talk."

"Is that a good or bad thing?" I asked.

"I'm not sure." He studied me with his penetrating stare.

"Why are you staring at me like that?" I asked.

"I'm trying to understand something," he said.

"What?" I asked, feeling heat rise again.

"Why I'm drawn to you."

"You said I seemed familiar to you," I responded.

"You do."

"Do I remind you of someone?"

He nodded.

I took a puff of my cigarette. "Is that why you want to paint me?"

"Maybe." He paused. "I feel like I can trust you."

I gulped back a guilty lump.

"Models I've used in the past have gossiped. I like that you're unconnected to this place, although I imagine Randall and the staff have probably revealed something of my history." He tilted his head as though to see me more clearly.

"It's only human nature to be curious," I responded.

"Have they spoken of my parents?"

I had to choose my words carefully. "I heard that your parents died, but I don't know how that happened. I haven't heard any details." Out of pure selfish need, I lied. Intensity I could do, but not that remote, bone-chilling mood.

He continued to gaze at me, and by this stage, I wanted to either run away to breathe properly or fall into his arms.

"I guess I best be going, then," I said hesitantly because I wanted to stay—if only to keep listening to his deep, sexy voice.

I went to turn away when he grabbed my hand. The heat from his palm rushed through me. Before I could think straight, his warm, sensuous mouth touched mine, and his pine, male-infused scent shot tingles through me.

As his caressing lips explored my mouth, I fell into a spell and my frame melted into his strong body.

Snapping out of the dream, I released myself from his arms. We looked at each other, and a smile touched his lips.

"I've been dying to do that for a while," he said.

I puckered my brow. "Really? But you could have anyone, and I'm older than you."

"So?" He cocked his beautiful head slightly.

He took me into his arms again. His hot, moist lips devoured mine. Luckily, he held my giddy body, because my legs had gone to putty.

His tongue traced my lips before ploughing into my mouth and tangling with mine in a dance of discovery. His desire grew against my leg and our bodies melded in a passionate embrace.

"Come inside with me," he said.

At that stage, I, the reptile phobic, would have followed him into a pit of pythons. Leaving all my fears behind, I moved along as though in a trance.

He led me up the forbidden stairs, where gloomy faces in golden frames seemed to watch us as we ascended to the second floor. His warm hand in mine shot electricity to my core.

I stepped into his bedroom, which was larger than my former apartment.

Daniel clapped his hands and lamps lit up.

An eclectic array of art, from impressionist and abstract to representational, graced his mint-green wallpapered walls.

"Are these yours?" I pointed at the art, taking a tour around the opulent bedroom.

He shook his head. "I don't hang my work."

Why didn't that surprise me?

Taking my hand, he led me onto the bed. I read hunger in his gaze. My body burned for him too.

Sitting on the bed, he took me into his arms, and our lips crushed in a long, exploring kiss that was as soft as it was urgent.

His hands travelled over my body and cupped my breasts.

"I need you naked," he said.

I removed my blouse and his eyes hooded.

Undoing my jeans, I regretted not wearing expensive matching lingerie, something I didn't possess. My budget didn't extend to such sexy frivolities.

He ran his hand over my thighs and along my waist as though discovering my contours. Maybe that was the artist, or was that the man?

He rose, then went to a drawer, pulled out a red scarf, and removed his pants. Aching desire shuddered through me as my gaze travelled up his long, muscular legs to a growing bulge.

I hadn't felt such an insistent swell between my legs for a long time. I'd even thought my libido had died. But then I'd never imagined a moment like this, sitting on a silk bedspread, watching a man who could have been a Greek god about to ravish me.

The ache to feel a man between my legs left me breathless.

Before I could protest, he blindfolded me, then his hands continued down my body, unclasping my bra and taking my nipples into his searing lips, teasing them and making my body tremble.

I started to giggle, more out of nerves. I'd never been blindfolded before and it felt odd—intimidating, but still hot and sexy like the man devouring me.

I went to remove it.

"No. Don't," he said. "Leave it on."

He pushed me down onto the bed and removed my panties. His tongue landed on my clit, and a bolt of electricity made my back arch. My mouth dropped open, and my legs tensed as he found that magic spot and took me over the edge. Sparks grew into a wildfire of sensation.

He ravaged me as though I were a delicious treat.

Being deprived of sight had heightened my senses.

Was that his intention?

The intensity of his lashing increased to a breaking point. I dug my nails into his shoulders, wishing him to stop, but craving to be ripped apart too—which is what happened as I trembled through an eruption equivalent to an erotic piñata bursting out embers. Each turning into one blaze after another. It felt like it would never end.

I ran my fingers over his muscular biceps and his hard-mounded chest as his lips ate at my mouth.

His hard cock rubbed against my leg. I opened wide. I wanted him inside of me desperately.

I stroked his enormous erection. Throbbing and hard as steel, his dick was bigger than any I'd encountered. It was mouth-wateringly thick and throbbed in my hand.

Lost at sea to lust, I let him take control.

I heard a wrapper, then he opened my legs wide and his finger slid inside me. "You feel beautiful," he uttered with that deep, caressing rasp.

My muscles gripped around his finger, the pain of arousal excruciating.

His dick entered me, and he was so big it hurt. I hadn't fucked for a long time.

I moaned as he filled me to the breaking point, a deliciously intense stretch.

His heart pounded against mine as he rode me.

Was I tripping on a fantasy?

His breathing grew rough in my ear and grasping my ass he pushed himself in deep.

My sex clung on tightly, contracting and threatening to erupt into uncontrollable spasms.

A deep guttural sigh left my lips.

I knew that once I surrendered, I'd never be the same again. How could one return to ordinary after this?

Each euphoric wave grew the deeper and harder he pounded.

The faster he pumped, the more guttural his breath. We writhed together in a crush of raw, primal need.

I craved his eyes. To indulge in his startling masculinity. To see his desire.

I went to remove my blindfold when he touched my wrist. "Don't."

His cock pulsated inside of me, groaning as he came. Joining him, I released my muscles and a golden light swallowed me up. I thought my heart would burst and I released a chest deflating groan.

He fell into my arms and held me.

Our wet and sated entwined bodies breathed as one.

And then we separated, and I missed him.

He sprung up off the bed and removed my blindfold.

I shook my head. "What just happened?" I laughed. I had to. Multiple orgasms, which I'd never thought possible, had melted my brain.

Much to my disappointment, he dressed in a robe. I remained naked on the bed watching him moving about the room. He headed to a crystal decanter of water and poured two glasses.

Passing me a glass, he stroked my cheek and smiled gently. It was the lightest I'd ever seen him. It was amazing what an orgasm did to a person's spirit.

I drained my glass, and then it became awkward. Was I to stay?

As I rose and went to change, my legs wobbled, almost giving way.

"Stay," he said with that low husk that had already registered deep in my burning core.

# CHAPTER 19

## *Daniel*

LIKE A MAN POSSESSED, I hadn't thought it through. How could I have let her stay the night?

One year without feeling a women's body had turned me into a mindless wreck. All it took for me to lose control was her soft, warm lips and her curves pressed against me.

I had to touch her, taste her, fuck her.

That screen of indifference I'd carefully erected came crashing down. On an impulse, driven by lust, I invited Scarlet into my inner sanctum.

My body burned remembering the way she felt. Her taste. The fit. Her full figure. Her responsiveness.

She moved and her ass pressed against my cock, sending a surge of blood down to my groin.

I hadn't wanted a woman this badly since Georgie. But this was different. There was something primal about my attraction to Scarlet. It started from the moment I saw her in that green gown, or even sooner—on the beach with her in that sheer camisole.

Perhaps it was because I hadn't fucked for over a year, or maybe because she reminded me of her. I couldn't say. But suddenly I wanted her awake so that I could be inside her again. I hungered for skin on skin. To soak up her moist heat.

The morning had broken, and although I hadn't slept much, I felt energized, along with a raging appetite for Scarlet.

When I did sleep, I dreamt of silky soft skin rubbing against mine, and it was the most peaceful and relaxed I'd been for longer than I could recall.

She rolled over and opened her eyes.

"Did I wake you?" I asked.

Shaking her head, she stretched her arms. With that mess of red hair splashed all over her face and those big green eyes, Scarlet was a beauty—even more so in the morning light.

Those sexy curves that had allured me as an artist also seduced me as a man.

I stroked her silky skin and kissed her neck, taking a deep breath of her feminine scent: a captivating blend of faded perfume and sex.

"I've had a blood test. Are you on the pill?" I asked, my dick governing the conversation.

"I'm not. But I can't have children."

"An accident?"

She shook her head. "My ex-husband injured me."

Her emotionless response contradicted the gravity of that confession. I frowned. "What—physically, you mean?"

She nodded. "I was pregnant at the time. He punched me so hard that I had a miscarriage. After that, the doctors told me I'd never have children."

I studied her face for signs of distress. Like her cool tone, she remained blank-faced. As a king of detachment, I recognized self-denial disguised as stoicism.

"He sounds like a cold, heartless bastard who shouldn't be alive."

She gazed into my eyes and a sad smile touched her lips.

I took her into my arms and rocked her gently and there we remained. Her warm body fitted perfectly into mine.

She ran her hands over my chest and all the way down to my dick, which quickly inflamed from her explorative strokes.

I rolled her on her side, ran my fingers between her thighs and parted them. I rubbed my dick against her curvy ass and entered her in one deep thrust. My lips parted with a sound of pleasure. "Aah . . ." Her welcoming pussy was wet, hot, and very cozy.

She wrapped her muscles tightly against my dick, which slid in and out, pumping into her as though starved, while I cupped her tits.

"You're one very sexy woman," I said.

"Oh . . ." she sighed as I rubbed her clit while grinding against her curvy ass.

The build-up came quickly. Too quickly. I was out of shape. Or was it because of Scarlet and how she felt? My orgasm was so intense, like my brain had exploded in a fireball of divine light.

I fell on my back and exhaled loudly. Who was this woman? How could I feel like this?

• • • • • • • • • •

AFTER WHAT HAD BEEN a night filled with delicious sexual surprises, I dragged myself reluctantly to the city for a couple of important appointments.

By late afternoon, I left my accountant with figures swimming in my head. My investments were thriving. I'd added another billion dollars to the family coffers that month alone. Playing the money market had paid off, and employing one of the best financial whiz kids as an advisor had helped.

A couple of women passed me on the street, and one winked at me. I smiled back. After Charlie and our loveless sham of a marriage, I stopped looking at pretty women, or even craving sex. But then Scarlet came along and reminded me of what being a hot-blooded male felt like. And now, the thought of rushing back to Starlington to seduce her sent a jolt of electricity through me.

First, I had one more errand.

In sharp contrast to the slick, ultra-modern building I'd spent the past few hours in, the run-down, dark-brick, thirties-era edifice should have been condemned.

Instead of riding the rickety elevator, I ran up the stairs to the fourth floor and tapped on the frosted-glass door. When I stepped in, I discovered the PI with his feet up on his desk chatting on his phone.

He gestured for me to sit.

After he got off the phone, he handed me a folder. "It's all there. This Milson character's a real piece of work. He's on the take, all right."

"What's the chance of him being caught?"

He shrugged. "Not sure. The black market needs crooked cops."

"Keep an eye on him. If you see him going anywhere near the East Ham address, let me know."

"I've already been there. Three times. There's surveillance going on."

Wondering if Scarlet had arranged that, I sat up. "How do you mean?"

"I noticed the same person, who was not Milson, sitting in a car there over the course of a few nights."

I nodded. "So this Kevin Milson keeps visiting the mother's house, then?"

"It would seem that way."

"Keep watching him."

"Will do." He studied me for a moment. "You do realize assholes like him are hard to get rid of."

I rubbed my spiky jaw. "What are you suggesting?"

He lifted his shoulders and opened his hands. "A hit."

I rose with a knot in my stomach. "Keep an eye on him."

As I left that dingy office feeling somewhat disturbed, I thought about how I'd never hated a stranger as much as I hated Scarlet's ex.

When I returned to Starlington, I found Scarlet outside her cottage chatting and laughing with Randall.

I didn't like how he'd suddenly become interested in her. On my approach, she looked over his shoulder and her face brightened.

The gardener turned and bowed his head. "Mr. Love."

I nodded. "Randall."

"Okay, then," he said, looking at Scarlet. "Better be off. Think about it."

She waved, then returned her attention to me. Her hair was out, and her cleavage sat seductively above her blouse. A rush of heat flushed through me.

"How was the city?" she asked.

"Smoggy and noisy."

She laughed at my curt response. "Would you like to come in?"

I stepped inside. Despite the cottage being part of the estate, I'd never been in there before.

"Are you comfortable in here?" I asked, noticing the dated furniture, which I imagined had been there from when my grandparents had the cottage built sixty or so years ago.

"I am, thanks." She smiled.

"Does he come by often?" I asked.

"Randall?" She shook her head. "I didn't ask him in." A slow smile grew on her lips. "Are you jealous?"

"He wants to fuck you, and I don't share."

A line formed between her brows.

It was too soon for me to claim her. And I didn't even recognize the man who uttered those words.

But as I regarded her intelligent, pretty green eyes with that twinkle of curiosity, and her thick red hair sitting provocatively over her milky cleavage, my dick had taken over.

It was lust. Pure and simple.

"I don't like him that way." She shrugged.

We stared into each other's eyes, then my mouth was all over hers. Ravaging her lips, I unclasped her bra and her tits fell into my mouth as I teased her nipples with my tongue and teeth.

"I can't stop thinking about you," I said.

"I can't stop thinking about you either."

Her soft voice caressed me. I'd never felt so consumed by desire.

She fell to her knees, unzipped my jeans, pulled out my hard dick, and placed it into her mouth. I fell into the chair and my head dropped back, drowning in stars as her mouth moved up and down my shaft. My heart pumped so hard it reached my throat. I was bewitched. My ex never sucked my dick.

I tried to pull away, but I'd become transfixed—especially seeing her naked tits bouncing while her big eyes stared up at me as her luscious lips sucked my cock.

Determined to go all the way, she swallowed everything I had.

It took me a moment to speak. She rose and wiped her lips.

"That was something else," I said, finally finding my voice.

"Isn't that why you visited?" she asked.

"I didn't expect you to blow me, no. But it was nice. Thank you." I smiled. "I actually dropped in to see if you wanted to come to dinner with me."

Her pretty face brightened. "Yes. Of course."

# CHAPTER 20

*Scarlet*

"WHY THE BLINDFOLD?" THANKS to a second glass of wine, I'd finally plucked the courage to ask that burning question as my gaze flitted between his gorgeous face and the harbor of swaying boats.

It was the fifth swish restaurant we'd visited that week.

"I'd just like to see you," I persisted, staring into those inscrutable eyes that had a habit of becoming impenetrably dark at will.

"Doesn't it intensify the experience?" he asked, cocking his head slightly.

"It does." I smiled. "But I can't think of a better way to heighten my senses than by staring at your handsome face especially when you're in the throes of passion."

He picked up his glass and sipped in silence. A glimmer of a smile formed on those lips that had tasted every inch of my flesh.

I continued, "Is it because you don't want me to see you vulnerable?"

His brow furrowed. "Why would you think that?"

"Doesn't sex makes us all a little vulnerable by revealing that shadow spirit we normally hide?"

A flicker of bemusement coated his eyes. "Shadow spirit?"

"We all have one."

He wiped his mouth. "That I don't dispute."

"I'm just trying to understand." I cut into my steak.

"No." His eyes fixed on my face.

"What do you mean, 'no'?" I asked.

"My blindfolding you has nothing to do with me wanting to hide my vulnerability from you."

Just as I was about to speak, my phone vibrated and made me start.

I removed the phone from my bag and, seeing that it was Detective Somers, turned it off. My nerves were close to snapping. She kept calling me.

"Not someone important?" he asked.

I shook my head, hoping the sudden drain of blood from my face hadn't been obvious.

"You haven't been painting much lately," I said, diverting the subject away from the call.

"I have been, but not late at night. I've been preoccupied." He cut into his steak. "How's your meal?"

"Very nice." For someone who'd subsisted on cheap takeaway and junk food before entering Love's privileged world, I found myself savoring every mouthful of the tender meat washed down with the finest wine I'd ever tasted.

Even though it had only been ten days of unbridled passion, it felt like I'd fallen perilously in love. And like a pressure cooker about to explode, I tried to squeeze a lid on the torrent of emotion swelling in my chest.

A fling. That's all it is.

How could I keep a man like Daniel Love interested?

And then there was the age difference.

He'd only get hotter, while I was on a downward spiral. Gravity was against me. We couldn't all be ageless beauties like Catherine Deneuve or Liz Hurley, who probably worked hard at it.

I lacked the discipline to work out or eat healthy, home-cooked, calorie-compliant meals. And the thought of someone sticking needles around my eyes turned me to ice.

I just had to remind my heart that this profoundly sexy experience should amply furnish me with enough fond memories to keep me warm during my winter years.

A month with Daniel Love beat a long, cold marriage.

There'd been a moment that afternoon as we walked along the beach when I'd come close to confessing. My brain hurt from thinking of ways to remove myself from this regrettable mission.

But if I hadn't signed up for it, I wouldn't have met him.

Which was worse: lying to him or never experiencing the kind of passion I thought only existed in romance novels?

"Do you think you can do without me this weekend?" I cleared my throat. That message reminded me I needed to visit London to see my mother and to beg Detective Somers to release me. "I'm referring to whether you'll be needing me to model." A grin twitched on my lips.

We hadn't worked much that week. The two sessions had descended into a sex romp with Daniel waltzing me against the wall, raising my slinky silk gown, and entering me in one deep, eye-watering thrust.

"I need to visit the city," I said.

His scrutinizing gaze held mine. If I weren't so bottled up with guilt, I would have enjoyed this game.

That's what made the tension between nascent lovers so compelling—the unraveling of layers in search of the soul. Sometimes the deeper we pried, the deeper the disappointment. Sometimes we were met with a void. And a soulless romance was like a meal without spice—mere sustenance to ward off loneliness.

Not so with Daniel. Just those searching, at times knowing, looks told me there was an ecosystem of emotion brewing deep. I wanted in because the glimpses I got seemed like home to me.

It was a difficult journey to take, nevertheless. Finding Daniel's soul would be like crossing Siberia on foot. Blustery. At times icy, and impenetrable.

"I should visit my mother. In fact, do you mind if I give her a quick call? I promised to call her."

"Of course," he said with a faint smile.

I rose. "I'll be back in a minute."

I stepped into the restroom and called Detective Somers.

"What's up?" I asked.

"Just my regular check-up."

"On a Friday night?"

"Why not? You're not staying in touch. That was the plan. Remember?"

"I'm coming to town tomorrow. I'll pay for my mother's protection. I'll move her if I have to. I've got nothing to tell you. He's a good man who couldn't have killed his wife."

"You're sleeping with him, aren't you?"

"Why would you think that?"

"Call it a hunch. He's sacked most of his staff but kept you on."

"We'll speak tomorrow."

"Two o'clock. Same place," she said.

I closed the call and exhaled slowly.

Studying my reflection, I wiped my brow. Who was that woman in the mirror? My cheeks were rosier than usual, my eyes wide and brimming with anticipation, or was that fear? Regardless, it was amazing what multiple star-spangled orgasms did for one's complexion.

• • • ● • ● • • •

DANIEL AGAIN OPENED THE door of his Tesla sports car for me.

"Thank you," I said as I stepped out. He smiled back and walked by my side, so close his heady scent mingled with the dewy night air.

A burning sensation settled in my core. The thought of us devouring each other made my body thrum with anticipation. I hated how addicted I'd become—because any minute now I could wake up from this dream, and my former, ordinary life would resemble a nightmare. Whereas once I was numb, I'd suddenly ignited a powerhouse of nerve endings, aroused to the point of sensory overload.

We walked across the grounds and his dogs came to greet us with wagging tails. Daniel rubbed their backs and they followed us into the house.

I settled down onto the leather settee in the front room and picked up a picture book on Venice. I wasn't sure if I was to stay or what Daniel had in mind for me. Whether fucking me or painting me, he called the shots. The fact he was paying me threw open a whole Pandora's box of implications.

I had to stop overthinking this situation or else I'd lose my mind.

We'd spent every night together except for one. That was the second night. I sensed it was Daniel's way of telling me it was a once-off moment of passion. However, after that afternoon visit when my inner vixen took control, and I got down on my knees and sucked that big, beautiful cock, we hadn't stayed apart.

He was a giving lover who couldn't take his hands off me. And I couldn't stop touching him. Only I wanted to see him, especially when he was buried deep inside of me.

He led me up to his bedroom and unzipped my dress—a new green silk one that he had bought for me in London. Like the others I'd worn for him, it was low-cut. He had exquisite taste.

"You have a thing for ballooning cleavage?" I'd asked.

My skin prickled under his caress. "The décolletage is the most beautiful part of the female anatomy along with the nape of the neck." His finger slid from my breasts to my neck and I nearly melted into a puddle.

"Is that the artist or the man talking?"

"Both." His eyes darkened into that shade of lust that made me ache with desire.

He trailed kisses up my body, making my skin prickle, then lifted me and carried me to bed.

The red scarf came out of the drawer.

I squirmed at the thought of being blinded again. "Am I the only woman who's worn that?"

He tied it behind my head. "No."

His cold, clipped response turned me to wood. I soon thawed, however, the moment his lips brushed my neck and took to my mouth with the same passionate hunger of our first kiss.

Daniel was right about the intensity of feeling because as his lips moved down my body, warm ripples turned into sizzling electrical currents of pleasure.

I winced from oversensitivity when his tongue lapped over my clit. My legs trembled and nearly crushed his head.

He entered me and the painfully pleasurable stretch made me sigh. I loved his dick—and what he did with it. I'd never orgasmed while penetrated before, and as I held on to his hard biceps, I moaned as he drove hard into me.

The release was overwhelming. For him too. With that blindfold on, I heard every grunt, gasp, and groan.

In the heat of the moment and driven with a desperate need to look into his eyes as we climaxed together, I removed my mask.

With hooded eyes and parted lips, his handsome face animated as a slow gasp dampened my cheek.

When it finally dawned on him that I'd removed my blindfold, he sprang off me as though I were poisonous.

He grabbed a robe and covered himself.

"Get out!" he yelled.

I started to shake. The warmth of his release still gushed through me, his seed dribbling down my leg. I rose and scrambled for my clothes. I couldn't find my shoes.

He kept yelling "Out!"

I raced out barefooted, impervious to the jabbing pebbles on the path as I scrambled along, numb and confused.

Once in the cottage, I fell onto the couch dazed.

What had just happened?

• • • • ● • ● • • •

THE FOLLOWING MORNING, I headed into the kitchen, where I found Jack puttering about and whistling. I entered with a pounding heart. I hadn't shopped, so my cupboards were bare. Since Daniel had insisted I take my meals in the house, there I was, nervous and unsure what to say should Daniel appear.

"Hey." I smiled.

"Morning. There's some fresh coffee."

"Perfect," I said.

He cast me a lingering stare, and I wondered if I'd worn my blouse inside out. Or perhaps he knew about Daniel and me.

I carried a plate with scones in one hand and held a cup of coffee in the other, choosing to sit by the pool to take advantage of the morning sun.

Having not slept after that tumultuous exit, I looked forward to leaving for the city straight after breakfast—if only for some space. I had to work on my next move. I sensed this odd but exciting chapter was about to end.

The thought of living in the city again punched fear in my belly. My ex had a sixth sense when seeking me out.

I heard splashing and discovered Daniel swimming in the heated pool. I knew he was an avid swimmer because one didn't get that kind of body from sitting around. And he didn't lift weights.

Instead of running away, as my gut instinct dictated, I decided to stay. After all, that whole blindfold thing was his issue, not mine.

Daniel looked like an Adonis in his speedo with those long, lean legs, and that firm, perfect ass that I'd clawed while he fucked me senseless. Talk about erotica incarnate. A swelling ache between my legs throbbed with a vengeance.

Had this steamy tryst been a dream? A provocative manifestation of some late-night fantasy?

"Oh?" He stopped toweling his hair. "What are you doing here?" Sounding scornful, he spoke as if I were a maid, not the woman he'd fucked that past fortnight in every position, all night long.

"I didn't realize you'd be here. This is the sunniest part of the estate. I craved some sunshine." My lips quivered into a smile.

His towel slipped and I went to pick it up, when he snapped, "Leave it."

Flinching at his scraping tone, I was about to respond with a middle finger, when I caught a glimpse of his scarred wrists.

I swallowed back shock. "Right, then. I'll leave as soon as I can for London."

He turned his back to me and walked away.

I remained frozen, gripped by choking pity. My heart sobbed and I could barely breathe.

Is that why he'd blindfolded me?

I wanted to follow him in and talk to him. Explain that I understood. Explain that I too had visited that dark, desolate void.

Intimidated by his stormy temper, however, I remained a dithering block of concrete. Years of my maniacal husband pushing me into a corner while heaping hysterical abuse had crippled me.

When I returned to the cottage, I walked around, unable to think straight while piling clothes into a suitcase. At least I'd found a way to extricate myself from this uncomfortable spying role.

Only my heart sank with each beat, feeling indescribable pain. I'd become attached—not only to Daniel, but to Starlington.

How would I deal with the bleakness of my former life?

A knock at the door made me jump.

It was Daniel.

His eyes were wide and almost haunted. I read shame, need. I wanted to hold him as a mother might, not as a woman possessed.

He stepped inside and, seeing my large luggage, said, "Don't leave yet."

My mouth opened, but I couldn't find a response.

"Walk with me. Then I can drive you to visit your mother." A faint smile warmed his face. "If you would let me."

"You would do that?" I asked, my head spinning. I had that meeting with the detective. Shit.

I quickly gathered my senses and followed him outside. "You really don't have to take me. I was planning on leaving in an hour."

"Leaving as in never returning?" He stopped and faced me squarely.

I gulped. "Um . . . well, you told me to leave."

He took my hand. "Let's walk."

We arrived at the edge of the cliff, where the turbulent ocean below smashed against rocks, spritzing the air with a fine mist.

As the wind massaged my face, Daniel turned to me.

He rolled his lips together. "When I was at college . . ." He expelled a breath. I could see this was difficult for him. "I tried to kill myself. My roommate found me."

"Why?" I asked.

"Unrequited love." He sniffed. "Cliché. I know."

I shook my head. "A broken heart causes relentless pain. Some people never recover."

"She looked like you." He fixed his eyes on me.

A tremor ran through me. "Is that why you wanted to paint me?"

He nodded.

"She must have been crazy. Was she gay?" I asked, trying to break the tension that even the wind couldn't dilute.

He shook his head. "She was married." Looking out to sea, he added,

"I was eighteen and she was thirty. She was married to my lecturer. She was my first, and I fell hard." He looked lost to his memories. "I wanted to marry her, but Georgie refused to leave her husband."

"Do you still speak?"

He nodded.

A knot of jealousy twisted in my stomach. "Are you still seeing each other?"

"No. That stopped when I was twenty-two. I was sick of sneaking around. I fell into a deep depression, and I did this." He showed me his wrists.

"I'm so sorry. But it's nothing to be ashamed of. I thought of doing it a few times."

His gaze returned to my face.

"Is that why you blindfolded me?"

He looked out to sea again and nodded.

"Hey, it was nice. I mean, it does intensify the experience." I smiled tightly.

"You and only one other knows," he said.

"I'd never tell anyone." I took his hand. "It's not something to be ashamed of."

"Wearing long sleeves everywhere can be a drag, particularly in France."

"What about your wife?"

He shrugged. "I managed to hide it from her."

"You didn't feel like sharing that? I mean . . ." I paused to choose my words carefully. "Isn't that what partners do?"

"Did you share all your innermost dark thoughts and experiences with your husband?"

"Some things. Maybe not everything." I took a deep breath. "I get it. We all have a right to our secrets."

"That's how I've lived my life. Guarding them." He looked deeply into my eyes and I prayed he couldn't read my guilt.

"What about holidays. At the beach?" I had to ask.

"I wore long-sleeved shirts, and always swam alone."

"Your grandmother?"

"She knew."

"That explains her overprotectiveness, I suppose." I smiled sadly. "Was it just unrequited love?"

His serious gaze remained fixed on mine, as though searching carefully for which version of his life he wished to share.

"I saw things growing up that no one should ever see."

"Have you seen someone about that?"

He nodded. "It didn't help. I hate questions." He squeezed my hand gently. "I feel like I can trust you. Unlike most people. That's why I got rid of the staff. There was too much gossip after Charlie's disappearance. I even suspected they were talking to the cops."

I released his hand in case he felt my tremor.

And there we remained in silence. I had nothing to add, listening only to the roar of the ocean and wind in the background as my mind filled with empty words.

What else could I say? And what was I to do next?

Especially now that we'd entered a deeper space.

"I should be off," I said, at last, painting a smile. "I promised my mother I'd be there for lunch."

"I'll drive you," he said. "I've got a friend I need to visit. His son's having a birthday. Perhaps you'd like to come after your lunch?"

My heart melted. His eyes had gone a tender shade of brown. He was allowing me into his inner sanctum by inviting me to a party.

I fell into his arms, and we held each other. The wind fusing our bodies together.

I wanted to cradle him. To remove his pain.

As we remained warm against each other, my eyes pricked with tears. We'd become emotionally intimate. Powerfully, almost frighteningly so, because at that moment I knew I'd never be the same again.

We kept holding each other. His body softening in my arms and our souls in communion. In that magical forest, surrounded by the sounds of the night and our hearts beating as one.

I reluctantly withdrew from his arms. It suddenly occurred to me that I had that appointment with the detective, the thought of which made me crash down to earth.

But what seemed to stress me even more was Daniel seeing my run-down childhood home.

# CHAPTER 21

## *Daniel*

THE POORER SUBURBS OF London seemed to have been forgotten. I couldn't help but notice the cracked pavement, the homes crumbling beyond repair, people shuffling along, and jumpy youth hanging together in packs.

I could almost smell Scarlet's insecurity—the way she kept crossing her legs, the pasted-on smile.

She thought I'd judge her for being brought up in a lowly neighborhood. But my inner snob faded the day I walked out of that police station. After my father murdered my mother, I came to the realization that no amount of wealth or nobility could help decontaminate one of shame. Shame that had seeped into my DNA. A wife-basher wearing a Rolex and designer suit was still a violent scumbag.

Scarlet turned and touched my hand. I liked feeling her soft warmth, even if I noted a slight tremble. "Thank you for the lift." She bit her lip. "Would you like to come in for a cup of tea?"

"Do you want me to?" I asked.

"I do. Only, we don't live . . ."

"Hey, I'm not expecting Windsor castle." I smiled. "I could do with a cup of tea, but if having me there will make you uneasy, I can just drop you off."

"No. It's fine. You're more than welcome." Her quivery smile reminded me that I was about to meet her mother.

With Charlie, I didn't meet her parents until just before we married. That's because after a month of dating, I decided Charlie wasn't for me—until she turned up and broke the news of her pregnancy. From then on, my spirit steadily anesthetized. The man I became, the one I saw in the mirror, was a stranger.

At least I could almost be myself around Scarlet.

Seeing her struggle with the front door, I stepped in and pushed it open.

"It's become stiff again. It's been kicked in one time too often." She gave an ironic chuckle.

Although Scarlet rarely spoke of the horrors she'd endured while married to a violent prick, I recognized the look she wore whenever he was mentioned. My mother's eyes also shone with that same apologetic glint on occasions, as though it were her fault she'd married an asshole.

As we entered, a pleasant aroma of cooking made my stomach rumble.

"Hey," Scarlet called out.

Her mother entered the hallway wiping her hands on her apron. "Darling, you're here." She smiled brightly, then she saw me, and her eyebrows flew up. "Oh, and you've brought a friend. How nice."

"This is Daniel Love, my . . ." She wore a questioning frown. "Boss."

I held out my hand. "Pleased to meet you. Excuse the intrusion."

"No. Not at all. How nice to meet you." She stepped away from the kitchen door for us to enter. "Ainsley hasn't told me much about her new position, only that she's staying by the coast on a beautiful estate."

"You'll have to come sometime," I said.

Had I just invited a complete stranger to my home? That was new for me.

"Oh, how lovely." She looked at her daughter as though she'd been offered a luxurious holiday. "Make yourself at home." She pulled out a chair. "I've cooked a shepherd's pie for lunch. Ainsley's favorite. There's plenty here."

We settled down at the table in the sunny room. Everything was clean, and despite the run-down nature of the house, it was still comfortable and welcoming.

Like her daughter, Marion didn't do small talk, a quality I admired in people. That said, we embarked on easy conversation, and I found myself enjoying my time there. It felt real and made me realize how much I missed my grandmother.

Half an hour later, I wiped my mouth after polishing off two servings of the hearty meal. "That was delicious. I'll have to get the recipe for my cook."

"It's very simple." Marion smiled, switching her focus from me to her daughter. I could see the similarity. She had the same expressive green eyes.

A knock came to the door. Marion looked at her daughter mystified. "I wonder who that could be."

Scarlet rose. "I'll go and see."

After Scarlet left to answer the door, her mother said, "My daughter's looking so much healthier and happier. I haven't seen her smile for a long time. Thanks for employing her."

If only she knew the smile that Scarlet had brought to me too. But it was way too soon for that.

I heard whispering and Marion threw me a puzzled frown.

"You were meant to be there," I heard a woman speak. Her voice sounded firm but familiar, which made my ears prick.

Scarlet whispered in a rushed tone as though trying to shoo something away.

"We had a deal. I got you in there and you haven't delivered."

"Please go," Scarlet implored.

I stepped into the hallway and saw Detective Somers standing at the door.

What the fuck?

Scarlet turned pale. Biting her lip, she looked at me, and her face crumpled with dismay.

"Who's that, darling?" Marion entered the hallway.

"It's about Kevin. She's making sure I'm okay." Her eyes slid from the detective to me.

The detective, meanwhile, seeing me there for the first time, looked just as shocked. She acknowledged me with a curt nod and departed.

"We need to talk," I said, my heart pumping fury through my veins. "Now."

Marion, who looked understandably baffled, left us alone.

I turned to Scarlet. "Where can we go?" It pained me to control my tone.

# CHAPTER 22

## Scarlet

WHY THE HELL HADN'T I called Somers to say I was running late? I'd lost all grip of reality. Living in this romantic bubble with Daniel Love had scrambled my mind.

I leaned against the wall to avoid falling. Daniel's dark, fuming eyes had me shriveling into a ball. I wanted to run and hide.

Barely able to walk, I led Daniel into the living room.

My eyes settled on the family photos. Who was that smiling girl in the pink dress standing in front of my father and mother? We were far from the happy family that picture conveyed. Why my mother even kept it on the mantle I couldn't understand.

Floral curtains matched the couch, and the streaming sun shone on a tidy room, where all the former bickering, violence and tears had been scrubbed with bleach. The walls remembered. Cracks had grown year by year. I, too, remembered. That's why I rarely stepped in there.

"What did she mean by getting you in there, Ainsley?" he asked.

The way he spat out my real name felt like an arctic blast on naked skin.

I was no longer Scarlet—that desirable woman who had been ravished by this handsome, complex man—but an ordinary, damaged woman, who, at that moment, wanted to crawl into a cupboard, just like when my ex came home drunk. Or when my father turned up in a shitty mood that quickly descended into mayhem.

Where was that blindfold now? I couldn't look at him. Those eyes I craved had now become repellent, filled with hatred. My body turned to stone.

I stared at my feet as a frenzy of colliding excuses toiled for a plausible answer.

"Tell me," he demanded. "The truth."

I fell into the old armchair. Springs scraped my spine, and a waft of stale tobacco reminded me of my grandfather pecking my cheek when I was little.

Taking the kind of eye-squeezing deep breath one would take to dive off a high platform, I said, "My casting agent offered me this job. I had to report to Detective Somers, who recruited me to observe you."

"To spy, you mean?" His brow creased. "Did you get to my computer?"

I shook my head. "I refused to do that. In fact, for the last month, especially since we..."

"Since we've been fucking, you mean?"

I nodded slowly, his eyes eating mine, but not devouringly like when he fucked me. I would have preferred a slap than to gaze at those eyes brimming with hate.

"I begged her to release me. But she forced my hand by offering round-the-clock surveillance. I couldn't have my ex torturing my mother." My mouth was so dry my tongue stuck to my palette.

"What else have they had you do?"

"Nothing. Only..."

"Speak."

I released a jagged breath. "They found a trace to the estate dealing in arms and drugs."

His face pinched. "What?"

I opened my hands. "That's why they wanted me to get to your computer. It was mainly that, not so much about your missing wife. But I swear I didn't go there. That's why she came here today—because I haven't been cooperating."

He stood intimidatingly close. "I trusted you."

"I was pushed into a corner. I had to escape London. This was my only way out. I had no money," I spoke in a rush of words, following him to the door. "I'm sorry."

Without turning to look at me, he stormed out.

I leaned against the wall and covered my eyes. Within a breath, my palms dripped with anguished tears.

My mother came to me, put her arms around me, and led me to the sofa. She held on to me as I cried and cried—tears of frustration and pain. My whole life's worth of sorrow pouring out.

Two months later...

I'd landed a role in a BBC crime series. Despite my initial resistance, I decided on taking the role of playing a battered wife. After all, wasn't that what method acting was, drawing on one's life experiences?

Since my break from Daniel, a few doors had opened for me in the acting world. I don't know what I would have done otherwise because life had gotten pretty bleak after that passionate encounter with Daniel.

Was it a dream? Or had I been on some party drug that lasted weeks with a savagely painful aftereffect?

Lucid and persistent memories of my time at Starlington in Daniel Love's arms followed my every waking moment, like some endless reel of a delicious banquet playing to someone whose mouth had been sewn up. Only a million times worse. Some days, I even craved a lobotomy.

On a brighter note, I'd managed to procure enough acting work to rent a studio apartment close to the city.

Apart from dreaming of Daniel virtually every night and wondering what would have happened if Somers hadn't arrived at my doorstep, I was slowly on the mend. If only my ex hadn't shown his weathered face on a few occasions. He hadn't resorted to violence though. Instead, he pleaded with me to take him back.

Arriving on the set of the show, I saluted the crew. The director sipped on coffee while instructing the cameraman on what angles he wanted.

Kirk, the actor playing the role of my husband, strutted over. "Do you want to go over some lines?"

"I would love that." I liked him, even though, like many actors, he was a little full of himself. But he made me laugh.

After we'd practiced our lines and had our makeup applied, we returned to the set. The makeup artist came and applied some more powder to my face after consulting the monitor, and Kirk poked his tongue at me and made me smile. He knew how tense this next scene was for me, and I appreciated the chance to loosen up.

He came over toward me, standing close by. "Are you sure you're okay with me going full throttle?"

I nodded. After the last scene, we'd shared a few drinks and I'd opened up about my abusive past.

We got into our places.

"Roll sound, camera and action."

"You're not meant to be here, Peter," my character said.

He came close and grabbed my arm. "This is my fucking house."

As I cast him a hateful glare, I saw Kevin, my ex. The part came naturally to me, even if the debrief involved drinking a few extra glasses of wine afterward. But for five thousand pounds, I would have agreed to sing a whiny tune in a diaper.

I shrugged out of his clutch. "You can't come storming in here like this."

"Don't tell me what I can't do. You're still my fucking wife."

"I'll call the police. I've got a restraining order on you!" I cried, grabbing my phone.

Taking the phone from my hand, he tossed it to the ground.

"Get out!" I yelled.

He hit me and I stumbled back. We'd choreographed that part over and over. The blood capsule burst from my nose as I crawled on the ground.

"Please don't." I cowered, covering my face.

He picked me up and shook me. Malevolence creased into his face. Kirk was a great actor to work opposite. I fought out of his arms like a tiger, then ran to the door and opened it. "Get out!"

He pushed past me. "This isn't the last of it. I've got my rights too. They're my kids."

"Out!" I screamed.

He stormed, out and I wiped the blood from my nose.

"And cut," said the director. He looked at me and nodded. "That was great. Got it in one, as always. You're both killing it."

After the shoot, while basking in a warm glow from receiving a pat on the back for a job well done, I met up with the cast and crew for a few drinks and a meal. It was fun talking about the show and all the latest showbiz gossip.

Feeling upbeat, and pleasantly lightheaded after a few drinks, I sprang back to my apartment, which happened to be within walking distance.

Just as I was about to enter my building, I felt someone grab my arm.

I'm not sure what happened, but the next thing I knew, I was in hospital.

My head ached, and as I opened my eyes, slowly a blurry image came before me.

Daniel stood by the bed.

Was I hallucinating? Had I died and perhaps ended up in heaven, or was I in hell with him sent there to torment me?

# CHAPTER 23

## *Daniel*

HER EYES OPENED AND the tangled knot in my chest unwound. Driven by a force virtually beyond my control, I went to the city that night. I already knew where to find her. I'd had my PI look for her.

It had been a bleak, desolate couple of months. Food had lost its flavor. Colors had lost their brightness. I could hardly move.

That's why I went to find Scarlet—to suggest we rewrite our past. Draw a line. Keep the sexy, romantic bits, and expunge the grimy bits.

Resentment had clung to me like asphyxiating plastic, bound so tightly I could barely move. Betrayal had turned me inside out. Eight weeks later, I'd had enough. I could no longer be that hollow man living on scraps of tender memories.

"Daniel?" Shock flickered in her eyes. Wincing, she tried to lift herself up.

"Hey, don't move. Let me call the doctor."

"What happened?" she asked.

"I'll explain in a minute. Just remain still while I call the doctor." I touched her hand. "Okay?"

She nodded while smiling faintly.

I found the doctor speaking to Scarlet's mother.

Marion turned to me, her eyes filled with tears. "She's going to be okay."

As my chest collapsed with relief, I turned to the doctor. "There's no internal bleeding," he said. "Her scans came up clear. She'll just be a bit bruised. We'll release her today."

After he left, Marion said, "She'll be so glad to see you. Poor girl's been really miserable after everything that happened. You do know that she's a good person. She only took that role because she was broke and needed to get away from Kevin."

"I know." I smiled tightly.

"Thank you for being there. You're an angel." She touched my arm and kissed me on the cheek. "I'll let you go in and have a chat with Ainsley. She'll love that."

I left her and entered Scarlet's room again, where I found her sitting up and sipping juice.

"Scarlet—I mean, Ainsley..."

"It's Scarlet. I relate more to her." She smiled meekly.

"Do you need more painkillers?" I asked after seeing her pained grimace.

"No, I'll be okay." She held my stare. "What happened?"

"You don't recall?"

"I remember someone shoving me from behind. They told me that you called the ambulance."

"It was your ex." I took a deep breath. "I got there too late. But I am now a witness."

She looked puzzled. "How did you happen to be there?"

"I found out where you were staying and came to see you." I swallowed tightly. "I missed you."

"And I missed you." She smiled sadly. "Why didn't you call?"

"What I had to say needed to be said face to face."

She kept staring at me as though trying to solve a cryptic puzzle.

I took a deep breath. "For weeks I stewed in anger and resentment. I didn't just hate you, but the world—and myself, in particular." I sniffed. "But then I confronted Detective Somers about the illegality of her line of inquiry, and she told me that you believed I hadn't murdered Charlie. That was all she got and nothing else."

I recall sitting in that cold room and glaring at the detective. Having grown up with a silver spoon, I'd never had to cross a moral line for money. Scarlet had little choice but to take that job. I only wished she'd have owned up to it. But then, Somers admitted, somewhat gingerly, that she had Scarlet over a barrel by having her ex watched.

That was when I forgave Scarlet. My heart insisted on it.

It helped immensely that Scarlet thought me innocent of a crime, even though I wasn't convinced of my own innocence

"Have they arrested Kevin?" she asked.

"He's been released on bail." I shook my head in disgust at how slippery and untouchable he was. I reflected on my late father, who, similarly, had managed to wriggle out of his charges for attacking my mother. By the time they took his crimes seriously and apprehended him, it was too late.

"Why doesn't that surprise me," she said.

"Don't worry. It will be different this time. I've got a new ally in Somers. I've threatened to have her head on the block."

"You think they'll arrest him this time?"

I nodded. "If not, I'll take the law into my own hands."

She reached out. "No. Please, promise me. He's not worth that."

"He's a worthless piece of shit. And the world would be a better place without him."

Her mouth twitched into a grin. "It's so nice to see you. Even if I'm still a little creeped out by you following me."

"It was like a voice told me I had to see you. I'm glad I listened."

She shook her head. "I owe you my life. God knows what he would have done had you not arrived."

I nodded, recalling my frustration at seeing that car drive off. If ever I was in the mood to put those hours spent punching a bag to use, it was then.

"The doctor said you can probably leave today. I don't want you to be alone. Would you consider coming back to Starlington? I can bring in a nurse."

"I've been working on a show. They'll be wondering what happened to me. What day is it?"

"It's Friday."

"So it must have happened two nights ago. I need to call my agent."

I rose. "Let me sort that out. Okay?"

"Thanks." She grimaced while touching my hand. "I've been a shadow since what happened. I wanted to explain . . ."

"Just come back. I need you there."

I'd never admitted to needing anyone before. With Georgie, it was lust and familiarity. With Scarlet, however, there was something deeper at play. I'd shared more with her than anyone else. Ever.

And we shared something sexy, raw, and profoundly sensual when making love. Her perfume on my pillow made my dick throb and my heart longed for her warm softness.

I looked into her green eyes and smiled. My heart unraveled like a butterfly from a cocoon.

# CHAPTER 24

## *Scarlet*

IT WAS LIKE HEAVEN being back at Starlington. I floated around as though in a dream. And the surprises kept coming. Daniel carried my suitcase to his bedroom. I'd expected to move into the cottage, but he told me that he wanted me in his bed. Every night.

While processing the magnitude of this new arrangement, I told myself to live each day as though it was a gift.

Lounging back on a velvet armchair in Daniel's room, I stared down desultorily at my book as the sun streamed in. I felt light, as though tranquilized. Had I died and been ferried to a parallel universe where only Daniel and I existed? The situation was so surreal that I started to believe that. Apart from Jack in the kitchen, and casual staff who came and went daily, we were alone in that huge house.

Daniel had started painting again. Although he was always happier after a session, he'd still have, on occasion, those remote moments of staring into the distance.

I spent my days reading, walking, and learning lines.

My star was rising, too. Much to my surprised delight, there were lots of roles for middle-aged actresses, even if my vanity recoiled at being described as such. Age was something that had never bothered me. But then, I'd never fallen for a younger man before.

• • • • • • • • •

WE WALKED THROUGH THE forest, hand in hand. Thor and Zeus ran ahead of us, and that magical forest, as always, seemed to pulse with energy. Heady, herbaceous scents wafted through the air, burning a glow onto my cheeks. Or was that from all the orgasms I'd indulged in earlier that morning?

"I've just scored a role in another series," I said.

"Oh?" He turned, and with the sun filtering through the tall trees his eyes had gone that soft melting brown that set my pulse racing.

"It came as a surprise, to be honest."

"You're a great talent. You were amazing in your last show."

My brow lowered. "You watched it?"

He nodded. "I Googled you and your name was linked to a show on Netflix, so I signed up and streamed it. You're a great actress. The camera loves you."

Basking in the warmth of a fine compliment, I smiled. "It hasn't always been like that. I struggled to get parts in my twenties and thirties, but the offers are suddenly flooding in."

"Will you be moving back to the city?" he asked, his gaze shifting to his feet.

"I've still got my apartment. I'll probably stay there while we're shooting."

"When does it start?"

"Next week. I won't go in until then. But I have some work to do. It's a meaty role. Lots of lines to learn."

"You'll still be able to model this week?" he asked.

"Of course." I smiled. "I'm so glad you're painting again."

He took hold of both my hands and stood before me. "My muse is back."

I shook my head in disbelief. "I could never have imagined being anyone's muse."

"You underestimate your allure," he said, leading me down the path to the bay.

"You can come and stay at my apartment anytime you'd like." I stopped walking to read his response.

I generally preferred my own space when working, but there was always space around Daniel. Comfortable space.

"The apartment's tiny, but it will only be for a few nights a week. It's a six-week call."

"I'm sure we can work something out," he said. Putting his arm around my waist, he drew me against his firm body.

Would I ever get used to being in the arms of this beautiful man?

This talk of my staying in town brought to mind my ex, sinking my mood in a breath. "I haven't heard from Kevin."

"He won't be bothering you again."

I frowned. "What do you mean?"

"Just that. He's being watched twenty-four-seven. Private surveillance. If he comes anywhere near your mother, he'll be locked up again. And he's out on bail. He'd be stupid to try and do anything now."

"I wish there were something I could do to repay you."

"Continue to pose for me. I've got this sudden surge of inspiration."

"Oh, I'm more than happy to." I grinned. "With clothes?"

"I don't paint nudes." His serious but direct response alerted me again to the mystery of his art.

"Will you ever let me see your work?"

"Mm . . . you'd be the first. I don't paint to share."

That cool response jolted me back to the reality of our tenuous relationship. Daniel Love was nothing but a sexy indulgence.

My heart would just have to stay out of it.

Impatient as I was to learn everything about him, especially his life growing up, I took baby steps. He guarded his privacy as someone protecting vulnerable children might.

We laid our towels on the ground, then Daniel tossed a ball for the dogs, who scampered about the shore.

"I love how secluded this little bay is." I removed my sandals and untied my wrap-around cotton dress.

"One can only get here through Wiching Wood."

"But that's open to the public," I said.

"Not many people visit. Only Oleander's cohort, teenagers, and colorful types during mushroom season."

"Ah. Of the magical variety." I giggled.

He smiled.

I thought about the mystical bookshop I'd seen Daniel leaving that evening. "Does this Oleander perform rituals in the wood?"

He nodded. "She was close to my mother."

"Like Beltane? I asked.

He nodded. "Like my late mother, they're committed Pagans."

"How romantic," I said.

He smiled and tossed the ball again.

"Do they sacrifice animals?"

He shook his head. "Nothing so gory. They dance around fires. It's all rather colorful."

"Do you attend these rituals?"

"I have in the past, but I'm not so inclined. They're mainly women . . ." He looked up at me and a glimmer of a smile warmed his face.

"Let me guess, they want you to remove those designer shirts."

I touched his firm chest and his eyes grinned back.

"They get a bit bacchanalian at times."

"And your mother was part of those romps?"

He shook his head. "No. It's a recent development since Eurydice Styx entered the scene."

I laughed at that theatrical name. "Let me guess, she's waiting to be taken by force by some dark, snakish man?"

His eyes flickered with amusement. "You've read your myths, I see."

"I studied Homer and Virgil at college. One can't embark on Shakespeare without some knowledge of the Greek myths."

"I studied Shakespeare for a semester," he said.

"Really? I thought you studied art?"

"I did, but literature was part of my electives."

"Did you finish your degree?" I asked.

"No. I got sick of the city. I don't do crowds. I didn't like college life."

"Being a committed artist and a social butterfly don't mix."

He nodded pensively. "Maybe."

"And Georgie?" I couldn't help but probe into his relationship with this much older woman.

"I was young. I hadn't been with a woman before." He raised a brow. "She came along with her bigger-than-life personality and take-no-bullshit approach. I've always had a thing for strong women."

Was I strong? At times I felt so feeble I could shrivel into a ball and hide. But I was also good at putting up a front.

Although I wanted to know more about his time with Georgie, I returned to our former conversation.

"I'm still interested in hearing about these local witches."

"It's not that interesting," he said soberly.

"Do they dance around in the nude?"

"The last Beltane they did," he said.

"Really? And you attended?" I asked.

"Yes." He looked at me. "It's a tradition. I don't strip down, however. Some choose to. It's not sexual for me, but more of a fascinating snapshot of history." He took my hand and looked seriously into my eyes. "It takes more than a naked woman to arouse me."

"Not even young, pretty women with firm breasts and tight . . ." I paused because we weren't into talking dirty... yet. His insistent body tended to do the talking.

"Tight pussies, you mean?" He ran his hand up my thigh and I went to liquid again.

"Well, isn't that the allure? A youthful body?"

"Experience is sexier. As is a smart, mature, and beautiful woman. What's erotic for me is not as stereotypical as a young, pretty girl with firm tits."

He ran his hand over my breasts. "In any case, you've got very sexy tits, so you have nothing to worry about."

"Have you been with lots of women?" I asked.

His eyebrows drew in sharply. I'd crossed the line again. This man hated questions about his past. "Have you been with lots of men?"

I swallowed tightly. Despite that being a fair question, I shrank.

"Depends how one measures lots."

"Then that tells me you have," he said. "I'd prefer not to know, by the way. And in response to your question, you're my third."

My jaw dropped. "Third ever? You mean you've only been with two women before me?"

He drew a circle in the sand. "I don't need sex."

"But you're so horny. You're insatiable. And you're an amazing lover."

A faint smile touched his lips. "Let's just say that I learned from an older, highly-experienced, and very adventurous woman."

"I just find it hard to believe . . . I mean, you're a hot, thirty-two-year-old man." I tilted my head. "Are you bisexual?"

A decisive shake of his head gave me my answer.

"It's just that you seem very sexual," I pressed.

"That's your doing." His eyes dripped with desire.

I had the sudden urge to strip bare and open my legs, just as I'd done the night before. After modelling, I allowed the dress to slink off me and parted my legs, if only to indulge in the shine of lust emanating from his hooded eyes.

"And then you married Charlie," I said. "She was younger."

"That was a mistake. As you already know."

"Do you want children?" I asked.

"Not really. And what with nature choking on plastic, I think one less being might give Mother Nature a chance to breathe."

"I understand. But a newborn can change that attitude in a flash."

"Do you want children?" he asked.

"I'm too old. And even if I weren't, I can't give birth." A lump formed in my throat.

He took me into his arms and kissed me tenderly. "You're not too old, by the way."

"It's okay. Really." A quivery smile touched my lips.

What had I to be sad about? Just being there on that secluded beach with the sun rippling on the blue sea erased any past woes.

I stretched out on my towel and enjoyed the warmth on my body. Daniel stroked my arm and my nipples hardened.

Drugged by his masculinity, I watched him strip down to his swimming trunks. I ogled his strong, masculine form. Even the smattering of hair on his chest inflamed me. I loved how it rubbed against my breasts when we made love.

My gaze settled on his bulge as that same burning, insistent throb returned. I'd become insatiable around him. I ran my tongue over my lips. I'd never liked sucking dicks before, but I wanted to devour Daniel. And he loved returning the favor.

"Let's have a swim," he said.

What a good idea—if only to douse the flame between my legs.

I followed him into the water, enjoying the way his muscular legs flexed in all the right places.

I winced and shuddered, clutching my arms at the coldness of the sea and taking tiny steps forward while I slowly acclimatized.

Daniel dived in and swam out far with powerful, effortless strokes. He was a strong swimmer. One didn't get those biceps from paddling about.

I swam close to shore, indulging in the refreshing, cleansing sensation of salty water on my skin. There was a slight sting in my cleft. I'd never fucked this much before.

Daniel swam over and parted my legs. Swimming between my legs, he lifted me above the water.

Wobbling slightly, I screamed and laughed at the same time. The last time I'd been on someone's shoulders like that was as a teenager in Blackpool, where I'd lost my virginity to a tough boy. Someone I'd thought of as cool because he was the leader of the pack. From that point on, my libido favored the rugged male—or, more specifically, the brute.

I gripped Daniel's shoulders. "I'm going to fall."

He laughed. "Stand up and dive in."

"I'm going to hurt you. I'm too heavy."

"You're light."

I jumped off him and screamed with laughter. He grabbed me around the waist and drew me close, his salty lips claiming my mouth.

# CHAPTER 25

I'D BEEN CAST AS a policewoman, of all roles. At least my time spent with Detective Somers had come to some use. Not least the fact I met Daniel due to this sticky, if not tense, arrangement.

After a big day on the set, I was in my city apartment stretched out on the sofa watching *Sanditon*, mainly because the leading man, Theo James, looked like Daniel.

The phone rang and I looked at the screen. Seeing it was the man that had stolen my heart, I took the call. "I was just thinking of you."

"Nice thoughts, I hope."

"Sexy ones, actually. I'm suffering from withdrawal symptoms. Only you're the drug," I said.

"My bed isn't the same without you."

I chuckled. "Have you been painting?"

"I have been working pretty hard."

With my phone to my ear, I indulged in his deep, resonant voice as one would a sexy crooner. Daniel could have recited the weather report, and I would have been close to coming.

"There's a party on Saturday. I'd like it if you were my partner."

I sat up. "Oh." An image flashed before me: women swaning around in designer wear while I stood out in discount formalwear like a weed among roses. "Will it be swish?"

"It's a black-tie event."

I thought of my maxed-out credit card. I'd helped my mother with a few necessary purchases and bills. I could hardly go to Oxfam for a gown.

"I'll be there Friday. A friend has invited me to dinner. We can catch up then, and if you let me, I can give you my credit card to buy yourself a gown."

"Oh." I shifted on the sofa. I hated taking his money. "I was wondering about what to wear. I don't exactly have much here. Unless I borrow that green dress?"

"No." His sharp response came as no surprise. He treated that session in his studio as something private, for his eyes only. And that gown was somewhat skimpy, especially with my full figure.

• • • ● • ● • • •

DANIEL KISSED ME ON the cheek, and I breathed him in as I would an elevating fragrance. I had missed him. It had only been five days, but I'd gotten used to being around him daily, which bothered me—that once fiercely independent woman.

He gazed into my eyes and smiled, unleashing a battalion of goosebumps.

"Shopping, then?" Cocking his head, Daniel looked so handsome I almost wanted to hit him.

"You don't wish to visit the gallery?" I pointed at the imposing Greek-columned edifice with Britannia sitting proudly at its peak, symbolizing art's conquering power.

He shook his head. "I've already been in. I make a habit of visiting each time I'm in the city."

Taking my hand, he squeezed it gently. Electricity sizzled right through me, and I fell even more heavily in love.

We jumped in a cab and ended up on Bond Street.

"Where's your car?" I asked.

"I left it at Mayfair."

"You have a home there?" I asked.

He nodded. "It belonged to my grandmother. I've just taken possession of it recently. It's a lovely double-story Edwardian house. That's where I'm staying this weekend—and you can join me, if you'd like to."

Always the gentleman with that formal tone of his. One would never have guessed that we'd fucked in every physically possible position.

I smiled. "That would be nice."

"Good." He looked into my eyes, which, as always, made me weak with desire.

People stared at us—mainly Daniel, who, in his dark-green slacks, linen shirt, and pale-blue blazer, exuded that effortless elegance that comes from a lifetime of privilege.

"You really don't need to do this," I said as we strolled along. "Wouldn't you prefer to be staring at art or talking to your accountant?"

He stopped walking and turned toward me. "I like being with you. And I visited my accountant this morning. I hate talking money."

"But you have to manage it, don't you?"

"Yes, I do. It's not that difficult when there's plenty to keep me and half of this country fed for a lifetime."

"Do I detect a hint of sarcasm?" I asked.

He shrugged. "At times, that amount of money overwhelms me."

"How did it amass?"

"It goes back centuries."

"No profligate offspring?" I asked.

"I'm sure there was the odd one here and there. And my father had a predilection for gambling and women. But, overall, there's been astute management."

That was the first time he mentioned his father, and though I was dying to probe further, I remained silent. With Daniel, one could ask the odd personal question here and there. I didn't want him clamming up on me. I loved chatting with him about anything and everything. He had an erudite mind and happily participated in discussions about books, philosophy, and history, but I'd lose him if the conversation veered toward gossip, the latest trends, or social media.

In the end, I settled on a blue silk Chanel. Flattering and slimming at the same time, the gown fitted me like a glove.

Daniel nodded. "It's lovely. It suits you."

My heart fluttered with anticipation as I looked at myself in the mirror. I felt like Cinderella.

At my age? This only happened to young women, not forty-year-old divorcées—which is what I was at last. Kevin begrudgingly signed the divorce papers, the only positive to come out of that attack, though he only did it because his legal team suggested it would help his case.

A few hours later, we were at Jerry's house, Daniel's college friend, who happened to live close to my mother's house.

"Do you come here very often?" I asked, surprised that we were in such a poor area.

"No. Only when I visited you."

"Does it shock you?" I asked, noticing a gang of youth smoking and poking at each other in the ribs.

"It's sad rather than confronting." He parked his car in front of an old warehouse. "I've offered to buy Jerry a house, but he won't take it."

"He must be a good friend," I said.

"He's my best friend. He's only just moved here. It's a studio. He likes to work where he lives."

Although it was run-down on the outside, the interior was a warm, inviting, open space with a potbelly stove. Brightly painted, the room boasted a clutter of interesting knickknacks and art.

Jerry met us at the door and showed us in. He hugged Daniel and kissed me on the cheek.

"It's nice to meet you." He wore a bright, welcoming smile.

A young boy ran out and wrapped his arms around Daniel's legs, then Daniel lifted the young boy and hugged him.

"This is Archie," his father said to me. "Dan's his godfather."

I smiled at the heart-warming sight.

Despite his compromised speech, the high-spirited boy expressed nothing but affection.

As the night progressed, I loved how attentive Daniel was toward the boy, taking time to look at the child's art and offer words of encouragement.

My heart melted. Despite his insistence on not craving fatherhood, Daniel would make a great dad, I reflected with a touch of sadness. I'd never be able to give him that gift.

After we'd taken a tour of Jerry's studio and viewed images of his latest mural in progress, we sat down to eat.

The stew went down well. I liked earthy cuisine—and my digestion preferred it too.

"So what brings you to London?" Jerry asked.

"A party. Georgie's turning fifty and she's throwing a big bash."

"Oh." He glanced at me quickly before returning his attention to Daniel. "Are you both going?"

Daniel took my hand and nodded. "Scarlet knows that Georgie and I have a past."

After dinner, while Daniel tucked Archie in bed and read him a story, which I found so adorable I nearly cried, Jerry went outside for a joint.

He passed it to me, but I declined and lit up a cigarette instead.

"You're an actress, Daniel tells me."

My eyebrows raised. "Oh, he's mentioned me?"

"He has."

"Did he tell you that I was a plant?" I asked.

He nodded. "After you left, he called me, sounding flat and lost. I convinced him to forgive you. From what he tells me, you've been through a difficult time."

"I've become his model," I said.

"How's that going? Have you seen his work?"

I shook my head. "But I've caught a glimpse. He wasn't too happy about it."

He returned my sniff with an eye roll and head shake. "I know. It doesn't make sense. He's a huge talent. At art school he used to get judged for being too technical. His draftsman skills are second to none. The teachers were trying to mold him into a contemporary artist."

"Oh, they thought his work too dated?" I asked.

"Art's never dated, in my opinion. But modern-day institutions tend to favor the next Tracey Emin or Lucian Freud."

"But why be so secretive? Did he have a bad experience at college?"

"He used to argue with the tutors all the time. Dan refused to play their game. He hated having his art judged. I think they were jealous of his precocious skills. I certainly was." He chuckled, then became serious. "What did you see?"

"I saw an image of the Folly by the pond."

He nodded slowly. "Ah . . . that doesn't surprise me. Tell me, was he listening to heavy metal?"

My eyes widened. "He was."

"While some might get plastered and do crazy things, Dan's outlet is his painting—like most artists, I suppose." He smiled. "His darker themes are in black and white."

I nodded. "Only the painting I saw had a confronting set of bleeding eyes. The splash of red drew you straight to the fear."

He shook his head, lost in contemplation for a moment. "You know about what happened to his mother and father, right? He's told you?"

"No. But the staff mentioned something about the father killing Daniel's mother, then his father being found dead."

He looked over my shoulder as Daniel came to join us.

"You two look lost in conversation," he said.

"We were just discussing your talent as an artist," Jerry said.

Daniel's gaze shifted from Jerry to me, remaining blank. "Mm . . . Archie's asleep."

"Thanks, Dan. He was so excited when I told him you were visiting."

"So where's your new girl?" Daniel asked.

"Melanie's taking care of her sick mother." He stretched out his arm for us to go back inside.

The rest of the night was spent looking at art, drinking fine wine, and getting to know Daniel a little more through the lens of his best friend.

# CHAPTER 26

FIRST, I FELT HIS hot breath, then his moist lips on my neck, as Daniel stood close behind me. Desire flushed through me, making my skin ripple in warmth as his drugging, pine-infused scent wafted over me.

"You look beautiful," he said.

I stared into the mirror at his handsome reflection. "As do you in that tux, although . . ." I smiled flirtatiously. "I rather like you in your painting gear. That half-open shirt and those tight, torn jeans make me all hot and steamy."

He studied me with his signature half smirk. "Is that why those nipples are always so provocatively perky?"

"Oh, you noticed?"

"As a painter, I notice everything," he said, adjusting his diamond cufflinks in the mirror.

"What about as a man?" I had to ask.

"Oh, he noticed too. Those tight jeans got a little tighter."

"Really?" I smiled seductively, stroking his dick. "Did you want to...?"

"Fuck?" he asked.

I nodded.

He came close to me and ran his hands over my breasts, then down my waist to my ass. "What do you think?"

"I don't know. You're not easy to read. And to be honest, I still don't get this. I mean, you're a young, stunning man."

"And you're a very beautiful, sexy woman."

I turned around and slid my hand down the silk trim of his black fitted jacket. With his thick, dark hair styled away from his handsome, tanned face, and those dark bedroom eyes, Daniel cut an irresistible male figure. "You'll have everyone swooning."

The butler knocked on the door, and I jumped. I'd forgotten that his home was fully staffed. Elizabeth insisted they remain, which meant that the house was always ready for when Daniel stayed at Mayfair.

"Your car's arrived, sir."

Feeling like a million dollars in my new Chanel gown, I draped a pale blue silk stole over my shoulders and followed Daniel to the door. Radiating heat, his hand rested on the middle of my back while he accompanied me to a shiny silver and burgundy Rolls Royce, where the uniformed driver opened the door for us, and I slid onto the green leather seat.

Daniel nodded to the driver. "Colin."

He bowed his head. "Sir."

"Chasterton House."

And off we went, gliding into the night with Daniel's warm hand on my thigh.

He turned to look at me. "Are you okay?"

"I'm a little shaky." I gave a tight smile.

"You look stunning." He kissed my hand, and I floated off into a dream. We were sitting so close that our shoulders touched, sending a flurry of tingles down my arm.

We arrived at a gated estate surrounded by white walls. The filigree iron gate opened, and the car drove to the entrance of a white, double-story, curvaceous Edwardian mansion. At its feet lay a garden in full bloom and a quaint pond with a bridge.

Colin held the car door open and out I stepped, trying to be as graceful as such an occasion demanded. My nerves were at fever pitch. What if I spoke in my street talk? Everyone in this upper-class scene, including Daniel, spoke with a plum in their mouths. An accent I could do in my sleep, given my theatre training. In real life, however, it made me sound pretentious.

Once inside, we entered a pink room embellished with carved white trimmings and a variety of paintings, ranging from classical to minimalist abstracts.

"Daniel," a woman's voice uttered from behind.

A woman with long red hair and big green eyes, who could have passed as my older sister, grinned back at me.

Daniel kissed her on the cheek.

He stretched his hand out. "I'd like to introduce Scarlet Black." He looked at me. "This is Georgina Preston."

She leaned in and kissed me. Her piercing musk perfume rushed up my nose. "Nice to meet you." As she studied me, I sensed her sizing me up, just like I was doing to her.

Georgina was one of those enviable few that at fifty didn't possess one wrinkle. She had such a flawless milky complexion that any cosmetic intervention was hard to spot. I'd been around many fading actresses to generally know the difference.

An older male, wearing an ostentatious purple suit and floral shirt, swanned over. "Georgie, darling, I didn't know you had a sister."

"She doesn't look anything like me," she said in a dismissive, bordering on disparaging, tone. "Scarlet Black, meet Quentin Slye."

I almost laughed. With those narrow, smirking eyes, he suited that name.

"Oh my . . . Let me guess, your parents were Stendhal tragics?" He touched his mouth and giggled.

I'd started to regret my name choice.

He turned to Daniel. "And aren't you looking like an Adonis in that fine Italian tux."

Daniel's lips lifted slightly at one end. The man didn't have a conceited bone in his body.

Small talk followed to which I didn't listen. Georgina's loud personality took center stage. She was one of those people who loved to hog the limelight. In the acting scene, there were tons like her, who, unsurprisingly, managed to swing the big parts.

Her earlier slap down still stung, and I sighed with relief when Daniel led me to another room, where the party was in full swing.

The large room, which I imagined was once a ballroom, had chandeliers, arched concave features housing statues, and wall-to-wall art. Pure sensory overload. No color had been spared, but it was beautifully composed by someone blessed with impeccable taste.

Laughter and chatter layered over a jazz quartet performing unobtrusive background music.

We mingled while I sipped on excellent champagne and watched Georgie flit from one person to another. All the while she'd look over at Daniel, either winking or pursing her lips on occasion. She was the proverbial social butterfly. Wearing a burgundy clingy velvet gown, she had curves in all the right places, and a twist of jealousy bit into my mood.

Daniel, meanwhile, stood by my side as guests dropped by for a chat and a peck of his swarthy cheeks.

Quentin kept hanging around. The hungry look in his eyes matched my own for Daniel. With that strong, upright, and quiet bearing, Daniel cut the kind of dishy, mysterious man that sent one's libido into overdrive.

Daniel leaned in close. "Would you like to step outside?"

A cigarette was just what I needed.

I followed him out to a large courtyard boasting ivy-clad walls and a charming fountain with a statue of Mercury.

Marijuana drifted over, and I saw Georgie taking a puff.

The joint came to us, and I shook my head. Daniel took a puff and passed it on.

"I didn't realize you smoked weed," I said.

"Occasionally. At parties."

Georgie sashayed over to us. Her attachment to Daniel was more than obvious. She didn't even try to hide the fact she was in love with him—either that, or she was competitive to a fault.

She whispered something into Daniel's ear, and he shook his head. Her plump lips turned down in a show of exaggerated disappointment.

As though sensing my insecurity, Daniel took my hand. I hoped she'd get the message and stop the shameless flirt act. I even noticed her running her tongue over her lips as she whispered into his ear.

When Georgie moved away, I asked Daniel, "Where's her husband?"

"He's probably in the study showing off his original editions."

"Oh, he's into literature?"

"Crofton is the dean of literature at Oxford."

My eyebrows lifted. "How interesting. He'd be great to chat with."

"Mention George Eliot and you'll have his ear all night." He smiled.

"Well then, I'll be sure to mention Middlemarch."

Daniel draped his arm around me and drew me close. "I hope you're wearing those silk panties."

His eyes flickered playfully. This was a new, sexy dynamic shift between us, and since I moved back, his guard had lowered. I was starting to see the man—still morose at times, but increasingly relaxed and smiling more often.

Georgie slithered over again. In that fitted dress, her movements were serpentine.

"You're both looking all loved up, I must say." Her eyes slid from me to Daniel and remained on him.

Daniel regarded me with a smile. "I'm happy."

Georgie's head jerked back with a frown. "Now, that's unlike you, Danny."

He shrugged. "I've changed." He took my hand and led me back inside.

The champagne had loosened my tongue. "Had she offered herself?"

He turned sharply to face me. "She'd never do that. She knows me too well."

"Oh?"

"I'm a one-woman man. Always have been."

I looked up lovingly into his warm brown eyes and couldn't wait to return to Mayfair and perform my version of seductress, a role I'd recently honed under Daniel's guidance. I'd discovered he had a thing for strip, while I had a thing for his big, beautiful cock. I couldn't get it out of my mouth.

While Daniel went over to chat with some of the older guests, who he relayed were friends of his late grandmother's, I hovered around a table, snacking on the fine array of finger food.

Georgina glided over and joined me.

She cut a slice of cheese and placed it on a cracker. "We normally do a sit-down meal for these events, but I felt like something a little more casual."

"It's a lovely party. Your house is exquisite. You've got great taste," I said.

"The house belongs to Crofton. A lot of what you see is him. He's rather into embellishments."

"And you're not?" I asked.

"I like to hang out at my ultra-minimalist apartment in Paddington. I'm drawn to simple lines." She tilted her head. "What about you, Scarlet? What are you drawn to? Other than handsome, younger men."

"I don't go out of my way to sleep with younger men."

"Why not?" She cocked her head. "They make the best lovers at our age."

"I'm not your age," I said, coolly.

"Still, it takes an adventurous woman to go there, especially with someone like Daniel."

"I'm not expecting long term," I said. "I'm just enjoying . . ."

"His nice big cock?" She smirked.

"That's personal."

"Oh. But we share something in common. And knowing Daniel's large appetite, I can't imagine you're there just for the conversation." She chuckled. "He's also not a man one forgets."

"Clearly. You haven't forgotten him."

She smiled. Her heavily kohled eyes wandered up and down my body. "I can understand his fascination with you given his predilection for bigger women." Her eyes settled on my cleavage. "But bulimic Charlie. That was one big mistake."

"He hasn't spoken much about her."

"That's understandable, considering the circumstances," she said, popping a grape in her mouth.

I studied her for a moment. "What do you mean?"

"Her mysterious disappearance. It's no secret that Daniel despised her." She shrugged. "His father murdered his mother, you know."

Despite that shocking inference, my heart went out to Daniel. Georgina was going straight for the throat.

"I don't think he's capable," I said.

"He fucked me on their wedding night." She pulled a mock smile.

"What?" I asked.

Daniel strode over and his eyes landed on my grimacing face, while Georgie's self-satisfied smirk mirrored that of someone having kicked the winning goal.

"What's happening here?"

"I just told Scarlet how we fucked on your wedding night."

His brow scrunched and anger darkened his eyes. "You're a fucking troublemaker, Georgie."

She ran her tongue lasciviously over her lips. "You're too irresistible a subject not to brag about."

Daniel cast me an apologetic look and flicked his head for us to leave Georgie alone.

I shook my head in disbelief. "Was she telling the truth?" I asked, following him outside.

He clicked open a gold case and offered me a cigarette, which I took. This was not the time to cut back on bad habits.

I stared expectantly at him.

"My wedding day was a farce. Charlie flirted in her typical fashion, and generally made a spectacle of herself. By the end of it, I was drunk. Georgina cornered me and..."

"You fucked," I said.

As someone who'd made some pretty bad choices, especially after a few drinks, I had no right to judge him. In this case, it was Georgina who'd hit the gutter.

"If you wish to leave, I'm happy to go." He wore a contrite half-smile.

"No. It's fine." I looked down at my drink.

He took my hand. "I like you being around. You have a calming quality."

When I didn't comment, his gaze remained fixed on me. How could I respond to that tepid explanation?

"Have I said something wrong?" he finally asked.

"No. I'm chuffed that you like my company." I tried to keep my tone neutral. But Daniel, whose brow creased, picked up on my subtle sarcasm.

"I'm not great at talking about my feelings. And I hate to share."

I rolled my eyes. Didn't I know it.

He brushed my arm tenderly. "All I can say is that when you're not around, I miss you. I like having you in my bed. I like the way you smell. I like the way you feel." His lopsided uncertain smile warmed my spirit. I could see he was trying. And for someone who didn't expect a lot from this arrangement, that was more than enough.

"I get it, Daniel. And if it helps, I'm not a fan of Charlie for roping you into marrying her under false pretenses. That was a low act. And we all fuck up."

"Have you ever cheated?" he asked.

I nodded slowly. "When I was younger, I did once. Booze and cast parties were a toxic mix. It was hard not to live in the moment." I stubbed out my cigarette.

"I am possessive to a fault," he said, after a moment of reflection.

"You're deep, Daniel. I get that. But after being married to a controlling man, the word 'possessive' scares me."

He remained silent.

"It's just that you mentioned earlier you're a one-woman man, that's all. Did you just say that because you thought I'd like to hear it?"

His face crumpled. "I don't play games, Scarlet."

"Are you still fucking her?" I had to ask.

He shook his head decisively.

"She's still in love with you," I said.

"Georgie craves the limelight. She loves to flirt. It's purely a game for her. In any case, she's too shallow to fall in deep."

While studying his face for signs of disappointment, I discovered nothing. "And you fell deeply for her?"

"I was young. I'm not that person anymore." He took my hand. "Let's go back in."

# CHAPTER 27

## *Daniel*

I HEADED INTO THE study and found Crofton waving his hands effusively, no doubt discussing some famous passage in a book. He turned and, seeing me there, his eyes lit up.

"Ah . . . Daniel. It's been too long." He shook my hand.

"This is Scarlet Black," I said, knowing full well what would follow.

Georgina's husband's eyes beamed with curiosity. "What a fetching name. Stendhal?" He cocked his head.

She nodded slowly.

"You could do worse. It's a perfect book."

"I know. I wrote an essay on it," she said.

"How interesting." He kept looking at her, then at me.

Unlike his wife, Crofton kept his thoughts to himself. Apart from his love of books and appetite for long discussions on that very subject, he rarely discussed people. And although he knew about my intimate history with Georgina, he always treated me respectfully.

At first, I couldn't look him in the eye without feeling guilt. But after a few dinner parties, where he treated me warmly, I established that Crofton didn't mind whom Georgie slept with.

Theirs was a marriage of convenience. For Georgie, it was his pedigree and super-wealth. As for Crofton, I sensed it was the companionship. Georgie doted on him, while he seemed to delight in her life-of-the-party antics. Georgina suspected him to be a closet homosexual. Regardless, the fact he didn't show any interest in the bedroom—and that his wife was a nymphomaniac—got tongues wagging.

Depressed from having married a woman I didn't love, I'd hit the bottle at my wedding. Georgie cornered me. She'd removed her panties, and I lost all sense of propriety. Other than Charlie, Georgina was the only woman I'd ever fucked. I'd lost my head over her. I thought she was the love of my life. But that was my dick talking. Georgie was the quintessential seductress.

Until Scarlet. She was something else. I'd never felt this kind of addictive sexual desire for a woman before. But it was more than sex. I also loved her company.

I'd even started to wonder if she was my soulmate. Or was it simply insatiable lust? Even at that party, with no shortage of pretty women—young women with curves in all the right places—I remained captivated by Scarlet.

Watching Scarlet chat with Crofton, I smiled at how passionate and expressive she became when discussing literature. And as predicted, they'd fallen into a deep discussion about nineteenth-century literature. I left them alone for a moment.

Georgie, who'd been following me around all night, cornered me.

"Hey, what were you thinking telling Scarlet about my wedding night?"

Her mouth lifted slowly at one end, an expression I once found adorable that now made her appear sly. "You know me, a few drinks and I can't help myself."

"Why do I get this feeling you're trying to sabotage my relationships?"

She flicked a wavy red lock over her shoulder. "I just like to stir the pot." She trapped me into a staring contest. "So, another older woman?"

"I didn't plan it that way. It just happened."

"Tell me, is she modeling for you in that green dress?"

I didn't answer her.

"You're going to have to tell her about what happened," she said.

"Scarlet doesn't try to get into my head about things. That's one of the reasons I like her."

"One of the reasons?" she asked.

I raised my eyebrows. "There's no need to spell it out, Georgie. You know me."

"Yes, I do." She stepped closer. "I know you well. Only I'm disappointed that you haven't called me. What with Charlie gone."

I breathed in deeply. "I've moved on. You had a chance."

"Would you have stayed?" I searched for that playful twinkle in her eyes but found only a hint of vulnerability.

"It's pointless to live in the past. To speculate about something that happened long ago."

"Then why do you?" she asked.

Because nightmares won't let me forget.

# CHAPTER 28

## *Scarlet*

DANIEL LOUNGED BACK IN a velvet armchair with his legs crossed, sipping scotch and smoking a cigarette. He would have made a great advertisement illustrating the charmed existence of the rich and powerful. It was after midnight, and we'd just arrived back to Mayfair after leaving the party.

"Sit there." He pointed at a sofa across from him. "And let out your hair."

Oh, so we were going to play this game. Seductress I could do.

I sat down and unraveled my bun, my hair cascading over my shoulders.

"Lower your strap," he said.

Holding his hooded gaze, I let it slide off and excitement sashayed through me.

"Remove your bra."

I unclasped my strapless bra and pulled it out from my armholes.

"Now you remove your shirt," I said, matching his bossy tone.

He unbuttoned his tailored white shirt. The hint of hair on his firm chest sent a shiver of arousal through me, setting off an insistent throb in my core, which had started in the car after he fondled me.

I licked my lips as my eyes settled on his growing bulge. "Now remove your trousers."

His searing gaze trapped mine as he unbuckled his designer belt.

In a lust-induced trance, I went to him and ran my hand over his dick tenting his cotton briefs.

I released his veiny, engorged dick and licked the salty head, widening my mouth to take him in deep.

He gasped as I moved up and down while he fondled my breasts. His sighs of pleasure inspired me to ravage him.

Removing himself from my mouth, he stood up, lifted me off the floor, and walked me to the wall.

Instead of recoiling at the tear of my very expensive gown, I burned as he turned me to the wall. He rubbed his hard, thick length against the crotch of my wet panties, and I nearly came on the spot.

He leaned against me, his hot breath against my neck. His finger looped inside my panties, and he stroked my swollen bud until my legs trembled.

As he entered me in one sharp thrust, I bit my lip to stymy a cry. It was so painfully full and pleasurable at the same time.

"I love your wet cunt," he said.

He rocked his hips in and out, every thick inch pumping in and out of me, his ragged breath in my ear until I came so hard that the walls of my pussy spasmed uncontrollably.

His own release was just as violent. As he growled, streams of cum gushed into me. It seemed like an endless flow.

He carried me to bed, his lips on mine.

• • • • ● • ● • • •

IT HAD NOW BEEN two months since I'd started living with Daniel as though we were married. Despite a burning desire to discuss our relationship, I remained tight-lipped, reluctant to burst our romantic bubble. And it was very romantic. Candlelit dinners, slow lovemaking that brought tears to my eyes, and hot, passionate moments that made my eyes roll to the back of my head. I was overdosing on orgasms.

"We're entertaining this weekend," Daniel said, as we walked through the forest with Thor and Zeus puffing at our heels.

"Oh?" I paused.

"It's the annual Beltane. The participants camp here for the night."

"Like, pitch tents, you mean?"

He grinned at my shocked tone. "Portable toilets should be arriving tomorrow. And Jack has arranged for food vans this year. It saves the house from being infiltrated by stragglers."

"By stragglers?" I frowned. "It doesn't sound like you to entertain strangers here."

"No. But my late mother had it written into her will. Starlington must always welcome those who wish to celebrate the Goddess."

"She sounded highly spiritual."

"My great-aunt Cordelia had been a close friend of Oleander's and my mother became interested also. She'd attend séances."

"How did your wife take all these festivities?"

"She loved it. It gave her a chance to fuck some young stud." He sniffed.

"Oh . . . Beltane." I thought about what I knew of that famous Pagan rite related to fertility and ancient Bacchanalias. "Do they have orgies?"

He shrugged. "Let's just say that people go wild. Some take hallucinogenic drugs."

"What did your father make of your mother's involvement with witchcraft?"

"He was too busy fucking the young staff."

His cool but dry delivery made my frown deepen. Questions kept mounting, far and beyond his mother's inclination to the paranormal.

"So are the revelers allowed in the house?" I asked, imagining a bunch of randy millennials bonking on the silk sofas and Persian rugs.

"No. They stay up all night, roaming through the wood."

"Aren't you worried they might fall off the cliff?"

He shrugged. "I get them to sign a waiver."

I laughed. "How incongruous. But probably wise in this highly litigious era."

• • • • • • • • • •

BY SATURDAY, EVERYTHING WAS in full swing. A motley, colorful array of people pitched tents while security guards ensured the house remained out of bounds.

The grounds were covered in tents and food trucks, and Randall hovered about directing people.

"You're not worried about the damage to your lawns?" I asked him, knowing how much pride he took in his manicured ground.

He just shrugged. "It's part of the job. I do as I'm asked. It's a fun weekend, anyway. Lots of pretty girls wearing very little or nothing." He chuckled. "I'm an old hippy at heart."

I walked around to the side of the estate, where Oleander, the spriteliest octogenarian I'd ever seen, made herself comfortable at a table in the courtyard by the rose garden.

As we shared afternoon tea, her grandson, Crowley—a warm, jolly guy with a hearty laugh—chatted with Daniel. Being the same age, they grew up together I was told.

After Daniel left us to take a call, and Crowley went for a walk, I was left alone with Oleander. Absorbing the pleasant afternoon sun, I watched butterflies fluttering over a pink and red rose bush. The scent from that part of the house always left me slightly intoxicated, especially during the evenings, when the moist night air trapped its sweet perfume.

Dressed in a purple robe, Oleander personified the New Age matriarch with her long white braid. She spoke with well-enunciated vowels and crisp diction, and her wide, probing, blue eyes shone with intelligence.

"I must say, Daniel is looking so much better. I haven't seen him smile for a long while," she said, setting her cup down on the table.

"He has his moments," I said.

Her scrutinizing gaze lingered as though reading my thoughts. "Tell me, is he still painting?"

"Yes. That's primarily my role here, to be his model."

"Is that so? I thought you were lovers."

"Is it that obvious?" I asked.

"It is to me." Her eyes held mine. "Have you seen his work?"

I shook my head. "Once. Uninvited, of course. He wasn't too pleased." I sniffed at how stupid that sounded.

"He treats his art as therapy, my darling. I wouldn't take it to heart. It's a sacred communion for him. Having observers is a desecration for Daniel. He's a fine talent. I attended his first-year college exhibition. But then Georgina Preston weaved her charms and he changed. Suddenly his art took a back seat."

"You speak as though she messed with his head," I said.

"Georgie's always the life of the party, however there's dark energy in there somewhere. I'd even say she's got a dark soul."

Having observed her sexy mind games with Daniel, Georgie was definitely a trouble-stirrer.

"He fell pretty hard for her though," I said.

Oleander nodded reflectively. "At that age, it's understandable. She was and still is, a voluptuous beauty. She has a magnetic way about her."

She studied me closely. "You're nothing like her, are you? You are, however, physically alike."

"I didn't go out of my way to seduce Daniel, if that's what you mean. I'm older and quite ordinary in many ways."

"Oh, you're far from ordinary." She smiled. "Daniel's not like men his age. He's an old soul—a kind being who's suffered greatly." She shook her head as though reliving something frightful.

I frowned. "You mean Charlotte's disappearance?"

Her decisive shake of head made my veins tighten. "His father was a bad man—a dark force that afflicted all who came near him. Cathy,

Daniel's mother, was like a daughter to me. A beautiful blithe spirit who'd been blessed by Terpsichore herself."

"The goddess of dance?" I asked.

She nodded. "She's one of my favorite muses. I was once a ballerina. I danced for the Royal Ballet."

Noting her long slender neck and upright bearing, I said, "I can still see the dancer in you."

She wore a faint, wistful smile. "Once it chooses us, art never leaves." She touched her heart. "We sacrifice everything for art. We reveal our naked souls for art. It's a spiritual communion."

There was something so powerful in what she said. I only wished I'd committed myself to the theatre in that same spiritually driven way. It was the other way for me. I'd sadly sacrificed art for men.

"You were saying something about Daniel's mother..."

"She traveled Europe working as a model. But deep down she was always a child of the forest."

"Daniel has shown me photos. She was very beautiful."

"A beautiful soul too." She looked into the distance as though seeing the woman herself. "Starlington was Cathy's. It belonged to her family. Despite being a woman of means, she still fell for that evil man." She sighed deeply. I felt Oleander's pain. I could see the passing of Daniel's mother had profoundly impacted her.

"Pan, whom it's believed Christians adopted to symbolize the devil, has always been the master of us women. One may have a night or two of pleasure with the Horned one, but one should never marry him."

I had to smile at that image. I wondered about the devil I'd married. He wasn't even good in the sack.

"Teddy Love had women swirling at his feet. A dark, tall, handsome man. Daniel has his looks. But that's the only thing they share." She continued to stare into the distance as though watching her memories on a screen. "Cathy fell hard for Teddy. I don't know why women like brutish men." She glanced at me, a question in her eyes.

Did she know about Kevin?

"Cathy was that masochist I'm afraid," she continued. "She had suitors coming from everywhere. But she went for the devil himself."

"So, are you saying that Cathy sacrificed herself to Teddy?"

"She sacrificed what may have been a healthy, long life for eighteen years with an abusive man."

"Did he hit her?" My body grew rigid.

"He did more than that. He had sex with any young, pretty thing that swayed his way. Took them to the folly. Didn't even cover his tracks. Poor Cathy. The brute would hit her if she complained." She paused for a breath. "And then one night he killed her." Her eyes had gone glassy.

Her sorrow touched me deeply.

"That must have broken Daniel."

"Oh yes. He retreated into himself. Elizabeth, whom I believe you met briefly, Goddess bless her soul, was really worried about him. And then he went and tried to . . ." She paused.

"I know about his suicide attempt. He told me."

Her eyebrows rose sharply. "That's a surprise. He's a very guarded man. No one was meant to know. Only Elizabeth. She was so understandably distraught that she confided in me." She regarded me warmly. "He must really trust you."

A bad taste of guilt made my mouth pasty. I wasn't prepared to share how I came to be at Starlington—and how I'd chanced upon his scarred wrists.

"He's the happiest I've seen him in a long time. I don't think I ever saw him smile once when he was married." She lifted the China cup. "Cathy's protecting him I believe."

"You mean his late mother's ghost?"

She nodded.

I swallowed some water. "Do you feel Charlie's energy?"

She shook her head. "Another poor choice. I warned Daniel about her. I told him she wasn't pregnant. I did a reading. The Nine of Swords, the Tower, and the Fool all lined up. Oh my Goddess, that augured badly."

Daniel and Crowley came and joined us just as the questions mounted. The more I heard, the more mysterious Daniel's family became.

"You look as though you're in a deep conversation," Daniel said, taking a seat.

"Well, you know me, love, I'm not one for small talk," Oleander said with a chuckle.

I liked her. She possessed the kind of wisdom and eccentric, albeit accurate, observations that I often admired in those who'd gone off life's beaten track.

• • • • • • • • •

BY EARLY EVENING, MY favorite fir tree had been dressed in lacing ribbons to represent a Maypole.

Flames danced in a cleared section of the forest, where a bonfire redolent of herbs raged, its smoke mingling with a cloud of marijuana.

A young woman danced over and hugged me, leaving behind a lingering scent of musk. "Hi, I'm Eurydice." Her pretty brown eyes sparkled with glee as she hugged me.

"Come and dance around the Maypole." She clutched my hand.

I glanced over at Daniel, who returned a smile. He seemed so heartwarmingly relaxed as he chatted with Crowley and a man in a black cloak, who looked like he'd stepped out of The Lord of the Rings.

Pleasantly lightheaded, I couldn't stop smiling after drinking a glass of mead—Oleander's magic brew—which I speculated contained more than just booze and honey.

Eurydice wouldn't take no for an answer as she dragged me along. "I'm not a maiden," I protested.

"Neither am I," she said with a cheeky grin. Dressed in a diaphanous dress that showed her naked frame, she was a stunning girl who I'd noticed had an audience of male admirers.

"No. Really. It's not me. I'm a non-believer. It wouldn't seem right. Let me just enjoy watching you and your friends. You all look gorgeous."

She shrugged and was intercepted by a young, striking, bare-chested man in tights. He drew her close and kissed her passionately. She'd found her Horned god for the night.

A smile touched my lips as I thought about Daniel, more a horny god than anything else. My core sizzled at the prospect of us alone and naked.

Timeless. That's how that moment seemed. Women in white. Flowers in their hair. Weaving in and out of each other, holding onto a bright ribbon. Their silky gowns floating in the air like an Isadora Duncan performance. Recalling the muses from ancient myths, I traveled back thousands of years as though watching a Greek frieze come to life.

The forest seemed to glow not only by the roaring bonfire but by moonbeams filtering through its leafy canopies.

Daniel came and draped his arm around my waist. I let him take the lead, his public display of affection touching.

Together we watched women swirling and leaping in floaty gowns.

"This is quite a performance," I said.

"It's a special night," he said.

Drumming built up to a crescendo and I felt my hips swaying. "I feel like dancing. The music's rather hypnotic."

I led him by the hand, where we joined a crowd of writhing bodies, lost in their own world, shaking, twirling, and leaping about to the primal beats.

"It feels like I've had E," I said.

Daniel smiled. "Oleander puts all kinds of herbal potions in her mead."

"I like the feeling." I started to giggle at Daniel's obvious intoxication. His dilated eyes twinkled with a hint of amusement. I hadn't seen him this relaxed before.

"Why are you laughing?" he asked.

"I'm stoned," I said while gyrating my hips.

"You're a great dancer," he said.

I grasped his hands and made him dance with me. He was a little unwilling at first, but he slowly started to loosen up.

We locked eyes and fell into each other's parallel universe.

After working up to a climax with sweat pouring down my face from the heat of the fire, we collapsed into each other's arms and laughed like children.

"It's so important to keep this tradition alive," I said. "I feel so blessed to have come here. To know you. Even putting aside the fact you make me see stars with that sexy body of yours." I slipped my finger through his loose shirt and slid down to his firm, smooth stomach. Arousal surged through me. The mead had heightened my already overstimulated libido.

He twisted a strand of my hair in his finger. "When we met on the path in the wood that first time, I was drawn to you. I'm not in the habit of chatting with people I don't know." His eyes shone with sincerity while tears burned at the back of mine.

He took my hand. "Come. Let's go back inside for a moment."

I stopped walking. "Tell me about the green dress."

# CHAPTER 29

*Daniel*

WE ENTERED THE BEDROOM and Scarlet giggled again, something she'd been doing all night. Normally I wasn't a fan of the mindless giggler, but her face came alive and made me smile.

"Why are you locking the door?" she asked.

"I don't want anyone bursting in."

She tilted her head with a challenging smirk. "Should I be frightened?"

I unbuttoned my shirt and walked toward her. "Aroused is the adjective we seek."

"I need to do something first." Before I could respond, she left the room.

I followed her up the stairs. "Where are you going?"

"To your studio," she said.

"But you know you're not allowed in there. And it's locked."

"Then you're going to open it and let me get something I left behind."

"Wait a minute, then," I said, walking in first so that I could cover my latest work of horror. "Okay, come in."

She headed behind the screen and after a few moments stepped out wearing the green dress. Something I should have expected. Scarlet wasn't going to stop quizzing me until I revealed my guilty obsession.

She sat on the chair, lowered her strap, and made my pulse pump. I pointed at the hem.

She raised it to her knee.

"Higher," I said. Sitting opposite her, I unzipped my pants.

"Were you hard while painting me?" She wore a teasing grin.

I nodded reluctantly. I'd broken that golden rule: An artist should always remain objective when painting an attractive model.

"Tell me about this dress."

"I had the family stylist buy it for me," I said.

She lowered the strap farther so that her breasts became half exposed. With her hair sitting over her shoulder and running her tongue coquettishly over her lips, the surge of blood to my dick turned volcanic.

Scarlet parted her legs, and I released my throbbing erection ripping a hole through my briefs.

"It's a silly boy's story," I said.

"Did Georgina wear a green dress when you lost your virginity?"

I shook my head slowly.

"Then please tell me."

There was no more hiding this little fetish. Scarlet would only keep asking. And maybe it was about time I shared my guilty little secret with someone.

I took a deep breath. "It was one of the family's many soirees. I was in the sitting room by the fire drawing when my aunt Hermione entered. She was married to my uncle Archie, my father's older brother." I needed a drink and, doing up my pants, walked over to the shelf and poured myself a generous measure. "Can I offer you one?"

She nodded.

I handed her a glass and sat down again. After taking a sip, I continued, "She was dressed in a green silk dress and very little else. She had big breasts that she liked to flaunt by dressing in low-cut blouses. It was no secret she liked men."

"How old was she?"

"She's still alive. At the time she was thirty."

"And you?"

"Fifteen," I said.

"Go on," she said.

"She swayed over to me, flirtatiously, and asked to see what I was drawing. I showed her—reluctantly, of course." I grinned. "I've always been private about my work. Anyway, she asked me if I would paint her. So, from then on, she arrived every afternoon for a week and requested that I draw her in a green dress, diamond necklace, and nothing else." I raised an eyebrow. "Being a young boy, I was..."

Scarlet said, "Horny?"

I nodded. "The second day, she lifted her dress to her knees, and the third day, all the way. Her pussy was naked."

"And you painted her pussy too?"

"Yep. The brush shook in my hand." I sniffed, shaking my head at that hormone-charged awakening. "After that, I was so aroused, I couldn't stop masturbating. I was confused and guilt-ridden. She was married to my father's brother."

"But you were a young man. Your sexual response was only natural. You didn't want to fuck a girl your age?"

I shook my head. "To be honest, I was only turned on by older women by that stage." I lit a cigarette.

"Mind if I have one?" she asked. I rose and lit her up. Our eyes met and hers seemed to reflect the burning heat between my legs.

"So, you painted her pussy. And you were hot for her, yes?"

"Overwhelmingly. On the third day, she looked at my creation for the first time and told me that she liked how I'd painted her face. She said it looked as though she was hungry for a cock."

"To a fifteen-year-old boy? My, how provocative."

"She rubbed my dick, which was already hard, then unzipped my pants, got on her knees, and sucked me off. My head nearly exploded. She made me come in her mouth. Anyway, the same thing happened the next day. Then she made me lick her cunt. She taught me how to use my tongue."

"She taught you well," Scarlet said, stubbing out her cigarette.

"So, for the rest of the week, she sucked me off and I licked her pussy. Then we got caught."

"Oh."

I relived the embarrassing moment my father stepped into the loft. "Luckily it was my reprobate father, who I'm sure was responsible for taking the painting I'd made of her."

"You didn't see her after that?" she asked.

I shook my head. "They moved to France. I'd heard that she was having some affair with a politician, and for the heat to go away, they had to leave quietly."

"You've never heard from her again?"

"No. I wasn't close to my uncle, especially after everything that happened here." I raised an eyebrow.

Steady. Don't open that can of worms.

I had to add, "It was a boyhood thing. By the time I met Georgina, I'd forgotten about Hermione."

"Well, not completely—because you've had me posing in a green dress."

"I'd already had a few models, but none of them sparked me up like you do—from the moment you stepped out from behind that curtain."

Her brow furrowed. "You had women modeling while you were with Charlie?"

I nodded. "We'd stopped fucking. I needed something to make me feel again. I was numb."

"And then you were aroused by me?"

"Oh God, yeah. You've even got the same fall to your breasts as Hermione had."

"What about my pussy?" she asked tilting her head. She lifted the dress all the way up and opened her legs.

A surge of fire made it to my dick.

"It's nicer. Tighter."

She frowned. "But you didn't fuck her."

"No. But I fingered her." My heart started to race. I was so hot to fuck after reliving that boy's dirty story that I crooked my finger.

She rose and walked over to me. She got on her knees, fisted my dick, and licked her lips.

"My... you're so hard."

Her fleshy, warm mouth sucked on the head of my dick, and I fell back and let out a sigh. "One could die of pleasure."

Up and down my shaft, her mouth gripped on tight; she was soft and hot, bringing me to the bursting point. Her eyes looked up at me as my dick filled her inviting mouth.

I needed to be inside of her. Badly.

Lifting her off the ground, I walked her to the wall, then hooked her knee under my arm and entered her in one ravenous thrust.

My heart raced like mad. I'd never felt so aroused.

"When you modeled for me that first time, I came really hard that night. I suddenly had a face for my fantasy."

"Oh?" She looked pleased. "You jerked off while fantasizing over me?"

I nodded as I pumped into her. "Your cunt is all juicy and open, like it is now. The green dress half hanging off you. Each time it was dangerous. Someone might come and find us."

"Did they?" I asked.

I nodded guiltily. "Yes, Charlotte would discover us. My cock in your mouth. Your tits in my hands."

"Aah . . ." Sharing my fantasy was not only making me want to erupt, but Scarlet's pussy was tightening in a frenzy as it contracted around my dick.

I turned her around and entered her again. My hands fondled her tits, which were sweaty and soft. "You feel so nice."

I came with such a thunder of a release that I yelled—something I'd never done before.

It was like I wasn't only releasing sperm, but also a guilty secret that once shared, had only intensified my hungry desire for Scarlet.

# CHAPTER 30

## *Scarlet*

AFTER DANIEL REVEALED THE origin of his green dress fetish, I refused to leave until seeing my painting.

"It's not finished. And I never share," he said.

"You've just shared an intimate detail of your life growing up. How could a painting of me be any more exposing?"

He released a deep breath, stepped in front of his easel, and lifted a sheet. "Come on, then."

Stepping away, he gave me space to look.

For some reason I expected to find something salacious, however the painting before me did little to shock. "You're an amazing draftsman. You've captured an expression I thought hidden."

His brows shifted. "How so?"

"Just that in my eyes there's this glint of uncertainty. I look insecure."

"I captured that the first day." He studied me. "You don't like it?"

"It's an astounding likeness." I shrugged. "But, sure, I wouldn't have minded coming across as more self-assured."

"But that's not you," he countered.

"It is me, but certain traumatic experiences have turned me into a shadow of my former self."

"Ainsley Alcott, you mean?"

I nodded slowly. It was a moot point. I wasn't sure if I'd ever be entirely comfortable in my own skin again. Although I felt physically safe around Daniel, emotionally, it often felt like I tiptoed along a flimsy rope bridge hanging over a rocky precipice.

A sad smile grew on his lips. "You've been through the wars, Scarlet. I'm sure that you'll heal with time. Just like I'm trying to do. It's easier said than done though."

That last comment was almost to himself. I switched from looking at his handsome face back to the painting. "You've only painted my upper torso and face."

"And?" He tilted his head.

"After hearing how you painted Hermione in all her glory"—I arched an eyebrow—"I expected something a little more salacious, I suppose."

"You sound disappointed."

"Do I?" I grinned. The ache between my legs fired up again. Who would have thought talking about art could be so arousing?

"I did fantasize about you posing with your exposed pretty cunt."

"'Pretty cunt'?" I laughed. I walked over to him and rubbed his semi-erect penis. It seemed he was aroused again too. "Mm . . . what have we got here?"

"Pose for me," he said.

"I thought you'd never ask." Falling into my position, I lowered my strap so that the bodice barely covered my tits. I then raised the silk gown and parted my legs. "How's that?"

His eyes darkened with lust. "Hot."

• • • • • • • • • •

IT HAD BEEN ONE week since Beltane, and we'd started to deepen our connection by exploring each other's erotic fantasies. By day, we took long walks while intellectualizing over anything and everything. Possessing a mercurial mind, Daniel enjoyed discussing worldly topics. As soon as it became personal, however, he'd clam up. Still, I'd gotten deeper into the man.

I was gazing at the rain-soaked window to a blurry vista of green meadows and red, yellow and purple flowers, reminiscent of a Monet, when a jarring, shrill voice snapped me out of my daydream.

I headed out to see what was happening when I came face to face with a blonde-haired woman of about thirty, done up to the nines. I assumed she was one of Daniel's friends because she reminded me of Camilla.

Daniel, meanwhile, looked bewildered, running his hands over his hair almost violently. He stopped suddenly when he saw me standing there with his visitor.

Speaking to me with his eyes, he wore the type of imploring look of someone pleading innocence. As though he were a man condemned.

I wondered if she was the law. But dressed like that? Wearing skin-tight designer jeans and a clingy pink blouse that matched her hot-pink pout, she didn't strike me as a cop.

A painful stretch of time followed. Silence screamed at me. Ambient sounds amplified as a tangle of questions thickened the air between us. All the while, Daniel's beseeching eyes continued to burn into mine.

"Well, aren't you going to introduce me?" she asked, wearing a dismissive smirk. Her high-pitched tone scraped at me like fingernails on a blackboard. All the while, she continued to run her cool blue eyes up and down my body.

Daniel released a jagged breath. He'd gone pale and I detected a hint of alarm in his eyes.

"This is Charlotte, my wife."

My eyebrows crashed. "Oh."

Her smirk, which seemed tattooed, remained etched on her heavily made-up face as she turned to Daniel. "She doesn't look pleased to see me. Neither do you, dear husband. You look like I've just come out of a grave." Her cold chuckle punched hard, sending a gush of bile to my throat.

Whether that visceral response was directly related to the love of my life's wife bursting through our romantic bubble or something more sinister, I couldn't decide.

Pointing at me, she cocked her head. "Let me guess, your latest girlfriend? You've always gone for the older, bigger women."

"Don't," Daniel snapped.

Her lips curled. She seemed to extract pleasure from taunting him.

"Well, is there a name? You both look stunned." She spoke with a nasally, high-pitched tone.

I couldn't understand how this woman could be married to Daniel. Putting aside her beautiful face, as manicured as the grounds of Versailles, there was an ugly heart buried inside. I gathered that from her haughty glare spitting scorn—not just at me, but also at her husband.

I held out my hand. "Scarlet."

Refusing to take my hand, she lifted her chin, then turned her back to me. "She goes."

Tottering on skyscraper stilettos, she clip-clopped out of the room, leaving behind a thick, invisible plume of asphyxiating perfume and tension.

My jaw dropped but words failed to follow.

Daniel looked at me and exhaled an audible breath. He opened his hands. "She just turned up."

My throat thickened, and a single tear escaped. I used all my might to avoid a scene out of respect for Daniel. Having gone pale, he looked like he'd seen a ghost. In this case, she was real. I would have preferred the dead kind.

What I found the most confronting, however, was Daniel struggling to speak. A knife could have sliced the air between us.

I waited for something: words of reassurance, anything, to remind me that there was an us. But nothing followed.

"Don't worry. I'll... grab my things and leave," I stammered.

He didn't stop me—which hurt.

What was I expecting?

Within two hours, I was in my old bomb of a car, heading to London. An eruption finally happened, and I cried like I'd never cried before. Like blood gushing from a severed artery to my heart, tears poured out of me.

• • • • ● • ● • • •

I WAS BACK IN my apartment in the city, and although losing myself in a crowd had proven helpful, I missed the space and the ever-changing beauty of Starlington, as I did Daniel.

For the first days, enshrouded by gloom, I barely moved from the sofa. More a lump of ice than flesh and blood, I stared out into space. Having been there before, I was well-practiced. Sadness was something I'd worn often, like that prickly pullover I'd possessed all my life.

Two weeks had passed since my hasty and emotional departure from Starlington. Although Daniel had called on numerous occasions, I couldn't bring myself to speak to him. His caressing, deep voice would have been torture. It would have dashed my resolve to shut him out for the sake of sanity.

Going through withdrawals, as though hooked on heroin, I shivered despite the sun on my skin. I couldn't eat, and burning tears intruded in awkward places—like on the street or visiting my mother, after she'd hugged me and I convulsed in her arms like a girl lost.

Late at night proved the hardest. I would hug my body and virtually drown under my blanket, tears splashing all over my pillow.

Daniel needed time to sort out his life, and I needed to focus. I'd lost myself to him.

It wasn't all completely bleak, however, because, within a few days of being back in town, I'd gotten a call about a role.

With that 'life must go on' platitude rotating in my head, the following morning, I scrambled out of bed.

While in front of my mirror, lavishing on foundation to hide my drawn, pale features, I painted on a stiff smile too. Although it was painful to look happy, I had to remind myself that emotions were to an actor what a palette was to a painter.

Channeling one of my happier moments, making sure it didn't feature Daniel, in case I should unconsciously start breathing heavily, I breezed into the interview. The next day I got a supporting role in a Netflix movie.

• • • ● • ● • • •

AFTER A LONG DAY on set, I was walking toward my apartment, when Kevin turned up out of nowhere, startling me.

I held up my palms. "Now, look, Kevin. Please . . ." I reached into my bag for my phone.

"I just want to talk," he said, his eyes pleading.

We were alone in a dark alleyway, and I knew he wouldn't budge.

"Not here," I said, pointing at a pub on the corner, which, luckily for me, was a few steps away. "In there. Around people, so you can't attack me."

He held my stare for a moment, his eyes devoid of expression.

I scooted ahead of him and stepped into the crowded pub, opting for a table surrounded by people.

While he went off to get the drinks, my heart raced. He was the last person I wanted to see. Just when things were starting to look up again. I loved my new role. The cast was supportive, and it had been such a welcome distraction.

I'd even had a day without Daniel's beautiful face in my head.

Now this. I sighed heavily as I watched my brutish ex lumbering over with drinks in his hands.

He set the drinks down and sat opposite me.

"You haven't been around for a while," he said.

"No."

He studied me again. "You're no longer with your boy toy?"

I sucked back anger and chose a calm tone instead. "Daniel was my employer."

"You were fucking him though."

"Look, what do you want, Kevin?"

"I just wanted to see you."

I released a noisy breath and shook my head. "Why can't you move on?"

"I have someone. But she's not you."

"Do you treat her roughly like you did me?" I asked.

He leaned in. "Only when she doesn't do what she's told." Wearing an irksome smirk, he was evil personified.

"How the fuck did they let you into the police force?" I rose. I couldn't stay there any longer. "This was a bad idea."

He grabbed my wrist. "Stay."

I sat down.

"I've just been released. I'm no longer in the force. Thanks to you."

"Thanks to me." My head jerked forward. "You put me in fucking hospital." I almost skulled my G&T.

How the hell was I going to get to my apartment with him hovering? My heart shriveled at the thought of what he might do. I felt cursed.

"I'm glad you've met someone else," I said, trying to sound calm and amicable. "Now perhaps this can stop."

"I've only ever loved you," he said.

He showed a glint of vulnerability. When his face softened, I caught a glimpse of the man I'd fallen for. Kevin had a certain rugged masculine appeal that, unfortunately, would turn ugly after a few drinks.

"Then why treat me like this?" I asked.

"Because you frustrate the shit out of me." He scowled before softening again. "If only you'd just been there for me."

"I was. But you would still come home and attack me."

"That's because you wouldn't let me fuck you. And then you were hanging out with all those men. You're a fucking flirt. You were cheating on me, weren't you?"

Shaking my head, I rolled my eyes. Kevin's need of psychiatric help for his delusional paranoia became more than apparent again.

"It's all in your mind. I never once cheated on you, Kevin." I picked up my bag. "I really have to go. Please don't follow me."

Of course, he did just that. I tried to act calm by taking deep breaths. I knew I couldn't walk to my apartment because the entrance was on a quiet street, so I headed for the main drag and, much to my relief, a policeman was on the corner.

I ran to him. "Please help me. He won't leave me alone. I'm too scared to walk home."

The constable looked at Kevin, who held up his hands and laughed. "She's crazy. I'm not doing anything."

Luckily, the policeman offered to walk me home. Kevin stayed away, but that sinking feeling in my stomach remained. I would have to move again.

"Thanks for helping me."

"Have you got a restraining order?" he asked.

I nodded. "He's an ex-cop. He's just been released from prison. The only time they'll take notice is when I'm dead."

The young policeman looked out of his depth. "I'm sorry to hear that, madam. I can put in a report if you'd like."

I gave him the details of my restraining order.

After making sure the entrance was locked, I climbed the stairs to my apartment, then entered and fell onto the sofa, where I buried my head in my hands and cried.

# CHAPTER 31

*Daniel*

POOR JAN, THE NEW maid, looked flustered. Barking orders, Charlie had her working around the clock arranging her new bedroom.

Although it felt longer, my wife had been back for two weeks. To say I was in hell was an understatement; it was more like crawling on my stomach in a dark tunnel with Charlie's screechy petulance chilling the air.

Apart from the feeling of relief that I hadn't pushed Charlie into the sea while I was sleepwalking, a recurring nightmare of mine that past year, I'd fallen into a deep depression. Divorce couldn't come quickly enough.

According to Charlie, she'd met someone a day before we'd planned to sail, and he told her that he'd help her escape by boat at midnight. After she ran out of money, she returned to Starlington. And now she wanted to make our marriage work.

I nearly laughed at that preposterous notion. "What do you mean?"

"I want to stay here," she said. "Don't worry, we don't have to fuck. I want my own room."

At least that was something we could agree on.

Charlie's parents turned up within hours of their daughter's arrival. Cecily, my mother-in-law, shot daggers at me. I could only assume her daughter had lied about me being an abusive husband.

"I met someone who offered to rescue me," Charlie concluded her story, without looking at her mother—something I thought strange at the time. "He looked after me. But it didn't work. So here I am."

"But why didn't you call? We thought you were dead," her mother said, shaking her head and regarding her husband, who hoed into the scotch without uttering a word.

Good fucking question.

Charlie shifted about and took a suspicious length of time to answer.

She turned to me, pointing in my face, and said, "Because I feared what he might do. I needed to escape."

I rolled my eyes. "That's bullshit, and you know it. I've never laid a finger on you."

"But what about the police?" Cecily appealed. "You could be charged for wasting their time."

Charlie just shrugged it off as she often did. She didn't give a shit about anyone but herself.

Although her parents stayed the night, I was glad to see them gone the following day. All night, her mother had fussed about while Charlie's father watched Survivor on TV, soaked to his eyeballs in scotch.

I wanted to ask them to take Charlie with them, but my wife was hellbent on making my life a misery by remaining at Starlington. It beggars belief why she wanted to stay with me.

And to make matters worse, Scarlet wouldn't take my calls.

I had to see her again—if only just to explain—and a trip away from Starlington was just what my nerves demanded.

Charlie was like a force of nature. She'd reinstated staff and my home had been invaded by noisy, unwanted strangers.

It was late afternoon when Charlie joined me in the sitting room dressed in white, skin-tight jeans, high heels, and a tight yellow blouse, more city wear than suiting a bucolic, relaxed lifestyle of the country.

"We need to talk," I said.

She fell onto the chair and shooed Thor away. The dog settled by my side, equally as perplexed by her boisterous presence, tantamount to a tornado tearing through the house. I stroked his silky fur and the canine looked up at me with his big sympathetic eyes. He understood my pain. And, like me, he missed Scarlet and their daily walks to the beach.

"You wanted to see me," she said, sliding on her shades.

"I want a divorce ASAP."

She cocked her head, wearing a smarmy grin. "No. I'm staying."

"But why?" I opened my hands. "This is a farce. You don't want me, and I don't want you."

"So? I like it here."

"You're a city girl. You've always hated Starlington."

"No, I haven't. I hated you and your stuffy old-fashioned ways, but I love this place. It just needs some redecorating."

"Oh no, you don't." Knowing Charlie's ultra-modern tastes, I baulked at the thought of our priceless antiques and art being relegated to storage again.

"It's my home too."

I thought of my other homes in Lake Como and Antibes, but how could I move away? And what about Scarlet?

Regardless of its dark history, Starlington was my home, having belonged to my family for generations. I couldn't lose it.

"How much do you want?" I asked.

"I want Starlington and half of everything on top. And then I'll sign."

"I'll give you half, which could buy at least ten Starlingtons with enough left over to feed a village for a lifetime."

"Then it's not a deal."

"Why does it have to be Starlington?"

"I like it here," she said with a petulant whine.

"Then it's a stalemate—because you'll get this place over my dead body."

She picked at her pink, claw-like nails. "Then I'm staying."

"You're going to try and wear me down. Is that your game?"

She nodded.

I swallowed my drink and slammed the door as I left. A punching bag at this stage would have come in handy. Instead, I stepped outside and yelled.

I jumped in my car and headed to London. Scarlet would see me, even if I had to wait outside her apartment all night.

Two hours later, I stood outside her modern apartment building, ringing the buzzer. There was no answer. But seeing that the lights were on, I waited before buzzing again, then, as luck would have it, a person was leaving. I grabbed hold of the glass door and slipped through.

I ran up two flights because I needed to get my head around what I wanted to say. What was I about to offer her?

I knocked on the door.

"Go away," she said from behind the door.

"Please let me in."

"Is that you, Daniel?"

"Yes."

She opened the door and stepped away as I entered.

Although her tiny one-room studio had that warm, lived-in feel, I decided I'd buy her a roomy apartment. That's if she'd allow me. Scarlet, unlike Charlie, didn't like taking my money.

"I'm sorry to turn up like this, but you weren't answering my calls," I said.

A watery sheen coated her soulful eyes as we remained trapped in each other's gaze. Words escaped me as I soaked her in. Relishing her scent as I would a jasmine-infused evening, I stepped close enough to feel her warm, jittery breath on my neck.

She fell into my arms and we held each other, her tears dampening my skin.

Scarlet unraveled from my arms. "I'm sorry I didn't answer the buzzer." She exhaled a strained breath. "I'm having a terrible time. I thought you were Kevin."

"Oh?" I frowned. "How did he find you?"

"He was a detective." She shook her head. "I can't take it anymore. I don't know where to go. He won't leave me alone."

Anger seared through me. I was at boiling point. Despite never having met him, I hated this man profoundly. "When did you see him?"

"Last night. He followed me here."

Her hands were shaking.

"Get your stuff," I said.

She opened her hands. "Where am I going?"

"You're coming back to Starlington."

"But what about your wife?" Her brow creased as she stared seriously into my eyes. "You led me to believe she was dead."

I rubbed my stubbled jaw. "I did think she was dead." What could I add to that? That I thought I'd murdered my wife by accident?

"Look, I'm glad she's alive... But..." I exhaled a frustrated breath. "Fuck ..." I buried my face in my hands. "It's been hell. I tried calling you over and over. To explain. But you wouldn't pick up."

I took her hand. "I miss you, Scarlet. You're the only woman I want in my life."

She removed her hand gently and walked to the other side of the room, and a long gap of silence followed.

"I couldn't bring myself to hear your voice," she said at last. "I needed the space. And what would you have said?"

I went over to her and looked into her eyes. "I would have said, I love you."

That shot out of nowhere. But it felt real. Like I'd finally removed my mask and I could breathe again.

I'd never told anyone I loved them before. My wedding vows were as though lifted off a Hallmark card. Propriety dragged me down that aisle. Not love.

Scarlet's eyes widened as though I'd admitted to a horrible crime.

"Why are you looking at me like that?" I asked.

Shaking her head, she stared down at her hands, as though I repelled her. "I just don't know what to say or do." Tears streamed down her face. Her green luminescent eyes reminded me of emeralds submerged in a pond. A sight of beauty. Even though I hated how much pain my fucked up situation had inflicted on her.

"I love you too," she murmured almost to herself. Her vulnerability had become mine. She too seemed frightened on those powerful words and their implication.

Our souls were now naked.

She turned away and grabbed a tissue.

"Sorry, I'm a mess," she said.

I stood close behind her and kissed her neck. Her head dropped onto my shoulder as I rocked her in my arms, breathing her in as I would a fragrant rose. And for the first time in weeks, my shriveled heart unraveled, and I could feel it beating warmth through me.

After a few minutes Scarlet removed herself from my arms.

"Would you like a drink? I know I could use one."

I nodded.

She passed me a glass.

"What will we do now?" she asked.

"I'd like you to come back to Starlington," I repeated. I figured she could stay at the cottage. At least that way we would be close.

"But what about your wife?"

"She's not interested in a relationship. She wants Starlington." I paced about sipping on my scotch like a man condemned.

"I wouldn't be cheating?" she asked, her voice wavering.

I shook my head. "No, you wouldn't be. Charlie and I are officially separated."

"Officially?" She tipped her head.

"She's not interested in sharing my bed. And I'm not interested in her being there either."

She nodded pensively. "But I need to remain here. This is our last week of shooting."

"Then let me buy a hotel for us for the week. Or we can stay at Mayfair."

While considering my proposition, she held my gaze. "We?"

I nodded. "Do you mind if I hang around?" My lips cracked into my first smile in weeks.

Her lips curled in response. "I think I could put up with you."

Scarlet had never looked so captivating as I indulged in her beauty.

I felt at home with her. I could share everything with this woman. I wanted her.

All of her. Her heart. Her body. Her soul.

# CHAPTER 32

*Scarlet*

OVERLOOKING THE THAMES, THE spacious hotel room boasted Victorian charm with its bird of paradise wallpaper and decorative fineries associated with that elegant period.

I'd opted for the hotel rather than Mayfair because it was close to the film set, and I needed us to be on neutral ground while processing me being the "other" woman. Despite Daniel declaring that they were no longer living like husband and wife, I still had to grapple with my inner censor. I hated the idea of cheating, and that clashing tug-of-war between morality and desire, which were at odds like a priest in a bordello.

But we shared more than just desire or passion. We were in love. Now that Daniel had opened his heart to me, the wall I'd erected to hide behind had come crashing down. How could I not be with him? I loved him so profoundly, I had little choice but to remain in his arms. My heart had become my dictator overriding these unexpected thorny ethical issues, pushing aside questions like what was Daniel going to do about Charlotte.

I'd seen how frigid she was toward her husband; that cold glare didn't reflect the gaze of a woman in love.

With only one scene to shoot, it was the last day of filming. That gave me time to spend with Daniel, lolling about making love, reading, and chatting. Daniel started to reveal his loquacious side. He was also a great listener, which I found unusual in my men, who normally preferred the sound of their own voices—unless it was dirty talk. And that's where Daniel had an edge because his direct, at times bossy, deep husk was like dousing smoldering embers with top-shelf gin.

Although the crew had invited us out for a wrap-up dinner, I'd opted out so that I could spend my last night in that grand hotel in the arms of the love of my life. It was either that or deny myself precious time with Daniel.

Those two weeks apart had been hell. Daniel had intruded my every thought and my dreams had me waking in a cold sweat. Some were related to my sadistic, omnipresent ex, while others were disturbingly lucid. Like one night when Daniel's grandmother whispered that he needed me now more than ever—that without me he would perish. I woke shaking.

"How was your day?" I asked, removing my boots.

Lounging in a green leather wing chair reading Brave New World, Daniel placed his book down. "I caught up with Jerry and had a long, tedious afternoon going over figures with my accountant and stockbroker."

I laughed and settled on the arm of his chair. "You find counting all that wealth of yours tedious?"

"In many ways, I do." He drew me onto his lap and kissed me, his lips soft and warm. We lingered as though it was our first kiss.

"I might take a bath," I said, unbuttoning my shirt.

His eyes hooded. "Shall I come and wash your back?" He tilted his head flirtatiously.

Standing up, I let my skirt pool at my feet and stepped out of it. Wearing the sexiest underwear I'd ever owned, I made a show of my scantily clad body. My gaze travelled down his sexy figure and noticed a bulge appear, and that throbbing ache between my legs fired up again.

• • • • • • • • • •

AS WE DROVE BACK into Starlington, my heart picked up in pace. I wasn't sure what I was doing, but to stay away would have been too difficult. And with Kevin finding me no matter where I lived in London, at least I was miles away. Daniel, with that big, considerate heart, had also arranged around-the-clock surveillance for my mother. I'm not sure what I would have done without his help. The law had well and truly let me down.

Daniel lifted my cases from the boot of his SUV. "I hope you don't mind the cottage?"

"Of course not. It's very comfortable." I stopped walking. "How are you going to explain me to your wife?"

"I'll tell her that you're my model, which is the truth." Despite his lips curling slightly, Daniel seemed understandably tense. His bossy wife's edgy attitude would've frazzled the nerves of even a Buddhist monk.

"I've got the divorce papers waiting for her to sign, but for some inexplicable reason she's stalling."

"You're really not sharing a bedroom?" I had to ask again.

He shook his head. "I know this is far from ideal. But I'll get her out of here somehow."

Everything about that situation was unusual, including this tall, dark and handsome billionaire wanting me—an ordinary older woman.

After Daniel left me to unpack and unwind, I made a cup of tea and stared out the window, as I often did. The folly caught my eye. Facing the pond and surrounded by willows, that enchanting corner of the estate made for a great photo, especially with graceful black swans gliding over the silvery water.

Daniel's macabre paintings came to mind, and instead of repelling me, the folly became a subject of my own fascination.

• • • ● • ● • • •

IT WAS EARLY EVENING and Daniel had invited me to dine with him.

"She's not here," he reassured, pulling a chair out for me.

As we ate, I noticed Daniel wince while the staff went about their work.

"Are you sure I'm not going to complicate things?" I wiped my mouth after polishing off a delicious salmon quiche.

"No. I need you here—if only to protect you from your ex."

I shook my head. "I don't know if I'm ever going to be free of him."

"I've got someone looking into it."

I bit into my cheek. "What do you mean?"

"There's a PI casing him. Should he attack anyone, then he'll have the evidence to take him down again. Hopefully they'll throw away the key and jail him for longer than six months this time."

"Thank you for everything you're doing. I think I'd have to leave the country otherwise."

He smiled sadly.

After dinner, Daniel asked me to model, and feeling frisky, I agreed. After that steamy session on the night of Beltane, I looked forward to wearing that green dress again—if only to have him ravage me.

With its white, pressed-metal-dome ceiling and panoramic windows that turned the night into panels of art, Daniel's studio was always a delight to visit.

I changed into the green dress and, seeing that Daniel had stepped out, my attention went to his easels, which were uncovered.

I allowed curiosity to get the better of me.

Once again, the folly was his subject. The four easels featured a series of scenes in cinematic layout, resembling a narrative of sorts.

The first image depicted the interior with the pond visible through the window. A pair of eyes peered through a crack in a wardrobe, while an angry-looking man scowled at a cowering woman covering her face. I moved to the next canvas, which showed the same scene, but this time he was pulling her hair. With her head fallen back, the woman's eyes were wide with terror.

My blood froze. The paintings were telling a story.

Ruminating over Daniel's parents' violent past, I heard his footsteps up the stairs and scurried over to the armchair.

I took a deep breath, not wanting him to know I'd seen the art—not yet, at least.

When he saw me in the chair, his eyes warmed, and my nerves ironed out.

I revealed a torn seam. "I'm afraid this dress is barely holding up after our last session." I raised an eyebrow and chuckled. At the pit of my belly, however, a knot remained.

"Good. It will make for a new theme. I'm starting afresh." He walked to the other side of the room to a stack of empty canvases and selected one.

"How do you want me?"

His brow lowered as he studied me. "Just as you are. Lift the skirt right up."

"Right up?" I asked, tilting my head flirtatiously.

His eyes hooded and he nodded. His arousal inflamed me.

"So we're going pornographic again?" I grinned.

"Yes. Are you comfortable with that?"

"I am, as long as no one sees it. Will you promise to destroy it when you're no longer . . . ?"

"All my art will be destroyed before I die."

His dry, sober tone defied that declaration's bone-chilling nature.

"That's a little radical. Don't you ever want people to see your work?"

He shook his head. "I have no need for attention. I do this for me."

"But art is something that should be shared."

"Scarlet." His tone went dark. "Let's not discuss this again." His eyes, revealing a dark, inscrutable soul, burned into mine.

I lifted my dress all the way, harnessing the erotic in the hope of easing this sudden tension.

He worked in silence for twenty minutes, before he set his brush down. "I can't do this."

Exhaling a tense breath, I lowered my dress as I watched him go to the window and light a cigarette.

I took one and joined him, staring out into the night. A cloudy halo enshrouded the crescent moon, mimicking the sudden mood shift in the studio.

"I'm sorry," I uttered.

He turned toward me wearing a sad smile. "It should be me apologizing. I'm heavily weighed down."

"You know you can share anything with me. I would never judge you."

He ran his hand up my arm and my skin puckered. "You grow more beautiful each time I see you."

Although this sudden shift in topic jarred, his compliment warmed my spirit. "I can't understand that. I've hardly slept from stress."

He fluttered his finger over my palm, sending a skin-prickling sensation over my body.

Our lips met for a caressing kiss, which quickly turned hungry. I savored the smoky flavor of his kiss as his tongue lapped over mine.

He pressed against me, and I felt his desire pulsate on my belly.

"Let's go to bed. I want to make love slowly," he said softly.

I melted at his touch, and I could barely feel my legs as we headed downstairs to his bedroom.

I wanted to ask about his wife. I knew they slept in different rooms, but the thought of us being in bed together and her finding us made me jumpy.

But as he fondled me, I pushed that thought aside. Especially with his hard dick rubbing against me, all I could think of was him making me burn and giving me endless orgasms. Consequences and addiction were as compatible as an environmentalist and an oil baron.

"Leave the green dress on," he said, just as I was about to remove it. "Just lie on the bed and lift it high up for me and touch yourself."

He removed his shirt and unzipped his pants. I licked my lips, hungry for him.

Lowering his briefs, he stroked his dick as I touched myself.

"That's it." He breathed heavily as he pulled at his cock. I ran my tongue over my lips.

"Do you want my dick in your mouth or your pussy?"

"Both," I whispered breathlessly.

He came toward me and stood at the side of the bed. I took his dick into my hand and ran it up and down the shaft. Slippery from his pre-cum, it throbbed in my hand. I placed it between my lips and sucked on it, moving my lips up and down. He grew steel-hard in my mouth.

His head tipped as he sighed loudly.

After I'd taken him deeply into my throat, he removed his dick, lowered my dress from the top, and sucked on my nipples while rubbing my clit.

I opened my legs wide to invite him in.

He traveled down the bed and nuzzled between my thighs.

As his tongue lapped over my clit in slow, tantalizing strokes, a hum of satisfaction parted my lips.

I experienced the pain of a release so intense, I unclenched muscles and a surge of heat rocketed through me.

He teased the folds of my creamy slit, soaking the head of his shaft before sliding in and making my eyes water from the fullness of his erection.

I rotated my pelvis slowly around his dick, burying my face in his neck, taking nips of his warm flesh while breathing his sex-infused scent.

"I'm all yours, Scarlet." His whisper flushed through my body, penetrating as deeply as his dick.

Our faces close and fingers laced, we moved in rhythm, fucking with the primal force of raw passion.

Breathing roughly, he let out a deep, tormented groan and, taking me with him, we exploded together.

As we held each other, breathing heavily, he whispered, "I love you."

My eyes burned with tears. "I love you too."

I fell asleep with my head on his warm chest.

# CHAPTER 33

CHARLIE RETURNED TO THE house the day after, much to our chagrin. I didn't run into her, thankfully, although it was close. We'd just showered, when her high-pitched voice rang through the air—making demands of Jan, I could only assume.

Although Daniel didn't show the slightest concern, my heart raced. When it came to confrontation, I was that person who always left the room first.

Amid Daniel's protests, I managed to sneak out the back way.

Kissing him, I said, "It's better this way. At least you can explain my presence to her first."

He shrugged. "Personally, I don't give a shit what she thinks. But sure, if it makes you feel better."

As I made my way through the back to the cottage, I wondered about this peculiar arrangement and how it would play out. I would just have to keep my distance from the house whenever she was there. At least the cottage was quite a distance from the house.

Soon after she arrived, I drove into the village to do my grocery shopping.

Being a sunny day, I sat outside a café delighting in the simple joy of coffee and apple pie.

I breathed in a lungful of fresh sea air while enjoying the fishing village's atmosphere. Locals and tourists ambled along the cobbled paths lined with heritage shops painted in bright colors, selling crafts, books, hand knitted pullovers and beanies. The air smelled of baking and the sea, and there were enough people for me to enjoy the spectacle of life.

For someone who craved privacy, I also welcomed the anonymity that came from being an occasional visitor to that historical village.

But over and above everything, I was miles away from Kevin.

For the first time in years, putting aside Charlie's unexpected return, and Daniel's dark art, I felt loose, almost agile. The incessant neck pain, which I put down to staring at a screen, had disappeared. I'd grown so used to carrying stress, I'd confused my aches and pains to a lack of exercise, given my aversion to gyms and jogging, when all along it was due to fear.

• • • • • • • • • •

AS THE DAYS WENT on, I had the space to finally start working on my writing.

Cozy and sunny, the cottage offered a relaxing environment to just be. I'd often sit at the table by the window, staring at the pond—which was frequented by elegant swans and amusing ducks—and daydream. It was hardly a chore to stay in there whenever Charlie returned.

Fortunately for us, she often stayed away. Like Daniel, I wondered why she was so stuck on Starlington when she seemed more drawn to London.

Daniel had even suggested redecorating the cottage. He needed me there, he kept saying. Surreal as this was, I had to believe him. Not least since he couldn't take his hands off me. His standing firm to keep Starlington made sense too. What didn't, however, were Charlie's ridiculous demands.

Happy to lose myself among nature, I had the sea and forest where I'd take strolls while contemplating the next chapter of my life. With ample savings enabling me to write, I'd lost my drive and ambition for film. While I once enjoyed the thrill of performing on stage, I found the stop-and-start nature of film acting tedious.

Due to Daniel's generosity, I moved my mother into a brand-new apartment. She insisted on remaining in the same area because her new man lived close. She was happy for the first time in years. If ever. I'd met her new man once and was thrilled to see how sweet and gentle he was around my very deserving mother.

One night I was alone in the cottage. Citing a headache, after Charlie's return from a week in London, Daniel had stayed away.

It was after midnight and, unable to sleep, I stepped outside of the cottage for a cigarette, when I noticed light flickering in the folly.

In respect of Daniel's wishes, I had resisted my urge to investigate until now, when curiosity got the better of me. I walked over to the pond, where the pearly moon's rippling reflection danced on the water.

With its gabled roof and gargoyles, at that hour, the folly looked spooky. Under the moonlight, those sculptured heads with their malevolent scowls had the intended repelling effect.

Sneaking up close, I crouched and peeked in the window. Through candlelight, I saw a silhouette of a tall, well-built male, who had a similar build to Daniel.

Despite his yelling, I couldn't make out words. A woman entered. It was Charlie—or so I thought, going on her slim frame and long tousled hair.

He pointed menacingly at her face, then lurched forward, grabbing her by the hair and tugging at it, making her head fall back. She screamed, and when he released her, she fell into his arms.

The man turned toward the window, and I ducked. Sensing him close by the window, I crawled off and hid behind a bush while steadying my breath.

After a few minutes, I snuck back the long way, through the bushes to the cottage.

I fell onto the sofa in a heap and picked up the glass of wine from earlier. As I sipped, my mind swam in so many directions trying to understand what I'd just witnessed. It felt like déjà vu.

My jaw dropped. It finally dawned on me. I'd seen that scene in one of Daniel's folly paintings.

How could that be?

Was that Daniel? And why was he in the folly, a place he'd sworn never to visit?

When he dropped in the following morning, I remained tight-lipped about what I'd seen, reluctant to stir further tension. His long ashen face told me that more drama was the last thing he needed.

"Are you okay?" I asked.

He exhaled an audible breath and shook his head. "No. I'm troubled. I'm sorry if I gave you the cold shoulder last night, but I needed some space."

"Hey, it's fine. I also need my own space sometimes," I said with an encouraging smile.

He stroked my cheek and his face warmed. "You're special."

Was I again giving into desire at the expense of sanity?

Was that Daniel in the folly?

We held each other and I bathed in his masculine scent, which was like a form of erotic Xanax. Drugged on his male muskiness, I surrendered to desire, unzipped his pants, lowered onto my knees, and devoured his dick.

"You don't have to . . ." His head fell back. "Aah . . ."

His velvety dick grew hard in my mouth.

I welcomed the fiery sensation sweeping through my body, which helped mute nagging questions as he shot hot cream down my throat.

Feeling opiated, having dosed up on testosterone, I grabbed the tissues and helped wipe him clean.

He shook his head. "I forgot what I came to say." Combing back his hair, he looked at me and laughed.

Oh, just to see that handsome face change from gloomy to happy was well worth the ache in my knees.

He took the glass of water I handed him. "I'm heading into the city to talk to my lawyer about suing Charlie for her fake disappearing act—and having to stomach months of interrogation as a result."

Just as I started to feel guilty again, he added, "You're the only good thing to come out of that. The mysterious hand of fate works in strange ways."

His forgiving words meant the world to me. At least that was one prickly situation I could lay to rest.

"What about suing her for faking pregnancy?" I asked.

He nodded, rubbing his jaw. "I'll do anything to get the bitch out of my life."

His chilling, acerbic tone woke me from a romantic stupor, and again, questions surrounding the violence in the folly bounded in.

"Did you fight last night?" I asked.

"I'll be back later this afternoon. We can have dinner." His mouth twitched into a faint smile, but it did little to allay my sudden temperature spike at his evasive response.

I walked with him to his car. The morning was crisp, and I gripped my arms.

After he drove off, I noticed Charlie from the corner of my eye, tottering along the path with a designer bag slung over her shoulder. She didn't see me because I was behind a bush, but I watched on, and when I saw her jumping into her BMW, I made a radical decision to enter the house.

Jan was around, which meant the door was open.

I slid in, and despite his studio no doubt being locked, I knew where Daniel kept the key.

I ran into the maid as I climbed the stairs.

"Morning," I said brightly.

"Oh, hello," she said, her brow creasing.

"I'm just going up to Daniel's room because I left my book in there. Is that okay?"

She nodded. I wondered what Jan made of this situation. She knew of my relationship with Daniel—as he hadn't exactly hidden his affection for me—and having heard the way Charlie spoke to the maid, I imagined the maid thought little of her.

I had in fact left a book in his room, so I was covered if she said something to Daniel.

"I'm just nipping out for the morning. Do you mind locking up when you leave?" she asked.

"No problem," I said, breathing a sigh of relief. I had the house to myself.

I entered the bedroom and made sure I removed my book from the side table. Tucking it under my arm, I headed to an antique gilded box on his dresser and removed the key to the loft.

With sweat trickling between my shoulder blades, I stepped into his studio and noticed six easels under sheets.

I lifted one of the sheets carefully and discovered a painting of me in the green dress.

I'd never seen myself so exposed. The dress was around my stomach, and my legs were wide apart, revealing my pink and moist sex, the anatomical detail masterfully produced.

My eyes had that glint of desire that I'd only ever felt around Daniel. The way he made my heart pound was something I'd never known before. And now, as I studied his vision of me, my heart pounded just as hard.

I covered it over. I hadn't come to see that, though I wondered what Charlie would say if she saw it. Georgina came to mind as I looked at his closet.

It wasn't locked, much to my delight, and a whoosh of oil paint hit me as I stuck my head inside to investigate.

I flicked through the canvases and saw that most were studies until I came across a series of models—all redheads in green gowns.

I started to question Daniel's sanity, as one might when reflecting on obsessive-compulsive types.

Georgina stood out, however. Her eyes brimmed with saucy playfulness. I'd seen that same expression at the party. Jealousy streaked through me. She was a beautiful woman, and each painting showed her in a different state of undress.

I stopped short of focusing too closely, reluctant to see her hungry vagina.

But I did come across a painting of Daniel. It wasn't signed, but then none of his other paintings were either, so I could only assume it was a self-portrait.

His face was dark, sallow, and remote, and I shivered as though seeing a man disturbed. It was so powerfully lifelike his eyes seemed to drill into me.

What I saw next, however, made my legs buckle. A shocked gasp shot onto my palm as it covered my mouth.

# CHAPTER 34

## *Daniel*

"I WANT YOU TO press ahead with the divorce."

My lawyer peered over his glasses at me. "If she decides to press charges on the abuse allegations, you'll have a major court case on your hands."

My neck heated. "That's ridiculous. I never touched her. It's her word against mine."

"But she has photos."

I released a tight breath. "That wasn't me."

He nodded slowly. "It will be a media frenzy. And then there's the case against your father."

Anger burned in my chest. "Why the hell should I have to wear that? I'm not my father."

"You certainly are not." He smiled gently. A close friend to my grandparents, Paul had been the family's lawyer for forty years. "It will be a trial by media, I'm afraid. The tabloids will devour this story. Dredge everything up."

"So, what do you suggest?"

"You say she wants Starlington?"

I nodded. My spirit sank at the mention of my irreplaceable home.

"What about her disappearing act?" I asked. "Surely I can sue for the pain that caused."

"Of course. But do you want her telling the world that she was hiding from an abusive husband?"

"If I'm so abusive, why is she back?"

"Good question. Have you asked her?"

"I have. She wants Starlington and half of everything."

"Starlington's worth about one hundred million. It's not an unfair demand given your substantial wealth. Only you don't have children so that would help your case. Look, Daniel, we can press ahead, but get ready for a tussle with the media. Charlotte's not camera shy." He raised an eyebrow.

I reflected back on Charlie at social events. Always the loudest one in the room. Always flirting. I should have run in the opposite direction. If it weren't for that fake pregnancy, I would have.

Lost in a battle of thoughts, I finally said, "I need to draft up a new will. And I'd like to set up two trust accounts."

He studied me closely. I could see his mind ticking away. I already had a list of benefactors: Jerry's son, animal welfare, the homeless, and marine life rescue.

"I want to add Scarlet Black, also known as Ainsley Alcott. Set up an account of twenty thousand a month for the rest of her life."

"I take it she's your girlfriend?" he asked.

"She's very important." I swallowed tightly. That said little about how I really felt about Scarlet. "And an account for her mother." I handed him the details. "Ten thousand a month."

He nodded. "I have the title documents of the apartment you purchased for her."

"Good. Send those off to her."

I thought of Scarlet's mother, whom I'd only met twice. The second time was when I opened the door to her new home. The tears and hugs. The kisses. I'd just made two people sleep well. And, unlike my own hold on my childhood home, Scarlet and her mother weren't sentimentally attached to their former home.

"I wish to include Scarlet in my will. If anything were to happen to me, she is to have Starlington."

He held my stare for a moment. "What about if there's a child?"

"I have no offspring."

He smiled. "I mean if a child comes forward from a past relationship."

"Scarlet's only the third woman I've been with." I took a deep breath. My private life wasn't something I felt comfortable sharing with anyone, let alone my lawyer.

He frowned. "I see. Are you sure you don't wish to add a clause just in case? Maybe the first partner..."

"We're still in touch. And I'm a hundred percent certain she isn't hiding an offspring somewhere."

"Okay. I'll draw these up for you."

I stood up and stretched out my hand. "Thank you."

# CHAPTER 35

## *Scarlet*

AS I CREPT DOWN the stairs, haunted by Daniel's gruesome art, Charlie confronted me.

I started, as she had taken me by surprise.

"Oh, it's you?" Blocking my passage, she stood before me with hands on her hips. "Why are you in my house?"

"I came to see if I could find a book I'd left . . ." I hesitated at mentioning Daniel's bedroom.

"Left behind after shagging my husband, you mean?"

Her face looked hard. Although a pretty woman, her scowl added years.

"Excuse me." I went to pass her.

She grabbed my arm roughly and pointed into my face. "I don't give a shit if you fuck him. But this house is out of bounds. I don't like the servants knowing that my husband has his mistress here. It makes me look bad. Got it?"

I pushed past her and walked to the door. Despite a tirade burning in my throat, I bit my lip. Dignified silence had the upper hand.

"You don't know him, do you? He's a horror to be with. A wife basher."

"I don't believe that." I stopped walking and faced her.

"That's because he's rich and good-looking." She looked me up and down. "You're not exactly from good stock, are you? And you're so much older. It shows."

Anger seethed through me. "You look like you're from a limited gene pool yourself. You're like any other bimbo."

She slapped my face.

My fists clenched, but I resisted. Instead, I brushed her shoulder while pushing her out of my way.

Rattled nerves left me shaking as I trudged back to the cottage—more from what I'd seen in Daniel's studio than from that nasty altercation with his wife.

The paintings, one frame at a time, showed a man attacking a woman. I recognized the stained-glass window from the folly.

One painting featured angry silhouetted figures of a woman and a man, along with a pair of frightened eyes watching from the cupboard, then those eyes were peering through the window in another painting.

Just as I'd done the night before.

Had Daniel attacked Charlie? The figures in the paintings, just as I'd witnessed in the folly, were difficult to distinguish.

I thought of his behavior toward me. When disturbed, he'd bury his anger and withdraw. The silent treatment. And why hadn't he become violent after discovering my undercover role? He just stormed out of my life. A spine-chilling glower was as brutal as he got.

I thought of Kevin. Even small things would set him off, like no milk in the fridge. That would earn me a slap or two. He looked for any reason to attack me.

Daniel wasn't anything like that. He bottled his anger. I wondered if the paintings were his coping mechanism. An outlet for rage. Art as therapy.

But why did the first frame emulate the scene I'd witnessed in the folly? The final frame, blood-splattered and depicting something fatal, was the most disturbing.

Was his art predicting something?

I found it difficult to believe that the paintings were prophesizing the future, like some domestic equivalent to Dorian Gray.

Then why did my legs feel like lead?

• • • • • • • • • •

LATER THAT NIGHT, DANIEL came knocking at my door.

"I hope I'm not disturbing." He smiled tightly. "You didn't respond to my message about dinner."

"I'm sorry. I fell asleep. I only just woke up," I said, stepping away for him to enter.

Carrying a box under one arm, he leaned in and kissed me before placing it down on the table. "I bought something for you."

"Oh." I lifted the cover and discovered a new green slinky gown.

"It's stunning."

"I think the size is right."

I held it against my body and stood before the mirror. The dress had a low-cut back and a side slit. "It's very sexy."

He stroked the same cheek that his wife had struck that afternoon. "Like you."

He kissed me tenderly, and all my earlier misgivings drifted away as we embraced.

"Do you want me to model it?" I asked with a smile.

"Later." He unbuttoned my blouse and ran his hands over my breasts.

Trailing kisses over my body, he made slow tender love to me, which soon turned into hot passion. I moved on top of him and gyrated over his dick. With deep, burning thrusts, I fucked him as though it was our last.

Trembling in each other's arms, we orgasmed together. Our lips fused. Our crushing bodies damp and sated.

Afterward, we shared a bottle of wine.

"I ran into Charlie today," I said tentatively. "I went to find a book I left in your room." I grimaced. "I hope you don't mind."

His initial frown softened. "Of course not."

"She wasn't very nice. To say the least."

"How unsurprising."

"She slapped me," I said.

His head jerked. "What?"

"I called her a bimbo." I bit a nail. "It was a knee-jerk reaction, I suppose. She said I was too old and common for you, and that you were a wife basher."

He ran his fingers through his hair. "I'm sorry."

"I can handle it. I've experienced far worse."

"I visited my lawyer. Relinquishing Starlington is my only way out." He exhaled a jagged breath.

"Oh." Although I didn't need reminding how much that home meant to him, the look on his face, as though he would have to remove a vital organ, made it plain to see. "I'll move if it will make it easier. I don't wish to stir trouble."

He took my hand. "No. I want you here. I'll speak to her."

"She's demanded I stay away from the house," I said.

"Maybe when I'm not around." His lips drew a tight line. "But I'll need you to model. It's still my house."

I held his gaze. "Will my modeling a green dress define this relationship?"

He held out his hand. "Let's walk. It's a nice night."

We ambled along in silence through the forest, where hooting owls, rustling branches, and scuttling creatures added to the mystical ambiance. The moon became our lantern, as our sight adjusted to the night.

Once we left the wood, it was only a hundred meters or so to the edge of the land. From there, a sheer drop threatened to swallow those who didn't watch their step, ending in a crushing fall onto ragged rocks thrashed by an unrelenting, and at times angry, ocean.

The chalky cliffs, a beacon to those journeying from afar, seemed to glow in the dark. I clutched my arms, my face tingling from the icy blast of sea air.

Daniel pointed up to a sparkling star. "Jupiter."

"It's colorful."

"Through a telescope, it radiates a spectrum of color. Quite the show." He smiled. "We have an observatory at the top of the house."

"Really?"

"It's at the back of the house, unnoticeable from the façade."

"There are so many rooms," I said.

"They're mainly closed. I get Jan to dust them from time to time."

"Rooms filled with memories?" I looked up at him.

He shrugged. "You could say that. The house is like a museum. So many possessions that go back many generations."

"Lots of ghosts," I said, almost to myself.

"Ghosts can't harm us."

"Even your father's?" I asked.

He looked away. His face hardened, as it did earlier after I asked about the dress.

"I'm sorry. I didn't mean to stir something," I added.

"I burnt everything of his." He faced me. "In answer to your question about modeling in a green dress: yes. I can't explain why I need it, but I do."

"Is that why you like me—or need me, as you put it?"

He took a deep breath. "You understand me, and our pasts are somewhat aligned."

"How?" I asked.

"Well, you have a violent husband, who I imagine wouldn't hesitate to kill. Neither did my father."

"So you feel sorry for me?" I asked.

"It's nothing like that." His voice had an edge.

Despite pushing buttons, I persisted. "Am I Georgina to you?"

"I don't want her. I want you."

"But why the green dress, then?"

"I explained it." He turned away and started walking. "I need to go back."

We walked back in silence as questions smoldered.

I paused at the path leading to my cottage. "Are you angry at me?"

"No." He pressed his cool, cushiony lips against mine, leaving behind a taste of smoke, sex, wine, and tension.

"I just need some space." He brushed my cheek, gazed deeply into my eyes, then walked off.

As I watched his tall figure skulk off, my heart shriveled. I wanted to chase after him. But like a lump of stone, I watched him walk back to that beguiling mansion with secrets bursting out of each cupboard.

What was I expecting: a happily ever after? I'd already woken from that fairy-tale dream only to find myself in a nightmare.

Couldn't I just be his mistress without needing to undress his soul? But what of my starved curiosity? Could I sustain that on crumbs?

Leaving Daniel would be as difficult as losing my soul.

Maybe I'd already lost it. Sold it in a moment of breathless euphoria.

I'd fallen so madly in love with him, I no longer recognized myself.

# CHAPTER 36

I HADN'T SEEN DANIEL again the next day or night. The fact he'd asked for space made me hesitant about pestering him through a call or text—something I didn't do often, given that he'd made all the moves in this pinch-me-am-I-dreaming situation.

I even entertained returning to the city to put physical distance between us, if only for the sake of my sanity. Knowing he was close made his silent treatment even more stifling. Despite identifying as an independent woman, I was acting more like a hormonally charged teenager obsessing over a crush.

After I cooked myself some instant noodles, which I found hard to swallow, I tried to watch television but was too distracted, so I decided on a walk instead.

This time, I deviated from my normal path to Wiching Wood and headed toward the pond instead.

As I approached the folly, I noticed light flickering again. Silencing my breath, I crept along. When I arrived at the grey building, which looked black under the shadow of night, I snuck around to the window and bent down.

Just like before, I saw a silhouetted male and female. Once again, she reminded me of Charlie. They seemed to be arguing, then he punched her. She stumbled and fell to the ground, holding her face and crying.

My body chilled. I'd seen that image. A woman on the ground, covering her eyes with her hands, and a man standing over her.

What was going on here? Were those paintings trying to tell me what was to come? If so, I knew the outcome. And it wasn't nice.

He turned toward the window, and I quickly crouched down, my heart in my throat. Had he seen me? Was it Daniel?

I hid behind a bush and, after a few minutes with my heart banging in my ears, I ran back to my cottage.

I buried my head in my hands; it felt as though I was losing my mind.

The following day, after a sleepless night, and no word from Daniel, I decided on a trip to the local village. My purpose was to drop into Crowley's bookshop in the hope of finding Oleander. I needed to talk to someone intimate with that family's history.

Crowley was on his phone playing a game, which jolted me back to the twenty-first century, even if stepping into that bookshop, redolent of decaying paper and herbs, made one forgot what year it was.

He looked up and smiled. "Aah . . . Scarlet."

I smiled. "Nice to see you again. I've been dying to drop in." I looked around at the shelves of hardbacks. "How's business?"

"Oleander's readings are always popular. They're what keep us going—along with Daniel's generosity." He chuckled.

I made the spontaneous decision to ask for a reading. "Does Oleander perform them?"

"She does. But only with people she feels a connection to."

"Would you mind asking her for me?" I asked. "I don't have her contact."

"Just give me a minute."

I gave him space and selected a hardback by Madame Blavatsky.

"You're in luck," he called out. "She's on her way. Five minutes or so."

"Oh, that's great. Thanks." I sat down on an armchair to wait.

I was reading half-heartedly about the mystical nature of Isis when Oleander arrived.

Looking up, I closed the book and greeted her.

She tilted her head to read the title. "Ah Madame Blavatsky. A great scholar. Unfairly maligned—as most powerful women were back then. Save Queen Victoria, of course." She chuckled.

I returned a smile.

Dressed in a burgundy velvet dress with her white hair up in a bun, she moved with the agility of someone half her age.

"How nice to see you again, Scarlet." She crooked her finger. "Come."

We settled into a curtained-off area, draped in black velvet and smelling of incense.

A crystal ball sat in the middle of the table along with a stack of cards.

"I know of Charlotte's return. Her scattered energy's everywhere," she said.

"It's not so much a reading I've come for. I just really needed to talk to you. I'm happy to pay for your time."

She frowned. "Nonsense. I don't want any money. And I'm happy to chat. Tell me, what's Daniel up to?"

Despite hesitating over how much to divulge, my nerves demanded I talk to someone. "Charlie wants Starlington and is refusing to leave until Daniel agrees." I bit my lip. "You will keep this between us?"

"Of course, my dear." She patted my hand. "He normally comes to me for a chat, but I haven't seen him since Beltane." She shook her head. "Starlington's his bloodline. Tell me," —she tilted her head slightly— "what have you seen?"

I swallowed tightly and told her about the folly and the art.

She knitted her fingers as sadness misted over her blue eyes. "He's seen things that nobody, especially at that tender age, should see—particularly before crossing over."

"Crossing over?"

"Saturn return, my dear. We really only become adults at twenty-seven."

"How old was Daniel?"

"He hasn't told you what happened?" she asked.

"I know that his father killed his mother, but Daniel has never really opened up about it. I'd heard about it from the staff."

She studied me for a moment. "He saw it all, the poor boy. He was in his late teens. He witnessed his father kill his mother in that dreadful folly—the scene of many a dark, wicked act." She paused for a breath. "His father took young girls there."

"Underage?" I asked.

She shrugged. "Mainly the staff. They were young. Teenagers. Many unwilling, I'm told. He plied them with alcohol. The family paid handsome sums for their silence."

"Rape?" My stomach tightened.

She nodded slowly. Her gaze remote as though seeing the horrors play out.

"I begged Cathy to burn the folly down, but Elizabeth's grandfather built it as a testimony of his love for his wife." She sniffed. "Sadly, it descended into an evil space."

My heart ached, as my face crumpled from shock. "Oh my God, it would have really affected Daniel to see his mother die in such a brutal way."

"Oh, it has. That's why he retreats into himself. I've tried to do healings, but he's not committed to our lore. One can't heal unless they believe. All the spells in the world can't cleanse the soul of darkness. Only true love can do that." Her eyes met mine.

By this stage, I was a lump of ice, but not numb enough for the deep pain in my heart to subside. "Do you think he might try to re-enact something in the folly?"

"That's not Daniel." Her brow creased. "However..."

I sat forward. "Yes?"

"His father was a somnambulist."

"A sleepwalker?"

"Yes. And Daniel, after that tragedy, was spotted in the wood, sleep walking. Luckily, the gardener was there with one of his ladies. Goodness knows what might have happened otherwise. Daniel wouldn't have been the first to plunge to his death from that treacherous cliff."

"But wasn't his father found dead in the wood while naked?"

"Yes. He died of a heart attack. It was speculated that he'd walked in his sleep."

"Do you think that could be Daniel in the folly? And why would Charlie be there with him? And then there are the paintings that seem to predict something..."

She closed her eyes. "The paintings tell the story of Daniel's past."

"So Daniel's art is, as already suggested, purely for self-healing?" That made sense. Especially to me. I'd used performance to deal with my father's absence.

"All art is, my dear."

"But what of the couple in the folly?" I asked.

"I'm not getting anything, my dear. Only that you should stay away."

How the hell could I do that?

"But was it Daniel whom I saw?" I pressed.

Her eyes remained closed. "My instincts say no."

I puffed out a trapped breath. "Should I leave?" I paused to consider my question. "I mean, does Daniel wish me to leave?"

"No. You need to stay. If you return to your former home you'll be in danger. A dark force wishes you harm. You're protected at Starlington."

"My ex, you mean?"

"He's evil. Stay well away." She opened her eyes and pointed to the cards.

"Shuffle the cards."

Although I didn't want a reading, Oleander's accurate reference to my ex had stirred curiosity.

"Cut them into three," she instructed. "Select a bundle."

She laid out the cards. I expected Tarot, but her cards resembled ancient playing cards.

"You are with child," she said.

I sat up. "What?"

"There is a child growing. It is but just a seed."

I shook my head in deep shock. "That's impossible. I'm unable to conceive."

"You're a healthy, fertile woman. Daniel needs you. You've come here to save him."

The rest of that session was a blur.

I went to pay her, but she refused.

Dazed, I could barely feel my legs as I walked out of the bookshop.

My period hadn't arrived. But that wasn't unusual. Stress tended to make it irregular.

Anxiety clung onto my shoulder blades as I purchased a pregnancy kit. My last test was a year into my marriage. Bliss, from discovering I was to be a mother, was soon usurped by mind-numbing depression, as I lay in hospital following a miscarriage not brought on by nature but by my insane husband.

# CHAPTER 37

DANIEL HADN'T RETURNED MY calls, but I wanted to see him. It had been two days. And while I stayed on the grounds, the cottage was far enough from the main house for me to remain isolated. Normally this kind of distance from people appealed to me, especially during periods of introspection. But I missed him.

Noticing Charlie's car gone, I decided to visit the house. I knocked even though the door was rarely locked.

Jan answered the door with a look of surprise. "Why are you knocking?"

"I thought I better. Charlotte's not exactly welcoming." I smiled tightly.

She rolled her eyes. "Tell me about it. I liked it better before she arrived."

"I trust she's out?"

"She is. Daniel's upstairs. In his studio, I think. He's had music blaring all day. It only just stopped."

"Oh, he's painting." I tilted my head. "Heavy metal music?"

She nodded. "I've even started wearing earplugs."

I smiled sympathetically. That confirmed Daniel had entered his dark zone again. I contemplated leaving when he appeared.

His eyes trapped mine.

Jan must have noticed the air thickening because she raised an eyebrow and scuttled off.

I opened my mouth to speak, when he said, "Come for a walk with me."

Being late afternoon, the fading sun dropped a veil over the distant forest.

Daniel whistled and Thor and Zeus came charging over. I bent down to pat the eager canines.

As always, we took the path through to the wood. "I hope you don't mind me dropping in. I tried calling you," I said.

He stared ahead. "Charlie's hanging around like a bad smell and I'm not the best company."

"I don't need you to chat mindlessly to me."

His lips curved at one end. "I know that, Scarlet. That's why I like you."

"So you're not angry or tired of me?"

"No." He stopped and picked up a stick to throw for the dogs.

"Would you prefer me gone?"

"I've told you I'm not in any state to be around anyone. But I don't want you gone either."

Although I winced at his sharp tone, I persisted. "Is that so you can paint me in the green dress when your mood calls for it?"

"It's more than that." He rubbed his neck, and as he looked into my eyes, I saw a troubled man who hadn't slept.

"I'm sorry." I looked down at my feet. "I'm a fucking emotional wreck." It just tumbled out. I wanted to speak about what I'd seen in the folly, but reluctant to dredge up his past and trigger a traumatic response, I stayed well away.

"I know it's not easy with Charlie around." He shook his head. "I'll do anything to see her gone. Not even over my fucking dead body will she get Starlington."

I frowned. "You're not going to resort to anything nasty, I hope."

"You don't know me, do you?" he said roughly.

"No, I don't know you, Daniel. I thought I did."

"I'm not my fucking father."

He walked off in a huff and I froze on the spot.

One thing I'd learned about men: The more one provoked a response, the more they retreated—or even worse, as in the case of Kevin, the more severe their blows.

I wanted to tell him about my pregnancy, but not while he was like that. His stormy mood made it hard to breathe, let alone think straight.

Hurrying back to the cottage, I convulsed in tears. Once inside, I buried my head in my hands and a frustrated scream burst from my chest.

I'd experienced far worse when it came to coping with emotional abuse, but somehow Daniel shutting me out hurt more than Kevin's tirades and punches.

Emotionally exhausted, I lay on the couch staring at the ceiling for some time, when the door sounded.

I answered it and stepped out of the way for Daniel to pass.

Combing back his hair with his fingers, he looked lost.

All it took was a whiff of his cologne and I fell into his arms. His lips, cool from the walk, claimed mine.

He walked me to the wall, while his tongue lashed mine, and ran his hands over my breasts. Our lips caressed, savoring angst and lust.

Lowering my leggings, he virtually ripped off my panties and got down on his knees. My legs trembled as his tongue lapped over my clit.

Taking me over the edge, I moaned as a spasm erupted and I flooded his tongue.

When I couldn't take it any longer, I lowered his zipper. His thick length—hot, heavy, and damp—fell into my palm.

He turned me to the wall and entered me in one deep, burning thrust. His chest reverberated with a groan as his mouth ate at my neck.

He rocked his hips, grinding his pelvis and pounding into me, as though starved, while fondling my breasts, his breath hot and noisy.

It didn't take long for colors to explode before me—one explosion after another while our damp, sticky bodies writhed.

"I need you to come," he said, as though someone was strangling him.

I nearly crashed to the floor. His seed gushed in as he made a guttural grunt.

Gripping his large biceps, a climactic seizure sent me flying. No man had ever made me come like this.

For some, it was see Venice and die. For me, it was fuck Daniel and die. I'd become a junkie. The more I tasted, the more I wanted.

After we'd settled back to earth and reverted to cool, collected individuals trying to negotiate a relationship of sorts, I poured Daniel a drink.

"You're not having one?" he asked.

I shook my head. My heart started to race again. This time it had nothing to do with animal lust.

Staring down at my hands, I felt his eyes burning into my face.

"Are you okay?" he asked. When I didn't respond, he said, "While Charlie's around, I might act like an asshole—and you do know me, I'm sure." He pulled a tight smile.

"I understand you need space, but it's not that." I took a deep breath. "Something strange has happened."

# CHAPTER 38

*Daniel*

"BUT I THOUGHT . . ." My head swam in so many directions, I was left speechless. "How do you know?"

"I did a test."

"It could be a mistake." I was close to hyperventilating.

"It's not."

"But I thought you couldn't. You told me you'd . . ."

"I thought that too. But then Oleander . . ."

My eyebrows rose. "Oleander? You saw Oleander?"

She looked away. "I did."

"Did you run into her?"

"No. I went to see her. I needed someone to talk to. I hoped she'd help me understand you more. You'd withdrawn. You hadn't spoken to me in days. I wanted to leave here, but she warned of danger if I returned to the city." She bit her lip. "And then she told me I was with child."

"But that's just from a reading."

"I did a test," she repeated, then shrugged. "I wouldn't just take the word of a psychic, although she was pretty accurate."

I rubbed my prickly jaw. "Did she help you understand me more?"

"Is that all that interests you?" Her scathing tone slapped me back to reality. I was to be a father.

"No, but I . . . What did she tell you?"

Scarlet bit into a nail. "That you witnessed your mother's death."

I puffed out a tight breath. My chest hurt from a memory that refused to take shape. But my emotions remembered something because the mere mention of my mother's brutal murder iced my veins.

"It's a blacked-out period in my life. That's why I paint." I poured half a glass of whisky and drank it like water. "Hoping that something buried in my subconscious might surface."

Pity reflected from her gaze. "Amnesia is a normal response to shock."

I had nothing to say to that. Only I wished whatever was trapped inside of me would let me go.

"Daniel." Her gentle tone brought me back to the present as I fell into her comforting green eyes. "I'm keeping this child."

Fatherhood. Me?

I exhaled a jagged breath. "Of course. It's just totally unexpected."

"You didn't expect to become a father?" Her brow furrowed.

"To be honest, the thought of it paralyzes me." I poured myself another triple shot and swallowed half in one gulp. "How the fuck am I going to love a child when I don't know how to?"

That confession spewed out of nowhere. Even the voice seemed foreign.

Scarlet shook her head with a pained grimace. "But you're kind and considerate. I saw how respectful and caring you were around your grandmother—and how shattered you were on her passing."

I ran my finger around the rim of the glass. "What I meant was that life's easier when I'm alone."

"But wouldn't that make you lonely?" she asked.

"After my mother died, I learned to subsist on loneliness. She stole my heart. Took it to her grave."

"Oh, Daniel." Taking my hand, she smiled sadly. "It doesn't have to stay that way. When I took this job, I was trapped in my own misery. And although I felt like shit for being here on false pretenses, I slowly started to find myself—thanks to you and the natural beauty of this place. Now, I have a life growing inside of me." She smiled. "To be honest, I'm warming to the idea of having someone else to think about for a change—to care for and love someone unconditionally."

"You're a lot more evolved than me," I murmured into my glass before draining it. "I need time to think. It's come as a big shock."

"If you wish me to leave Starlington, I'll understand."

"No. I want you here. Close. Especially now. I just need some space and time alone. I will always need that. You do understand." I took a breath. "I'm claustrophobic."

She gave me an understanding nod. "So am I. I'm just grateful to be here. You know how much I love this place."

I stroked her cheek and kissed her. "Give me time. And then there's the Charlie issue."

"About that..." She looked burdened again.

"Don't worry. We'll work through this together." I took her hand. "I won't abandon you."

I could see she wanted to continue the discussion, but I needed to close myself off.

"We'll speak tomorrow." I kissed her, then almost collapsed into the night as I made my way back to the inner sanctum of my studio.

# CHAPTER 39

## *Scarlet*

THAT FOLLY INCIDENT WAS akin to one of those horror movies that lingered like an unwelcomed creepy guest. Possessing a vivid imagination didn't help. I'd started to cook up all kinds of explanations, like perhaps they were squatters. Or was it some twisted game between Daniel and Charlie?

As all-consuming as this mystery had become, I gave Daniel the space he desired, and hoped that an explanation would materialize without stirring the air between us. The chicken's way out. I just wasn't in a state for a confrontation. Even the mere mention of the folly and Daniel's face darkened. And by visiting that forbidden place, I'd broken his trust.

Rather than speaking to my mother on the phone about my pregnancy, I decided to visit her instead. In many ways, I needed some space from Starlington.

After the long drive through thick traffic, I finally arrived at my mother's new apartment: a jaw-dropping gift from Daniel. When he passed over the keys, I looked at my mother and her shock mirrored mine. Shaking my head, I insisted it was too generous. But with my ex hanging around our old home and my mother subsisting on a meager pension, we eventually accepted the shining new first-floor apartment, boasting state-of-the-art security, with the same good grace with which it was given.

Meeting Daniel was like winning a lottery, even though the ticket was purchased with tainted money borrowed from the devil. I'd happily repay it a thousand times over if it meant a healthy child and Daniel freeing himself from his inner demons.

I now understood his obsession with the green dress. It represented a time when life offered everything and anything his young heart and imagination desired. All that vaporized the night he saw his mother murdered—not by a stranger, but by the one person who should have protected them.

I found my mother on her knees, painting the cupboards in her new kitchen.

"Why are you doing that? This place is brand new." I opened the window to release the fumes.

"I know, love. I just didn't like the color." She smiled.

After she cleaned herself up and we made tea, we sat in the living room.

"You're looking well," she said, holding a willow-patterned teacup passed down from my grandparents. Only two cups remained after my father smashed the rest in one his drunken tirades.

"I'm pregnant."

I might have told her I was having a sex change by the shock on her face. "But how?"

I opened my palms and cocked my head.

"With that dishy man, your boss? Is it Daniel's?" she asked.

I nodded slowly.

As she processed my life-changing announcement, my mother went from wearing a crumpled brow to a bright smile.

She rose from her seat and hugged me. "Darling, that's such marvelous news."

And then the immensity of becoming a single mother and what that would mean hit me. My mother's presence had lowered my guard. Around Daniel, it was hormones, desire, hot sex, and goodness knows what else that took center stage, but here with my mother, the façade dropped. My emotions erupted, bursting forth—and there I stood, alone and naked.

She placed her arm around me. "If you're worried about caring for the child. I'll be there, by your side, all the way."

Tears spilled all over my palms.

"Does he know?" she asked.

I nodded, biting a fingernail.

"I take it he wasn't supportive?"

"He's in shock. As I am still. I wasn't meant to conceive. After that pig Kevin . . ." My voice choked up. I couldn't even bring myself to talk about my ex without paralyzing fear taking grip. What if he hurt me while I was carrying? He'd done it once. Killed my baby. I couldn't have him do it again.

"He hasn't been around. Daniel's been an angel. He is an angel, darling. He won't abandon the child. I don't think so. He's a good man."

I gulped back a lump in my throat. "You're right. It's just that I can't stop seeing the horror on his face after I told him."

"Maybe it was just shock, love." She passed me a tissue.

I blew my nose. "He's got so many issues. That's why I need to stay here for a couple of days. Is that okay?"

"Of course. This is your home too."

"I've got the apartment in town, but I'm terrified Kevin will come and find me. He's got this sixth sense. He seems to know when I'm in town."

I told my mother about everything that had happened at Starlington. The folly. The art. Oleander's predictions.

"Daniel can't remember seeing his father killing his mother, despite being present."

My mother nodded reflectively. "You know that's not uncommon. It's obviously still having a major impact on him. As it would. Oh, my goodness. Poor love."

I smiled sadly and tears splashed down my cheeks, the pathos of Daniel's past pulling at me again.

"I want to suggest hypnotherapy but he's too tender at the moment, especially with Charlie hanging around."

"What does that house mean to him, I wonder?" my mother asked.

I nodded. "Great question. Daniel's offered her over three billion dollars. You could buy ten Starlingtons and still have plenty cash left."

"Maybe you should get Oleander to look into it. There might be something about that place. Some hidden gold?"

My mother and her novels.

"Why would that matter? Three billion is more than plenty."

She opened her palms. "The super-rich are known for their greed."

Daniel was generous beyond belief, so he didn't fit that description.

"The father's death in the forest sounds interesting," she said, fascinated by my story. "This would make a great movie."

I chuckled. "Wouldn't it? Weird how tragedies make the best stories and movies."

"But only when there's a happy ending, love. I do need my happy endings."

I smiled and nodded reflectively, wondering if my life would find its happy ending. "Yes. The battles that lead to that final victory, just as Joseph Campbell talks about. The hero or heroine battling obstacles to finally arrive at their true self—open, revealed, and ready to love."

"That's a little too intellectual for me, sweetie. Just give me Pierce Brosnan saving the world while rescuing a woman from a dull life."

I giggled at my mother's obsession with the Irish actor and romance stories that repeated the same plot.

"I guess a whole film devoted to a happy couple would bore us to death," I said.

"It wouldn't in real life though," she said, tilting her head.

She was right. After what we'd endured with horrible, violent husbands, an easy life in marital bliss would be the ultimate prize. For me, however, it wasn't so simple. I was a sucker for complex men. And when it came to issues, Daniel had enough to keep Sigmund Freud up at night.

My phone pinged.

I looked at it and the message read: "I hope I didn't push you away. Where are you?"

"I'm at my mother's," I wrote, wearing a big smile.

"When are you returning? We need to work this out together."

"I thought you needed space."

"Just come back. I need you."

"I'll see you tomorrow."

"I love you, Scarlet."

My finger trembled as I wrote, "I love you too. And I love what's growing inside of me. Created from passion and love. Even if you decide against being involved, I feel blessed that we've created something magical."

"I will try. I am new to this. I am new to love."

"I'll be there tomorrow, my love."

• • • • • • • • • •

STARLINGTON SHONE LIKE A jewel in the sunlight as I drove into the parking lot. It was late afternoon. The excitement bubbling away in my stomach soon turned acidic on seeing Charlie's BMW. I missed visiting the house and all its beautiful art and objects, especially the sunroom at the back with the flourishing garden in full view.

I entered the cottage and filled the fridge and cupboards with my shopping. Through online recipes, I'd learned to cook a decent stew and some roasts. Domesticity suited me at this stage of my life.

I was no longer that restless spirit that hated being trapped between four walls, a quirk of personality that drove Kevin crazy. While he slumped on the couch draining bottles of beer, glued to watching football, I preferred to visit museums or go to the theatre.

He couldn't stand me not being that domesticated wife who'd open her legs when he said and wear his insults as comfortably as cotton underwear.

I sent Daniel a message and within five minutes a knock came to the door.

We didn't speak; we just made love. It wasn't raunchy like it normally was, but slow, caressing, and tender.

My head rested on his cushiony chest, and he stroked my hair.

"I'll do everything to be a good father. You'll both be looked after, but I can't promise marriage. I'm not sure if I can do that again," he said.

Daniel's hesitancy was understandable if not predictable. In my case, I would have swum the English Channel during a tempest to marry him.

"It's okay," I said gently. "I don't expect you to marry me."

"You've made a big difference in my life. When you weren't here yesterday, I thought I'd driven you away. When I asked for some space, I didn't mean for you to leave. I missed you. I know it's far from ideal around here at the moment."

"Let's just take it one day at a time."

He turned to look at me and we shared a smile.

After that, we ate some chicken and salad I'd picked up.

"You seem very hungry," I said as he polished off his plate.

"I didn't eat much yesterday. Charlie was hanging around and giving me the shits."

"She's hell-bent on Starlington?"

He nodded. "I even offered her more cash."

"Have you been painting?" I asked.

He shook his head. "No. I've lacked inspiration."

"I'm happy to model," I said, thinking of the green dress I'd yet to try on.

"Later." He rose. "I should leave you."

"Why don't you stay?" I asked. "We can watch a movie or . . ."

A smile touched his lips. "Or . . . ?"

"I can put on that green dress now . . ."

He nodded slowly. "I haven't got my sketch pad."

I rummaged in the drawer and found a pad and some pencils. "Will this do?"

"Mm . . . sure." He took the pad, which he'd left behind at some earlier point. There were studies of birds and botanicals in there, which I planned to frame one day, if he allowed. Even done in pencil, they were masterpieces.

As he flicked through them, I said, "They're so well done."

"I like to loosen my hand and sharpen my eye. Nature's a great way of doing that. It was through drawing birds and plants, not to mention cadavers, that Leonardo developed into the greatest artist in history," he said.

His smile lit up my world. And for that moment, we were just us.

# CHAPTER 40

THE FOLLOWING DAY I ran into Charlie. I was about to jump into my car to go shopping when I noticed her black eye and my heart froze.

I must have worn my shock because she cocked her head with a smirk that soon turned into a sneer. "Are you still here?"

Instead of commenting on her eye, I drove off, deeply disturbed.

That night, after dinner with Daniel, we made love. I noticed he was gentler, which got me wondering if he was atoning for something. I hadn't brought up Charlie's eye only because, rather selfishly, I wanted to indulge in his affection.

"Do you feel differently because of the baby?" I asked.

He shook his head. "I'm not sure why, but I feel like we've entered a different place together. I've developed deep feelings for you."

My heart melted because underneath his sad smile, his eyes shone with affection.

"I feel the same, and I have for a long time." I looked down at my fingers. "I just hope it's not only because of the child."

He frowned. "I stopped wearing those kinds of masks after my last marriage."

"Which masks are those?"

"The bullshit kind." He rubbed his jaw, which was covered in a dark stubble. His eyes held mine, as if seeking the right words. "I need you close. I'm not the same when you're away from me."

"Then why does it sound like you're struggling?"

"Look at this situation. I can't have you in the house because of Charlie and her fucking hissy fits. I hate her being there. Every day I have to tolerate her awful music, and she keeps moving my favorite things, hiding family heirlooms, whereas you and I are on the same wavelength. I like having you around."

"I like being around." My lips trembled into a smile. "Charlie's got a black eye."

His brow creased. "If you're insinuating that I'm responsible for that, then you really don't know me."

I winced at his biting tone. "That's not what I meant. I'm just wondering how she got it."

"Probably one of her rough lovers. Charlie likes to be bashed around. That's one of many reasons why we didn't work. I detest any kind of violence, especially toward women."

He poured himself a scotch and gulped it down. "She probably had some brainless brute hit her to show the world I'm the abusive husband she's accusing me of being—to add more weight to her ridiculous demands."

"Is she laying charges?" I asked.

He shook his head. "Not yet. She's got no fucking proof. I've never laid a hand on her. She used to try and goad me. Push buttons. She's heavily into S&M."

I thought of the folly. I felt trapped. If I told him, I'd push him away. If I didn't, I'd go crazy.

He walked to the door. "I need to do something. I'll be back later."

"But it's ten o'clock," I said.

He kissed him. "I feel like painting."

"Do you want me to pose? Is Charlie there?"

He shook his head. "No. But look, I need some more time alone. I hope you understand."

"Sure." I smiled tightly. Daniel was an enigma to me, however my need for him outweighed any fantasy of what our relationship should look like.

As I watched his dark figure diminish into the distance, my heart continued to race. It hadn't returned to a steady beat since moving to Starlington. It was either all-consuming suspense or burning-hot arousal.

I thought of the crippling, white-knuckled fear of living with Kevin. In comparison, this was like a holiday at a sunny resort with endless free cocktails and massages from men named Javier.

Was I just a pleasure junkie?

Would I finally grow up now that I was to become a mother?

Anyone in their right mind wouldn't be living in a cottage on an estate owned by her unborn child's father, who also lived there with his current wife.

So what did that make me? Mad? Besotted? Both.

An hour after Daniel left, I couldn't sleep, so I got out of bed, and—missing cigarettes like one would a cozy pair of slippers—I headed to the cupboard for a sugar hit instead. A chocolate biscuit was hardly a stimulant, but it had become my latest compulsion. Going cold turkey on cigarettes and my evening drink had proved agonizing.

I stepped outside and drew in the damp, earth-rich air as I would a cigarette, and my cheeks flushed from the cool blast.

Buttoning up my coat, I decided on a stroll. I grabbed my cell just in case Daniel texted late at night as he'd done before, telling me he needed me in his arms or something just as romantic.

I walked along the path to the folly.

In what was an eerily riveting image, the gabled building's shadow rippled over the silvery pond. Magical under the veil of night, the Gothic structure conjured up images of an occupying witch stirring a smoldering cauldron while chanting about frogs and princes' hearts.

Despite itching curiosity, I decided on a walk through the woods instead.

Just as I deviated, I heard a scream.

I snuck back along the path to the folly. Within a few steps, I heard a woman and man arguing.

I crouched down, peeping through the window at their silhouettes. The male was pointing and yelling at her.

He placed his hands around her throat and looked to be strangling her.

Although my legs felt like ice, I scampered off to call the police, when I slipped and fell into a noisy bush.

Within a breath, the big bulky figure came toward me.

It wasn't Daniel.

Despite a surge of relief, fear soon had me scrambling out of the bush's clutches.

I dashed off, one eye on the ground to avoid holes and obstacles, the other straight ahead. Sensing him close, I scurried off into thick scrub.

Gripping on to my arms and squeezing myself into a ball, I heard rustling getting louder.

Dizzy from fear. I felt my heart thump against my hand.

I snuck a peek. He had his back to me, and he was encouragingly far enough for me to make a dash.

But where?

I couldn't go back to the cottage because that path was exposed. My only option was to continue through the thicket that led to the bay.

For a second, I thought of staying put, but when he turned in my direction, instinct had me crawling along the scratchy scrub.

Despite the moonlight aiding my navigation, it also threatened to expose me.

From a distance, I eyed the monolithic rock I'd often admired, which—much to my luck—was exposed due to a low tide. Rushing down the steep path, trying not to stumble, I finally got onto the beach and virtually staggered over to hide behind it.

There was a chance he'd spotted me—or, I kept telling myself, he might have given up and left. If only.

Clutching my phone, I went to make a call for help, when—through a crack in the rock—I noticed him lumbering toward me.

With my heart pumping in my ears, and virtually hyperventilating from fear, I suddenly remembered the hidden cave that Daniel had shown me. I had access to it, given the low tide. The only problem was that I could potentially injure myself on sharp reef.

But flesh wounds would be the least of my problems because he'd see me as I splashed along the shallows. But once I got around the rock wall that partitioned the neighboring bay, the cave was hidden.

That was my only hope. At least I could call for help once I got there.

But for now, I remained pitched against the rock as I tried to gather my senses.

First a shadow, then the bulky figure came into view. He looked about him, obviously unable to see me.

Discharging trapped air from my chest, I leaned against the damp rock. My clammy hands gripped my cell as sharp edges dug into me. Fear had become my morphine. My body was numb to pain.

When I noticed the stalker looking in the opposite direction, my muscles eased. I managed to press on Daniel's number. Of course he didn't pick up, which made me want to scream.

I whispered a rushed message, then called the police.

"Your location," asked the operator.

"I'm at Starlington . . ." He was heading toward me. He must have heard. "Help. I'm on the beach and I'm being followed by a dangerous man . . ." I must have sounded crazy. I didn't even know the name of that bay. "It's by Wiching Wood, just outside of Deal."

I had to get to that cave. My mouth was dry and bitter, and I could barely swallow.

I ran to the shore to the jutting rock wall.

Glancing over my shoulder, I spied him descending the rocky stairs. Unless he was short-sighted, I'd been detected.

Without time to lose, I paddled in the cold water. Luckily it was calm. No smashing waves or swallowing rips.

I hurried along, stumbling every now and then from embedded rocks as jagged reef stabbed at me.

I finally made it to the other side of the rock wall and raced onto the shore. Tripping over a hidden rock, I landed on my knees, and a sharp, eye-watering pain rang through me.

Searching for the cave's hidden entrance, I spotted what was to the naked eye an extension of the chalky cliff face, its only visitor the sea at high tide.

Thanking the day that Daniel had rather whimsically shown me the cave, I touched my stomach and rubbed it to reassure the growing life that no harm would come to it.

I finally entered the dark, dank chamber, and lowered myself onto the hard, wet ground.

My fatigued legs collapsed beneath me, and my body slumped.

With my teeth chattering so loudly they echoed in that confined space, I was too frightened to appreciate the arched image of the dark-green sea, the shimmering moonbeams over it looked like a metallic escalator to the heavens.

After I tried calling Daniel again, I heard splashing and froze. Taking some comfort in the cave's obscurity, I tried to breathe calmly, but it was cold and creepy, and it smelled of rotting fish.

Then my phone sounded. And the next thing I knew, I heard the splashing sound come closer, then nothing. He must have landed on the beach by the cave.

I tried calling Daniel again. This time he picked up.

"I'm in the cave," I whispered. "Please come and save me. Call the police."

"I'm close. The police are on their way too. Are you okay?" he asked.

"I am. He's violent," I whispered. The cave's echo magnified my voice. "He might be armed."

"Stay calm. I'm on the beach. Just stay there. Hide."

A minute or so later, I heard splashing.

I clutched on to my arms as my body trembled. I couldn't stand it—waiting there and wondering.

I went to the edge of the cave but couldn't see anything.

Hearing voices and yelling, I had to look outside. The suspense was killing me.

I stepped out of the cave and saw Daniel in a scuffle with the man. I noticed a gun lying on the sand. I ran over and picked it up.

I could hear sickening cracks as they both rolled on the sand.

My hand trembled.

Taking a deep breath, I channeled the police character I'd played in my last role and fired into the air.

# CHAPTER 41

## *Daniel*

THE NAUSEATING STENCH OF antiseptic mixed with decay and excrement clung to the air. It hurt to breathe—and to move—but I was alive. Just barely. My mind was a frazzled mess of loose wires as endless thoughts kept rotating around and around, searching for answers.

A nurse entered and said, "The doctor won't be long."

I glanced at Scarlet's mother, whose hands moved deftly. I'd never seen anyone knit before. I thought it was an antiquated pastime that only existed before the internet and sweatshops. It was strangely meditative. My late grandmothers didn't knit. They used their time arranging social gatherings, like garden parties, the hunt, and cricket matches—anything that upheld tradition. That's all that ever mattered at Starlington. Tradition. I too was keen on upholding an element of the past. Whitewashing it, of course. Distance of time was good at that— keeping the romance of Starlington but expunging the darkness. And here I was yet again, faced with another dramatic chapter right at my feet.

Marion looked up and smiled. She was a calming influence.

The doctor entered, carrying a clipboard. "Ah . . . good. You're family, I take it?"

I looked at Marion and she nodded.

Scarlet stirred and we all turned our attention to her.

"Good timing," the doctor said smiling as he went to her side.

She touched her forehead. "Where am I?"

"You're in hospital," he replied.

She noticed me by the bed. I took her hand. "Daniel." Then she looked over to her mother.

"What happened?" she asked.

"You passed out," I replied stroking her hand, and smiling for the first time in days.

The doctor said, "Can you just give me a minute to check on her? Just step outside and I'll be with you soon."

We stepped out of the room and into the passageway.

Marion held my hand. "I'm sure she's going to be just fine."

I nodded. The tight knot in my gut started to unwind at last. It had been a harrowing twenty-four hours.

Ten minutes later, the doctor stepped out and said, "You can go in and speak to her. She's good to go. Everything's fine. She was depleted of iron. We've given her an infusion and she'll bounce back. Only..."

My heart squeezed. "Only?"

"She'll need to put her feet up for a while. No more excitement until the baby's born."

"Oh... the baby's okay?" I asked.

"She's in perfect shape."

"The baby's a 'she'?" Marion asked, beating me to it.

"Do you want to know the sex?" The doctor asked me.

I nodded slowly.

"Then yes, it's a girl."

I felt such a visceral sense of relief that all the aches and pains I'd sustained wrestling that maniacal thug miraculously vanished.

• • • ● • ● • • •

MARION ACCOMPANIED US TO Starlington at my request. She seemed like a child at a theme park, oohing and aahing as we drove into the estate.

Everything looked the same—undulating green meadows glowing in the sunlight, the lush garden in all its myriad textures, colors, and heady perfumes.

Only things had changed. Dramatically.

I glanced over at the once sleepy folly, now cordoned off as men in dark uniforms and protective clothing carried out paper bags filled with contraband and illegal weapons.

Detective Somers watched on, waving and upon seeing us.

I turned to Scarlet. "Are you okay to take your mother to the house?"

"I'd like to hang around. I'm feeling totally fine." Her cheeks had gained color. Scarlet looked the picture of health.

"I promise to tell you all about it." I touched her arm. "Just go inside and put your feet up. You heard the doctor. Your mother could probably use a drink too."

Marion giggled. "You're not just handsome, you're a mind reader too."

I gave her a smile. I liked Marion. She was down to earth.

Scarlet twisted her lips as she often did when disappointed. Her expressive face made me smile.

Holding firm, I tipped my head toward the house and she left me to it.

I went over and joined Detective Somers.

"It explains everything," she said.

I studied her for a moment. "I take it you're referring to Charlie's disappearing act?"

"She said you beat her and fearing for her life, she hid."

"That's bullshit."

She held my stare, trying to read me as usual. I had nothing to hide. For once.

"Yeah, well. Between Charlotte and her thug boyfriend, their IQs don't make it past fifty." She chuckled. "Must be all those steroids he was on. Made his brain shrink."

I thought about my last conversation with Charlie. Just before picking Scarlet up from the hospital, I visited my now ex-wife at her family home to finalize the divorce—something the solicitor could have done, but I needed proper closure. I was also curious to hear her side of the story, away from the police.

Charlie signed the document and shoved it away. "There. Now you can marry your commoner."

I shook my head.

"What?" she asked.

"I'm just wondering why," I said.

As I studied those cold blue eyes that rarely smiled—or even softened, for that matter—I felt nothing but pity for her. Her wispy blonde lifeless hair hung around her sullen features.

What happened to this woman? Was it because she was spoiled rotten as an only child in a rich family? That was the simple, clichéd explanation. Or was it something more sinister?

"You're wondering why I married you?" she asked, wearing a scornful smirk.

"No. That's easy enough. You wanted my money." I pulled a mock smile.

She rolled her eyes.

"Why the fuck did you disappear?" I asked. "Why not just come back and do what you'd planned with that thug?"

"He's not a thug."

"Last I heard, he was strangling you."

She stared down at her hands. "I asked for it."

I rolled my eyes. "Don't feed me that crap." I hated that argument women used to justify a partner's brutality.

"I wanted to get away from you. From this. I missed Tyson."

"But you would always have to return. The drugs and money were found in the folly."

"I didn't know about that. Once I'd spent my inheritance, Tyson convinced me to return. I actually wanted to stay away and get a divorce, but Tyson pushed me to fight for the estate. He wanted to set up his empire in Starlington. And you, being a stick-in-the-mud bore, wouldn't budge."

"Great empire, killing teenagers through drugs."

"People will always take drugs. They need to buy them from somewhere." She picked at her nails. "Not everyone's boring like you."

As much as I resented Charlie for all her deception, I still hated the idea of her going to jail. I left her at her family home feeling conflicted—while I was now a free man, I could have done without the secrets and lies, not to mention the danger to Scarlet. If anything had happened to her and our baby, I would have committed a crime myself.

Now I was back at Starlington and ready to start a fresh chapter. But first I needed to deal with the cops.

The detective seemed riveted as we continued to watch the police clearing out the folly.

She opened her hands. "Why hide here?"

"Charlie knew I never went near the folly." I took a deep breath. "If it were up to me that building would be dust by now."

"Oh, you want to knock it down?" She squinted as though trying to get into my head again. As she kept eyeing me, her mouth dropped open. "It's where your father..."

I exhaled tightly. "Let's not go there."

"And you never saw anything taking place there after Charlotte's reappearance?"

I shook my head. A knot twisted in my stomach. Scarlet had sidestepped my question about how she came to be there that night. I sensed there was more to it, but due to her delicate condition, I remained silent, despite my unsettling questions.

"As I said, it's far from the house."

"It's a pretty setting with that pond of swans."

Didn't I know it. My childhood was spent playing there. I even had a little boat I drifted around in. It was my own little boy's paradise. Until that blood-curdling day. The loss of a playground didn't compare to losing my mother and discovering my father was a murderer.

"It explains why your wife insisted on staying, I suppose," she said.

"I offered her two billion dollars to sign the divorce papers, but she insisted on clinging on. She wanted Starlington."

"I'm not surprised."

I tilted my head. "How so?"

"Well, it's an ideal location: ensconced in a sleepy village and virtually in the middle of a forest with a port within a couple of miles. Perfect set-up for smuggling."

I thought of the drug empire Charlie's boyfriend had planned for Starlington, which made my skin crawl.

"We found buried weapons, gold, and drugs. Going on the dust, the cache had been stashed for a while. One of the floorboards was lifted when we arrived. He'd obviously been disturbed when he ran off after Ainsley."

"Her name's now officially Scarlet."

A slow grin grew on her face. "That's right, you're now together." She shook her head. "When this is all done and dusted, I think Hollywood could be interested in this story."

"It's a nice ending to an otherwise sleazy story. You aren't completely exonerated, but as you point out, I wouldn't have met her otherwise." I raised an eyebrow.

"One of the main reasons for planting Ainsley—I mean, Scarlet—here . . ." She gave me a sheepish, crooked smile. "Wasn't so much because of your wife's suspicious disappearance, even though I was convinced you did it. Husbands often do." She paused. "This property was tracked through activity to the dark web. That stalled when the hacker we'd employed was killed."

"So you're telling me that Tyson had set this up before we left for France?"

She nodded.

"Then why didn't the police come in sooner?" I asked.

"Resources, mainly. It was vague at best. We need a ton more evidence before committing to that kind of investigation. It wasn't until your wife disappeared that we discovered some dark-web activity. But when the signals paused, the department lost interest."

"So, when did this dark-web activity start?" I asked.

"It goes back to a couple of years ago, to an Eastern European mob. This is a significant bust for us. If we can cut a deal with Tyson Drill, we'll have a foothold into a major trafficking ring."

"So, while Tyson was my security guard, apart from screwing my wife, he was also running a drug operation from the folly?"

"Yep."

"Just drugs?" I asked. "I saw weapons too."

"Automatics, pistols, you name it. There's at least a million in gold bullion. The coke we found is worth a few million on the street. Crystal meth too." She studied me for a minute. "You need to get better security."

"You're right. The folly, as you can see, is about half a mile from the house, with easy access through the forest. I have my dogs, but they would have been familiar with Tyson from when he worked here."

"Okay. Let's leave it there for now. We'll have to talk again soon," she said.

# CHAPTER 42

## Scarlet

DANIEL ENTERED AND HANDED me a bottle of water.

The silky green gown barely fit me. "It's a little tight. I've put on weight, I'm afraid."

His gaze hooded. "In all the right places. You're a very sexy woman."

"So, on the chair, strap down?" I asked with a teasing smile.

Nodding, he pointed to my legs. "Lift it."

"All the way?"

"Yes."

He ran his tongue over his lips. That gesture alone inflamed me.

"Will you ever just paint nice pictures, like trees and bowls of fruit?"

He laughed. "That would bore me to tears."

"I meant subjects other than me, like portraits of our daughter." I smiled. My body warmed at the mere mention of my baby, especially now that Daniel seemed just as emotionally invested. The glint of relief in his eyes upon learning our baby was healthy revealed that.

"A picture of you would be nice," I persisted. "Dressed like that." I pointed at his painting attire—a major turn-on for me with those torn jeans, which allowed me to slide my hands inside.

"Mm . . . maybe. For now, quiet. I need to capture you in all your libidinous glory."

I laughed. We'd finally found a nice place to park our relationship. Everything was now out in the open—barring one incident.

I couldn't bring myself to confess sneaking into his studio to snoop about like some suspicious nosy parker. Those paintings represented Daniel's subconscious and his trapped memories. His desire for privacy was more than justified.

That he'd depicted violent scenes similar to those I'd observed was purely coincidental, not some spine-chilling prophecy, as my colorful imagination had speculated.

After my mother returned home and I'd fully recuperated, Daniel asked that uncomfortable—though inevitable—question about my presence at the folly that night.

"I went for a walk, and I heard a scream," I said.

"I know that bit. What else?"

Biting my lip, I looked up at him like a child who'd been caught smoking or something just as noxious. "It wasn't my first visit."

A line formed between his brows.

I stammered through an account of how I'd seen the shadowed figures arguing on my two earlier visits.

"Why the hell didn't you tell me?"

Taking a nervous breath, I chose my words carefully. "Because, at first, I thought it was you."

His unblinking gaze made me shrink.

"You thought me capable of that?" He spoke quietly, despite the fire in his eyes. "Why would we even be there?"

"I know. It didn't make sense." I sighed. "It was selfish of me. I didn't want to stir the air between us."

He shook his head and walked off.

I clutched my arms, even though the warm sun shone down on me.

He returned with a tumbler half-filled with scotch and sat down, drinking it in silence.

"If you want me gone, I understand." Biting into a nail, I spoke with a tremor.

"No." He cast me a penetrating stare. "But you should have told me. I'd never hit a woman." He stared down at his glass. "Charlie liked it rough. One of the many reasons our marriage died."

I released the air trapped in my lungs. "I'm sorry for not telling you."

After a long painful gap, he said, "I can understand why you kept it to yourself. I'm not the easiest person sometimes." He brushed back his hair. "It doesn't sit well, you thinking that was me."

I touched his hand. "I'm sorry for thinking that."

After that, we sat in silence, waiting for the air to settle. It was a difficult admission, but an important one, nevertheless.

A wall had finally come down now that Daniel had shared that dark episode in his early life. He looked more relaxed. The tightness in his face had smoothed out.

It was as though the chain around his heart had finally snapped.

Maybe I read too much into it, but as a slow, sad smile grew on his face, all I wanted to do was take Daniel into my arms and hold him.

He beat me to it. He reached in and took my hand. "I love you, Scarlet."

"I love you too. I always have. I always will." I stroked his chiseled jaw. "In all your shades of eccentricity."

A playful smirk shaped his lips. "And I've always had a thing for quirky women."

"Here I was, thinking I was ordinary and overweight." I chuckled nervously. It wasn't easy owning up to low self-esteem.

"You're far from ordinary, Scarlet." His lips curved. "And you're voluptuous. Deliciously so." His smile faded. "It's not just about how sexy you are though. I felt a deep connection from the beginning." He shrugged. "I'm comfortable around you. There's no expectation. And you know more about me than anyone else."

"I'll always be here for you, Daniel. Please know that."

His gaze warmed my face as we stared into each other's eyes. I released a deep breath and my spirit broke into a waltz.

I melted into his arms and let him lead me into the bedroom for an afternoon of unbridled, passionate lovemaking.

Rummaging through my collection of sexy lace costumes, I lifted a white teddy, which Daniel had, one steamy night, received an image of on his phone.

"This?" I dangled the skimpy lace garment. "Or this?" A green lace crotchless version.

Running his tongue over his lips, he pointed to the green. Of course.

Daniel unbuttoned his shirt and lowered his jeans. With those smoldering, dark eyes, and lips that were made for sex, Daniel Love had me in the grip of burning lust.

But more importantly, he'd made me feel good about myself—not just as an attractive woman, but also as an intelligent being with plenty to contribute to the world at large.

After copping so many cruel blows during my disastrous marriage, I'd started to blame myself for my ex's venom. Kevin's relentless putdowns had seeped deeply into my psyche, to the extent that I started to believe I possessed the ugly flaws he accused me of. I wore self-loathing as one would a tattered, oversized coat in the hope of being invisible, not only to him but also to myself and anyone that came close to me.

• • • • • • • • • •

A MONTH HAD PASSED, and we'd learned that Charlotte was out on bail, while her boyfriend remained behind bars.

One night, Daniel asked me to pose in the green gown for a session in the loft.

"What happens when I'm no longer attractive?"

He put down his brush. "You're a part of me now, so what will be will be."

I grimaced. "You make me sound like an appendage."

He came to me, and I relaxed my pose as he massaged my shoulders.

I dropped back my head. "Mm..."

"I've never felt easy around people, but silence comes easy with you, and our conversations are effortless." He continued to expertly knead my shoulders. "Married to Charlie, I was the loneliest I'd ever been. Being with the wrong person seems to heighten desolation."

I thought of my horrible marriage to Kevin. I turned to look at him and nodded. "That was me too."

"That's not going to be us." His eyes burned into mine, and his intensity melted into a gentle smile.

As he stood before me, I sensed there was something else he wanted to say.

"What is it?" I asked.

"Will you marry me?" he asked.

My jaw dropped. "But, I thought, you didn't want to marry again."

He knelt down before me, lifted my chin and kissed me sweetly on the lips and rose.

"I've changed. You've changed me." His mouth lifted slightly at one end. "In a good way. Love has changed me. And I love you."

My heart exploded like fireworks.

Tears splashed down my cheeks. Sniffling away, I could barely talk let alone declare undying love.

I wiped my tears and taking a deep, composing breath, I uttered, "And I love you."

I fell into his arms, and there we remained. Our bodies crushed in a bond of love—our hearts dancing together.

"So is that a 'yes'?" he asked while staring deeply into my eyes.

Without any qualm whatsoever, I said, "It's a yes."

We exchanged a smile that quickly fired up to a giggle. Yep, we liked to laugh. At times, even at nothing. A sign of true happiness.

• • • • • • • • • •

TWO YEARS LATER...

Lake Como sparkled in the afternoon sun. Vibrating in a celebration of color, the garden resembled a Monet, with roses creeping over a honey-bricked archway. The floral-infused air filled my lungs and made me high, as did the overwhelming aesthetics of that Italian village.

My first visit was after Catherine was born and I fell in love at first sight. I loved the relaxed and easy vibe of the locals too.

Some days were lazy, while others were filled with activities, like walking or playing with Catherine, who kept me active at the capricious age of two.

The neoclassical home with its columns and balustraded balconies took my breath away. It was one of a few homes that Daniel owned, and now they were my homes too. Although we would always live at Starlington, Lake Como had become our second home and the perfect location for our wedding ceremony.

Was I really about to become Scarlet Love?

The wedding guests had arrived. It was to be a small affair. I wouldn't have minded a registry office, but Daniel felt like a celebration. And who was I to quibble? I would have gone to Afghanistan for a wedding ceremony if it meant being with him.

Georgina wasn't exactly on my list of favored guests, but I understood Daniel's decision to invite her. At least her whimsical husband, Crofton, was always a joy to be around. I loved our chats about George Eliot's freakish grasp of language and her timeless, profound insights on human nature.

It was late afternoon and being Springtime, we couldn't have wished for nicer weather.

My mother entered my bedroom and found me at the mirror applying lipstick.

"You look half your age, darling," she said, peering at my reflection.

As a woman marrying a younger man, her fine compliment made me smile.

Catherine came skipping in and my mother lifted her up and kissed her on the cheek. "Look at this pretty princess."

I smiled so much my face hurt.

My daughter hadn't arrived easily. Despite the long, painful labor, it was worth every teeth-clenching second for that beautiful dark-haired angel.

I ran my hands down my fitted, knee-length dress that I'd purchased in Milan. Nothing slinky or inappropriately revealing, just a flattering cross-over bodice, the only embellishment a ruffle on the sleeves.

"Green's always been your color," my mother said.

If only she knew how much that color meant to this relationship.

Daniel entered and Catherine ran to her father. "Daddy."

He lifted her up and swung her around. They were the image of each other, with their large, loving brown eyes.

Wearing a black velvet jacket with silk lapels, and a burgundy silk scarf, Daniel could have been a model in Vogue.

"The guests are seated and we're ready to go," he said, holding my hand. He kissed me on the cheek. "You look beautiful."

Our eyes met, and that warmth and understanding we shared touched my soul.

He left the room with Catherine skipping along.

My mother shook her head in wonder. "Is this real?"

I shrugged. "I keep asking myself that." We looked at each other and laughed. I really wanted to cry. But mindful of my makeup, I resisted, despite the lump in my throat.

The courtyard where the ceremony was to be held overlooked the majestic lake, which, streaked with the late afternoon sun, seemed to shimmer in gold.

That historic setting with the golden-walled villa draped in pink and red roses, jasmine, and fragrant blooms sent me back to a time when technology didn't exist. I almost expected a draped nymph, like the statues gracing the courtyard, to float past.

Words of love and devotion kissed the perfumed air as Daniel's shoulder touched my arm.

"I do," he murmured without a breath's pause. "Forever to love and protect."

I couldn't even recall my own response because I'd fallen into his soulful eyes and flown off to paradise.

We kissed, the seated guests clapped and cheered, and the champagne flowed.

A string quartet played in the background as people milled about chatting, laughing, drinking, and eating.

It was a colorful turn-out, but no one was more colorful than Oleander, who looked spectacular against the pink bougainvillea in her deep-purple gown as she chatted to Crofton.

Jerry gave Daniel a hug, followed by a kiss on my cheek.

He whispered, "I've never seen Dan so happy."

I smiled and had to fight back the tears, which had threatened to erupt into a face-contorting wail since those heart-swelling vows. I sucked it back with a fine glass of champagne. There wasn't much that excellent bubbly couldn't fix—like nipping the urge to bawl like a lunatic.

After what had been a sit-down banquet meal that had delivered everyone to culinary heaven, the party began.

At my request, Daniel had reinstated Stephanie and she was there with Randall, who she'd started seeing again. Jack was also present, as was Jan. Some of the guests who had been at Starlington the day of the hunt were invited, Camilla included. She was now married to her own rich guy, and she seemed happy enough.

A band playing dance favorites had set up in the domed ballroom, where a dazzling fresco of the three Graces emblazoned the ceiling.

Dressed in a figure-hugging red gown, Georgina slunk over to me.

"You designed it well," she said, her eyes sliding from me to Daniel.

"Yes, it's been a great day." I wasn't sure if that's what she meant. Her signature smirk hinted at a dig.

"I meant Daniel. You achieved what half of London's elite lusted after from the moment his voice broke."

"I didn't design anything."

She cocked her head. "No need to be humble."

"It was destiny's design. Speak to her about it. Not me. Now, if you'll excuse me. I love this song."

I left her standing there wearing her smug grin. There were plenty of young, handsome locals present to keep her toes warm for the weekend.

Joining my husband, I said, "Let's dance."

Although he wasn't a keen dancer, he soon relaxed, staring into my eyes as he held me close. "Thank you."

"It's me who should be thanking you," I said.

"I'd be half the man without you, Scarlet. Thank you for taking that job."

I laughed and we glided along as though in the air.

# EPILOGUE

## Daniel

FIVE YEARS LATER...

"Bramwell," I called out to my two-year-old son, who was running through the scrub.

In the distance, builders had put the finishing touches on a folly that I'd commissioned—a small children's castle by the pond.

Resting a pad on my knees, I sketched the pond with its family of swans, where Catherine skipped about, enchanted by the romance of nature.

After the loft burned down, with me arriving just in time to save Starlington, it was like a fresh start.

How the studio caught alight remained a mystery. An electrical fault was the vague but unsubstantiated explanation.

In any case, the time had come to lay to rest that hidden world I'd once inhabited—a world that only my imagination allowed entrance to.

After Bramwell arrived, I made a pact to bring light and art out into the open.

Surrounded by a magical world, we had it all.

I had it all.

Scarlet had brought me more gifts than I could ever have imagined possible.

She came over carrying a couple of G&Ts.

"Here, love." She passed me a glass.

In the sunshine, with her red hair free and blowing in the wind, my wife was more beautiful than ever. Her beauty just grew and grew.

Her full figure still excited me, maybe even more now than it had before.

We sat back and sipped our drinks as the sun's warmth rippled through me.

Bramwell and Catherine rolled around in the grass, giggling and finding magic everywhere.

Scarlet laughed as she watched them play. "They're mischievous little angels."

"Aren't they," I said.

"Are you happy?" she asked.

I nodded with a smile.

So much had happened.

After a short stint in jail, Charlie had gone to the United States. Her boyfriend was jailed for twenty years for drug dealing and apparently a murder. His DNA matched a cold case. A young woman. Charlie had been lucky that wasn't her. That much I did tell her. She just returned glazed indifference and that was the end of that sad chapter.

"The folly's so magical," Scarlet said, pointing at the golden castle.

"The children are crazy about it," I replied.

She stared at me for a moment. "You don't feel guilty for going against your great-grandfather's wishes by demolishing it?"

"Nope. It was an easy decision to make."

"I would've done the same." She smiled sadly. "Hopefully Oleander's ritual cleansed that area of any evil spirits."

I turned to look at her. "Thanks for suggesting it."

"I'm surprised you agreed." She chuckled. "Especially with Eurydice turning up with that horned god of a boyfriend and their fascinating ritual." She raised an eyebrow.

I laughed. "They're a colorful bunch. My mother liked them, and they're an important part of Starlington. I'm a firm believer in tradition, and they bring protection."

"I would never have thought you a believer of witchcraft."

"Hey, I never believed in love either. It was a complete mystery to me."

"I didn't either." She wore a tender smile. "Until I met you. By uncovering you, I discovered love."

I leaned in and kissed her soft, beautiful lips. "I love you."

"And I love you."

Our love was eternal.

I was as certain of that as I was of love.

THE END

**jjsorel.com**

# ALSO BY J. J. SOREL

THORNHILL TRILOGY
**Book One Entrance**
**Book Two Enlighten**
**Book Three Enfold**
MALIBU SERIES
**A Taste of Peace**
**Devoured by Peace**
**It Started in Venice**

**The Importance of Being Wild**
**The Importance of Being Bella**
**Take My Heart**
**Dark Descent into Desire**
**Uncovering Love**
BEAUTIFUL BUT STRANGE SERIES
**Flooded**
**Flirted**
**Flourished**

Printed in Great Britain
by Amazon